For my mother, father, wife, and daughter
and to whoever happens upon this book

Contents

1   PRELUDE TO THE DARKNESS

"Better to fight and fall than to live without hope." Lying down in the tall grass, calling to mind the words and memory of her father, she had been reminiscing every night for the past fortnight. She missed and loved him without reservation. It had been several years since his untimely death. Haunted by that day of great battle, pondering the mystery that was the end of an era and the nightmares that followed. Alone in the dark and silent as the grave, Alex gazed up to the stars. Mesmerized by the flickering heavenly bodies; disappearing but for a moment as the wind gusts tossed and bent the high grass above her.

"Alex! join us by the fire," a voice in the dark cried out.

It was Gudrun, one of her closest friends and leader of the warriors. Alex slowly climbed to her feet and crept through the high grass towards the dancing flames in the distance; never stepping foot on the windswept path leading out from the village but walking through the swaying grass which was nearly as tall as she was. There in the tree line, she joined her friend and the unexpected visitors.

"Easy, Easy!" Gudrun scolded his dog as it emitted a low, lengthy growl.

Moving slowly and imperceptibly, Alex could see four shadowy figures by the fire. Gudrun's dog, Flux, jumped on Alex as she approached them, licking her face and gently whimpering in excitement. Standing upright, the dog was nearly the height of her. It was more beast than dog, a magnificent animal with a coat of solid black with various shades of red and a lengthy mane.

"Hello, care for some mead?" asked one of the men but Alex seemed to all but ignore him.

"She doesn't drink," said Gudrun as he quickly took the mead from the man's hand and began to drink. Seemingly annoyed, he sat close to the fire and prodded it with a short, flimsy stick which gave way to misty, grey smoke and tiny, red flickers of light which rose into the midnights sky.

"My name is Oslaf, and this is Weohstan. We are traders and have recently passed through Harrogate to the south. We are travelling to the Frozen Wastes to trade for furs, but your chieftain won't allow us to pass and demanded we return to Harrogate at once," said Oslaf.

Oslaf and Weohstan both were busy about setting up large animal furs on the ground preparing to rest for the night, adding leaves and branches to the fire when Gudrun seemingly became more and more agitated.

"You should return to your caravan!" shouted Gudrun.

Alex sat down next to Gudrun, smiling, and elbowing his side playfully as they warmed themselves by the fire. Fall or not, it seemed far colder. The winds from the north howled through the forest and the moonlit mountain peaks shined in the nights sky. The western side of the mountains hadn't seen rain in a month and the village had already begun to bring in the harvest for the season.

The flames of the fire danced, and the ring of smoke rose high up above the trees.

"Why won't you let us pass?" asked Weohstan seemingly frustrated but curious.

Alex was prodding the fire as Gudrun, glancing ominously at Alex, stood up and started looting the trader's provisions. They wanted to stop him but how could they. Gudrun was known as the Bear of Grom, both for his size and his ravenous appetite. Gudrun was a formidable man, he inspired both fear and respect from everyone. He had long hair and a short beard; he was impressively large and powerful. Over his tunic, he was clothed in a wool jacket and a bear skin mantle which covered the better part of his torso. He had a large cuirass breastplate which was stained red from battle; this connected into a second piece of armor protecting his neck and shoulders. He wore gleaming shin guards and gauntlets which were made up of several plates intricately locked. His greatsword was as long as a man and the blade measured two palms in width.

Finding some mead, Gudrun's agitation turned to cheerfulness as he sat back down next to Alex with a grin on his face. Flux, who had seemed anxious and alert, now sat beside Alex as he nudged his way under her tiny arm to be petted but was far too big and simply knocked Alex over.

"One year," replied Alex, as she continued to pet and play with Flux as he gently bit and nibbled on her arm with an open mouth full of sharp, white teeth and a large red tongue that dangled out to the side.

"One year?" asked Weohstan as he looked back and forth between Gudrun and Alex with a perplexed expression on his troubled face.

Gudrun stood up and helped himself to some more of the trader's mead. He probed their encampment for any manner of luxury items he could find, all the while looking through the darkness uneasily as the dark trees bent and swayed in the growing wind around them.

"It has been nearly a year since Stormgarden was burned, and what was once a home to a great many warriors has been reduced to a ruin full of cinder and ash. Of the other settlements, we have not received any word, not for some months," replied Alex with a troubled brow.

Staring into the fire, her mind turned against her and all manner of evil, foul, and loathsome memories of the past came to life. The deep dark lair with the loud shrill cries from within, and the sinister laughter that followed. The dread of that place, the memories of the battle that followed and the long journey through the dark haunted her day and night. Alex closed her eyes and turned away from the fire, straining her neck and head this way and that, but there was no forgetting the past. Upon seeing her torment, Gudrun sat back down next to Alex, placing his hand on her shoulder.

Weohstan and Oslaf who were previously lively and undeterred were now nervous about their journey to the north. Looking at one another with concern, they sat by the fire apposite Alex and Gudrun. Weohstan put a kettle of tea on the fire. It was made from the root bark of a tree commonly found in the south combined with other herbs, ginger, cinnamon, and cloves.

Weohstan and Oslaf were of normal stature, wearing the furs of many animals and having an abundant supplies and provisions for their journey. Their horses were solid black and tethered to a large tree some ten paces away from their campsite.

Oslaf, sipping on some tea glanced at Gudrun nervously and said, "We lost many ships crossing the sea to reach you. The Leviathan there destroyed most of our company. Tomorrow, with luck, our ship will return to deliver us back across the sea to the south to rejoin our caravan. We will make another plead to your chieftain in the morning to allow us to journey north. We were told your chieftain is a most generous and gracious host, so we were dismayed to find he will not allow us to take rest inside your fortified walls," he concluded while putting his cup of tea down and now looked on at Alex.

"We carry scrolls from the four kings in the south granting us safe passage through these lands. The king of Durga, of Vikhyat, of Gulzar, and of Hazade will want to know that Stormgarden has fallen," said Oslaf while glancing at Gudrun.

"In our trading caravan is a company of emissaries. They were sent to inquire why the southern kings have not received word from the chieftains of the north. If what you say is true, and that Stormgarden is no more, this will be most troubling news," said Oslaf with a pat on his knees as he warmed himself by the fire.

Weohstan, taking some tea from the kettle asked inquisitively, "how did Stromgarden fall, raiders? What happened to the chieftain there and what of the other settlements?" but before Alex could answer, Gudrun stood up and grabbed the kettle of tea out of Weohstans hand, pouring it on the fire.

"Raiders, trolls, giants, ghouls, or demons, what difference does it make! Leave now before the mist is upon us and maybe you'll survive the night," exclaimed Gudrun.

Frightened, Weohstan and Oslaf sat by the now half extinguished fire, fixed as stone as Gudrun untethered one of their horses and motioned for Alex to join him. Alex stood up and whistled for Flux, Gudrun's dog, as they began walking back to the village; there was but a single path from the village which led deep into the forest and abruptly ends without warning.

Glancing back, Alex could see Weohstan and Oslaf rekindle the fire and it appeared but a flicker of light there in the darkness. A heavy mist slowly crept into the land and Alex and Gudrun's pace quickened. Shaking her head in sorrow, Alex looked towards Gudrun who was gently guiding the horse who neighed softly.

"Nothing a fine woman and a cup of mead can't fix," said Gudrun in a quiet, soft voice.

Gudrun looked around them apprehensively, glancing at Alex with a grin all the while peering into the depths of the forest.

"Another restless night? I had hoped you would rest tonight but suspected you wouldn't. I'm glad you joined me tonight to see what became of our visitors," said Gudrun as he moved low hanging tree branches out of his way.

They continued on, now walking across a small opening in the forest, the same area in which Alex laid upon the cold earth and gazed up at the stars in the swaying high grass. Alex looked behind them every few steps as her and Gudrun were both on edge. She could hardly see the visitors fire in the distance as she peered into the forest. Heavy gusts of wind and the moonlight turned the high grass around them into what seemed to be a sea of glass as it passed over and swept through the field.

"You don't get them?" asked Alex with sincerity.

"Bad dreams?" replied Gudrun with a shrug of his shoulders as he gently led the magnificent steed onward.

As they continued, they could see the village and when in sight, motioned to one of the guards in the watchtower high above to let them through a concealed, narrow pathway which was positioned at the edge of the sea. Gudrun handed the horse over to a guardsman just inside the narrow pathway and he and Alex entered the village through the concealed entrance.

The village was some five hundred paces wide and equally long, fortified by high wooden walls with watchtowers and a moat which was most treacherous; the moat consisted of a shallow section filled with water which hid holes dug at various depths between one to three feet followed by a steep twelve-foot trench. Inside the fortified village walls were several long houses which all resembled an overturned boat. There was a single entrance to each home, it was a small door that would require all who entered to crouch and lean in headfirst upon entry. This was deliberate, for if the village was attacked and the walls breached, a single man could defend the home and cut the heads off all who enter. It was a village built for battle with the only opening facing the sea and it was heavily guarded and fortified.

"After the war, I saw many broken warriors who drank away their guilt and fears, many men who now live a life of solitude, unable to live with themselves for the things they did and the things they saw. It all started with lies and lies and lies. Was it worth it? What did we accomplish? My father back then and now my uncle last year. We do not know the fate of either and nobody, including our chief is doing anything about it," exclaimed Alex with great lament.

They walked through that narrow pass, passing guards who had been at their post since dusk. There were several small fires with heavily armed guards sitting around them, each giving a nod to Gudrun as they passed through. They kept several dogs with them, all the like of Flux, having reddish, blue-grayish, and solid black coats with large wild manes.

"What are you on about?" asked Gudrun. "Go have a rest. Just dreams, nothing more. We have been at peace now for some time. You dispatched of those foul devils long ago and all the northern kingdom have you to thank for it," said Gudrun as he nudged her warmly with his elbow.

As they walked, the mist rolled over the high walls of the village; the mist was thick, very thick. It seemed unnatural as they could see it rolling down from the mountains like a strong gale at sea. It covered the ground, and they could no longer see Flux, only hearing him panting heavily as they walked up through the center of the village towards the great hall. Alex whistled to Flux and with an endearing pat on his head she veered off away from Gudrun, bidding him a good night's rest. As Gudrun went towards the nights guard rest house, he called out to Alex.

"What of Weohstan and Oslaf, the traders?" asked Gudrun. "Do you think they will make it back to their caravan tomorrow?" asked Gudrun as he was all but consumed by the heavy, white mist.

Gudrun watched as Alex continued into the darkness and without turning around, "A heavy fog… they won't survive the night!" yelled Alex from a great distance away.

Gudrun stood and listened as Alex continued through the heavy mist. The mist consumed them both completely and Flux brushed up against Gudrun, frightening him, as he forgot that he was there. Flux whimpered and Gudrun comforted him with a few pats to his side. Gudrun stood in the dark and wondered, could Alex be right? The recent events seemed all too familiar, much like the prelude to the horrors that once fell upon them several years ago. Gudrun had an all too familiar shiver run up his spine as he quickly ran inside his humble, comfy home to rest for the night.

Gudrun put on a fire which would last him for the remainder of the night, adding a few logs and several branches for good measure as the nights air had chilled his bones after staying out for too long beyond the village walls. Laying down in his bed, covered in layers of animal furs, he looked forward to seeing the sun rise in a few hours. There in the dark, in the cold pitch black, he glared out the window into the mist and fell asleep with Flux laying down near his side, enjoying the warmth and comfort of the fire.

Alex could not sleep, having found her way to one of the watchtowers, she gazed out across the sea. She imagined a different time where sunshine and clear blue skies were commonplace with crystal blue waters and white sands. It was nice to imagine if even for but a moment. The harsh waves crashed and crashed against those jagged rocks as the wind moved swiftly and smoothly through her hair. She became dispirited as her mind wandered back into that dreadful place of whispers and shadows. That place where she was hailed a hero and the bravest of warriors, to be lifted up with songs of praise and victory only to suffer in torment every day thereafter with the memories of the horrors she had endured.

Sometime later out in the distance, in the pitch black of night, she heard screams and groans of despair that penetrated the cool nights air. The nights guard looked at one another, curious and puzzled. Alex with a sense of foreboding, surveyed the forests to the east, already knowing the poor fate of Weohstan and Oslaf and what she would find in the twilight. Succumbing to exhaustion, Alex rested up against the wall under the dim light of a torch and was joined by two of the village dogs. They fell asleep there as the mysterious, heavy white mist enveloped them.

2 A QUEST FOR HEROES

There in the mist, before the twilight hour where the golden sun would rise and give comfort to those inside the fortified walls, it happened. *"Arm yourself!"* screamed one of the guardsmen from a watchtower some forty paces away. Alex turned away from the sea and dashed forward towards the blood-curdling cry. The mist was thick, and she couldn't see more than a few paces away. As she ran down the wooden ramparts towards the nearest watchtower, she heard groans of despair and the clanging of weapons. Screams were muffled and Alex edged closer as it now went silent.

She could see the flicker of a torch which now lay on the ground and in its light, a shadowy figure moved away into the depths of the mist. She charged down that misty rampart free of fear, but tripped and hit the ground hard. Picking herself up off the ground, she realized she had tripped over the body of a guard, and it was torn limb from limb. No sooner was she struck with a mighty blow from behind while trying to stand up, sending her into the air and into the wall. Dazed and confused, Alex glanced up and a large dark figure shrouded in the mist descended upon her.

A spear whooshed in the air and struck the beast, followed by another spear as the sharpened tip pierced its fiendish hide. The beast let out a deep growl that filled the nights air. Alex seeing a stack of pikes on the ground, picked one up and drove it into the silhouette. It passed clean through the beast, but to no avail and the beast lifted Alex up and flung her into the air some five paces away. The pitter-patter of heavily armed guards came up the rampart. Alex grabbed another pike, meaning to pierce the beast again, but with another loud growl it knocked Alex off her feet and pinned her to the ground.

In the pitch black of night and in the heavy mist, she couldn't see its face. She could see the steam vapor come out of its mouth with every breath, and then the large, jagged teeth that followed with slimy drool dripping from its mouth. It had eyes like glowing red and orange embers that pierced her soul as its mouth opened and tried to bite her neck. Reaching for one of the pikes on the ground, she heard a familiar voice cry out in the dark.

"Alex, what are you doing!" demanded Gudrun.

Gudrun grabbed the pike from Alex's hands and tossed it to the side. Flux was energetically and affectionately licking Alex on her face, nudging her with his head and brushing up against her as she lay there against the wall.

"What happened?" asked Alex with a bewildered face.

She looked around and down the rampart at the nearest watchtower as Gudrun stood above her. The Sun was high in the sky with clouds on the horizon. A gentle breeze blew through her hair, and she felt the warmth of the sun touch her face as she looked up with her eyes closed.

"You were dreaming, I hope of something other than this harsh, bleak place," replied Gudrun as he helped Alex to her feet.

Gudrun was drinking mead and was very cheerful. He carried a golden cup of mead in one hand and was eating some soft bread with the other. Joyful and well rested with the darkness of night behind him and the warmth and comfort of the burning sun ahead, he motioned to some of the guards along the ramparts that Alex was in good condition, and he passed some soft, delicious bread to her.

"Chieftain Grom is requesting you in the great hall," said Gudrun.

Together they walked down the ramparts through the courtyard back towards the center of the village. Alex looked around the village, and it was lively that day and most of the villagers seemed to be enjoying the unseasonably warm weather as they approached the winter months.

"You seem to be in high spirits," said Alex.

"I just paid a visit to our dear friends Weohstan and Oslaf. They are most hospitable and generous guests," replied Gudrun with a grin and laugh.

Gudrun took a bite of bread and a drink of mead, as some spilled down his chin and beard as he nodded to a group of beautiful women who passed them by.

"Where are they? We should let them speak with the chieftain before they leave," replied Alex.

"I found them, well what's left of them, torn asunder and missing their heads. Oddly their horse remained unscathed, and their provisions were intact," said Gudrun motioning to his bread and mead.

"What tears a man limb from limb but leaves all his goods? The nights guard said they heard screaming in the dark, out there in the forest," said Gudrun as he ate and drank to his heart's content.

Alex looked at him but said nothing, she didn't need to. Both of their countenance fell as they walked through the village up towards the great hall, not knowing what evil lurks in the night, but evil it was for sure.

As they approached the great hall the sun was shielded by clouds and a furious wind swept through the village. They were received by the chieftain's herald and were admitted into the great hall. It was the largest dwelling and situated in the center of the village, serving as the chieftain and his kins residence, a meeting place for visitors and a gathering place for events.

There was already a large gathering inside. Seated at some of the many tables, which could comfortably seat six, were some of the nights guard, prestigious warriors from the village and a few passerby's which were not permitted to leave due to the mist. There was a large, blazing fire in the center of the hall. The roof directly above the fire had a small opening which let the smoke escape and some sunlight enter. A large cauldron with an abundant amount of mead was off to the side and Gudrun stopped for a moment to fill his cup as they walked up towards the chieftain. Alex and Gudrun approached and with a nod, acknowledged Chieftain Grom as they took their seats at one of the tables closest to him.

Grom, the chieftain for which the village was named after, had served in the previous great war when Alex and Gudrun were still young in mind and spirit. He fought in the high north against an army of unknown assailants, venturing into the Frozen Wastes to do battle with the inhabitants there. A great warrior and leader of men, he was ill prepared for those ferocious, vile, and ill-disposed beasts which pursued him day and night as he managed to escape south back into the lands of his forefathers. Surrounded and outnumbered, it was Alex who saved him and a great company of his warriors. His armor rent, with wounds that oozed blood, maimed and clinging to life, it was Alex who pushed the beasts deep into that Abyss while Chieftain Grom, although badly wounded, and his company of warriors escaped with their lives.

Chieftain Grom had endured many battles, conflicts and wars which had aged his face and silvered his hair. He sat on his great chair, hunched to one side leaning towards the warmth of a fire. His silvered hair was long, and mead spilled down his braided beard as he was tended to by servants. He was stern, wise beyond measure and respected by all; not a single person could speak ill of him. Several servants entered the main hall and served food and drink to those in attendance while the remaining kin of the chieftain sat at their tables closest to Chieftain Grom.

"There!" pointing to Alex. "The bravest and most cunning of all the warriors I've known. It was she who saved a great many of us some time ago. She who entered with many strong arms, their bravery and strength unmatched, diving deep into the Abyss to vanquish those foul beasts from the unknown and she alone who survived. Tonight, we drink in their honor, those who did not return and fell in battle," exclaimed Chieftain Grom.

The hall was filled with cheers and merrymaking at these words and Gudrun slapped Alex on the back, but Alex paid no mind to the words of praise. Servants were busy brining all manner of food and drink around to the tables. An ample serving of breads with fruits and meat, pork, lamb, and mutton were served. A servant girl poured Gudrun and Alex some mead from a large tankard. Gudrun quickly grabbed Alex's drinking cup and with a grin drank it down to the last drop.

"This mead is excellent," said Gudrun to Alex. "To our honorable chieftain," he said as he stood up and shouted with his cup raised.

With a large cheer the warriors and servants gave praise to Chieftain Grom for he was a most loved chieftain and very kind to his people. The mead being served was a specialty and visitors would come from near and as far away as Stormgarden for it. It was made from raw honey, honeycomb and contained parts of the beehive as well as the bees.

The feast went on for quite some time and passed into the early evening. Alex looked at Chieftain Grom and behind his smile, she could sense he was troubled. The better part of the nights guard in attendance looked troubled, as well as the chieftain's kin who sat at a long, large table below the chieftains grand, ornate chair. Servants were still brining food and drink and began to light the various candles and torches throughout the hall as twilight approached. One of the passersby's there came and sat next to Alex and greeted her warmly.

"My name is Ødger," the man said as he kept drinking some mead from his silver cup while taking a piece of fruit from a passing servant.

He was a young man dressed in fine clothes. He wore dark fabric pants and boots, and a bright red tunic. He was tall and thin, having long hair and no beard.

"How fortuitous that we arrived in your little village when we did, confined here only to enjoy banquets like these from our most generous host," said Ødger while raising his cup to Chieftain Grom with a sincere smile.

The chieftain was encircled by several heavily armored men who were giving glancing looks back and forth at Alex. While eating some bread and blueberries, Gudrun was called over to the chieftain by one of his kin.

As Gudrun stood up, he asked, "Are you finished with that?" and took the drink from Ødger's hand and winked at Alex as he passed on to meet with the chieftain.

"Such lovely company," said Ødger to Alex with scornful laughter. I did not have the heart to tell him I was still drinking."

"It's not manners you lack but courage," replied Alex as she leaned back and gazed into the fire as she had no interest in conversation with the traveler. "You're welcome to leave at any time, you and your company are not imprisoned here," said Alex as she began to look on inquisitively at Chieftain Grom and Gudrun.

"Ha!" exclaimed Ødger. "And what of the mist?" He questioned.

"What of it?" replied Alex as she looked on at Gudrun who had an unsettled expression on his weary face.

Gudrun motioned for Alex to join him, and servants began to tend to Chieftain Grom in his great chair, for he was very weak and fragile.

"They say a man doesn't survive the night should he find himself outside these walls. They say that evil has now a foothold in these lands and more so further north. It has been three months and I haven't seen any visitors arrive. Whether it be traders by land or sea, or messengers from the southern kingdoms. Are we to rot here, hidden away as the mist consumes us? I have heard of your exploits and truly you are a brave and courageous woman, but do you not fear what is out there in the mist?" said Ødger in a quiet but frightened voice.

"The only thing I fear is your constant prate," replied Alex with a small smile as she took a cup of mead from one of the servant girls and handed it to Ødger.

Seeing that Alex said this in Jest, his spirits were lifted, and he began to drink.

"Think no more of these things. You are safe here, evil has not lurked this far south in ages," said Alex.

At this, she saw a beautiful woman staring affectionately with a smile towards Ødger. When Ødger's eyes met hers with a sideways glance, she stood up and came towards him and sat in his lap provocatively.

Alex bid him a good evening and said, "a terrible place to be confined indeed, perhaps you'll consider staying a bit longer," as she stood with a smirk and left the table to join Gudrun and Chieftain Grom.

She walked through the large gathering passing by many drunken warriors. They were laughing and reminiscing about days of glory and valor. Despite being a rather joyful event, Alex could tell many of them were apprehensive as the day turned to night. For it was there in the dark where men's minds are left to their imaginations, dreaming of all manner of foul, loathsome, and menacing thoughts.

Gudrun turned away from the small gathering around the chieftain and walked over to Alex. He leaned down and whispered, "I'll meet you in the courtyard by the gate," before grabbing a large cup of mead and exiting the great hall in haste.

As Alex approached the chieftain, the small gathering around him drifted back to their seats and into the crowd. Alex kneeled beside the chieftain as servants stoked the fire near them to keep the chieftain warm.

"I take this to be a farewell party, is it not?" said Alex while looking out the window into the dark, cloudy sky.

The chieftain leaned towards her and placed his old, rough hand upon hers.

"Nothing can be concealed from you! For in this merriment there is much sorrow and misery. Men's hearts are failing Alex, apprehensive of what is coming out there in the night," said Chieftain Grom as he coughed and hacked, for he was old and weak.

The chieftain gripped Alex tightly, wheezing and coughing as he leaned in closer towards her.

"Look around you, these are all brave men. Many served with me in the north and owe you their lives, as do I. They are all afraid, dismayed, and anxious. Truly I tell you, last night a great number of us were killed, we can delay no longer," exclaimed Chieftain Grom.

"Here? Inside our walls?" replied Alex for she was surprised and alarmed. "Who else knows?" she questioned.

Her eyes darted around the hall as several onlookers exchanged whispers and glances towards them.

"Gudrun, a number of the nights guard, and now you. We found them all bashed, bruised, and torn apart. Not a shout nor a cry of battle, they all fell in silence, Alex. I fear this is the work of something beyond us, something from the past that has returned. Do you remember the Abyss?" asked Chieftain Grom.

Alex's countenance fell and she was deeply troubled.

"I prefer not to think upon such things," said Alex softly while looking deep into the fire.

She closed her eyes firmly and covered her face with her hand, for she was indeed haunted by the memories of that dreadful place.

"I find it troubling to remember so very little, given that I was there for quite some time and the only one to survive," said Alex as she looked at Chieftain Grom with glowing eyes.

"Yes," replied Chieftain Grom. "That is why you must return to the north, to seek answers and find out if this evil has indeed returned and what has become of the northern kingdom. Perhaps you will learn what became of your father and uncle. It may bring you some peace, for I see your torment which you bear day after day since we returned here. You were a young woman full of life and joy, and I would see those days again," said Chieftain Grom as he leaned away and sat upright to the best he could.

"If I had your authority and power, I would choose another to send on this task. If I had your wisdom, I know that it must be so," said Alex as she stood upright and brushed her hair away from her face.

She looked out the window as the clouds slowly revealed a bright crescent moon. Chieftain Grom was helped to his feet by servants, for his left leg was maimed and his right arm had been severed some years ago in battle. Alex looked on and wondered how she had survived when so many were left crippled or dead, for the battle on that day was relentless against a fierce and unknown horde from the Frozen Wastes.

"Alex, look at me. The last few winters have grown harsh, and I will not survive another. I have lived long enough, and the people here look to you for courage. Should you return, you will become a chieftain. I bid you farewell and luck in battle," said Chieftain Grom as he was helped away to his sleeping chambers, as he was most tired from the evening's activities.

After pausing for a moment, Alex walked slowly out of the mead hall; exchanging looks with Ødger who was now staring at her. Alex walked down through the dark, quiet village towards the open courtyard by the concealed gate. She soaked in the brisk, clean mountain smell and the refreshing cold air pierced her lungs. It was crisp air, the earthy dirt, and the smell of pinecones that she had enjoyed there. It had a quietness that she had grown fond of, as it reminded her of home. Gudrun was there, waiting for her next to the horse that he had taken from Weohstan and Oslaf.

Alex gazed at the shimmering stars and could hear the faint sound of waves slamming against the rocky shore from beyond the village walls. She thought of home, but it was faraway across the sea. A land of gentle rolling plains, deep and verdant forests with innumerable rivers. She remembered her father and uncle who took her fishing in the summer and hunted buffalo in the fall. They were both brave and cunning warriors who fought to protect their own lands when war came.

For it was in that time, when Alex was still a girl, a terror from the north casted its shadow across their lands and a myriad of demons fell upon them. Alex thought to herself, could this really be happening again? First as a young girl and now here, across the sea among these brave and fierce peoples. To be chieftain, it was an encouraging proposal, but Alex wasn't enticed.

Looking down from the stars with a clenched fist, her bright azure eyes met Gudrun's gaze. Gudrun was drinking a large cup of mead and was pale as snow; he was clearly unnerved and rightfully so.

"You asked me about bad dreams," said Gudrun with his head held low. "I get them too, Alex," he said while throwing his now empty cup of mead to the side. "They started soon after we returned from the north. That was many years ago, but it might as well have been yesterday for the memories are vivid and etched in my mind. Are you not afraid of what horrors await us, do you not fear death?" he asked with a frightened voice.

"Eaten by trolls, heads crushed by ogres, robbed and hanged by bandits, hunted by ghouls, goblins and the undead. Or perhaps it will be demons who devour us in the darkness, or the terrors from beyond the Frozen Wastes who will come and slay us before our time has come," replied Alex with a large smile.

"I'm not kidding Alex," said Gudrun seemingly aggravated as he clutched his sword tightly.

Alex, without breaking a smile, said "Who's kidding? At any rate I hear the mead in the north is made with the sweetest honey around, so if your courage fails you, try to look forward to the mead. Soon, we will see if your worrying is warranted or not."

3 THEY COME AT NIGHT

"Prepare yourself," said Gudrun. "We leave tonight, and with haste."

Gudrun mounted his horse and motioned for some of the nights guard to bring Alex her battle garments, but she refused. Alex wore a shirt, pants, boots, and a dark hood made from fabric which covered her head save an opening around her eyes. She then covered herself in a grass and straw cloak, which was good protection for when it rained. Her cloak completely concealed her with a small opening in the front; inside she had a bow with a quiver of arrows made with stone arrowheads, a short sword, and short axe which could be thrown. All the warriors were amused, always urging her to wear a more proper set of armor forged in fire, but she held onto what was customary in her own lands save a few of their weapons.

"I didn't plan on sleeping tonight anyways but couldn't this wait till the morning?" asked Alex, frustrated at the chieftain's decision to send them on their way in the dark and coldness of the night.

Gudrun took another drink of mead from one of the nights guards and was looking into the distance.

"More good news," joked Gudrun. "We are taking the Chieftains daughter with us."

The chieftain's daughter, Reis, was coming down from the great hall on a solid white horse. Reis had long, flowing, blond hair bound in a ponytail which was adorned with a ribbon. She wore fabric gloves and boots with a beautiful colored dress. She had a large animal fur which she wore as a cloak and a necklace which hung a small, bright crystal of magnificent shades of blue, red, black, and orange.

"I'm coming too!" shouted Ødger.

He rode his horse up besides Reis as they came trotting down the pathway. Alex and Gudrun looked stoic, glancing at one another as Reis and Ødger came closer.

"The chieftain requested I join you, and should we reach the northern plains I am to take my leave and return south on the Volda river to rejoin my kingdom and send word of what has happened here," said Ødger who seemed most overjoyed being able to finally leave the village.

He smiled warmly at Reis and continued to speak, but she paid him no mind. Alex and Gudrun looked at one another with raised eyebrows and turned to exit the village through the narrow corridor and out towards the long wind-swept path which led deep into the forest.

"The leader of the nights guard and all the warriors of Grom, the woman from across the sea who saved him, and his own daughter," said Gudrun. "Ødger I understand, he poisons the air with his constant chatter. With any luck every ghost, goblin, demon, and troll will come to devour him and rid us of his irritation, as I'm sure was the chieftain's desire," said Gudrun who was half serious.

Alex smiled and could not help but laugh as the horse gently neighed and continued on into the night.

"Why us, and his own daughter!" exclaimed Gudrun quietly while looking back at Reis. Has he gone mad? The nearest settlement is three days ride and none of our scouts survive a single night's travel beyond our walls. Surely, he knows we will not survive. Why destine his daughter to such an inescapable doom. I had planned to die in battle, a most honorable death fitting of a warrior, not to be slaughtered like a sheep out here in the dark," said Gudrun as he patted his horse who wobbled and struggled to carry Gudrun's weight.

"I'm sure he has his reasons," said Alex while looking back at the village walls and through the treetops ahead.

The four of them continued down that dark path, and at its end they began to move carefully through the forest saying very little for fear was in their hearts and the impending terror in their minds.

"At least no mist, no fog. Pray we can move unseen until dawn," said Alex as she kept looking back to Reis, Ødger and out in the forest.

The trees were an endless sea of pine, spruce, and fir. It was nearly pitch black and they could only see the shapes and shadows of one another moving between the tress and branches. Some moonlight would breach the treetops, as the wind swept through the forest with a furious anger. It was cold, the vapor was coming from the horse's mouths and Alex breathed into her hands to keep them from freezing. They travelled on, silently for quite some time, hearing howls which they took to be from wolves.

"Can we take a rest? It has been hours and I need to stretch my legs," said Ødger with outstretched arms giving a yawn.

They were all tired, having left shortly after dusk, travelling for what seemed like an eternity in the dark. They were fighting sleep, and in their exhaustion had almost forgot about the dangers of their journey north.

"I know you must be as uncomfortable as me, Gudrun," said Ødger as he fidgeted atop his horse.

"It's not safe here," replied Gudrun. "Daybreak will be upon us soon."

Gudrun's horse was wobbling for he was considered a giant amongst men, the largest and most powerful in these northern parts and his horse neighed and wobbled under his weight.

"Where are we heading exactly?" asked Ødger.

Clouds slowly blanketed the sky and the glimmering light from the spectacular moon was all but lost. The mist slowly enveloped them, and they could no longer see anything below the horse's belly.

"Quiet!" Alex cried out.

He turned to Gudrun and motioned for him to look back behind them, deep into the forest. A figure appeared, and then another along the horizon.

"We are being followed, I can see at least two of them, their eyes red like fire there in the distance. Can you see it?" asked Alex, looking back and forth between Gudrun and the forest.

"Aye, I see at least two, theres no mistaking it. It is the Vollgarim," said Gudrun as he motioned for them to all stop the horses and they did so, staring back at the figures behind them in disbelief.

"They stopped too, no doubt having seen us. What do you think? If they give chase, we will not make it," said Gudrun.

"Light your torch, each of you," said Alex in a quiet, whispering voice as she pulled out a torch and a small flint.

She struck the flint against the blade of her short sword and the flame of her torch lit up the darkness around them. In turn, they each lit their torches and looked around frantically searching for any more Vollgarim.

Vollgarim were a thing of folklore and legend. These creatures only appeared at night and resembled the mating of a man and a beast. Their skin was dark or grey, appeared smooth in some places and yet they had scales in others. They were taller than any man and walked hunched over. They had no ears, hair, or nose; some had eyes, and some did not. They had a mouth that was filled with fangs upon fangs with a large red tongue. Some of them had one head, while others had two or even three. Their hands and feet were abnormally large, and it was said they ran on two legs and sometimes on all four. They were a detestable and terrifying sight, and none had been seen in nearly one hundred years, so they say.

"Fasten your torch to your horse, and stay close," said Alex as she moved forward into the mist.

The mist was now heavy and covered them completely. They could not see more than a few paces away, save the glow of the torches that was fastened onto the horse's saddle. They moved silently for a time until they reached a small river.

"Get what provisions and goods you can, we leave the horses here," said Alex as the others removed some of the bags of goods, food, and drink.

"Gudrun," said Alex as she looked and nodded to the horses.

Gudrun gave each horse a heavy smack on its rear, sending them running up along the river while they hid in the heavy mist there along the hard, earthy ground. They could not see anything except the light of the torches which moved further and further away from them as the horses ran to their doom. Then, in an instant they heard the horses squeal, scream and neigh; the loud shrill cries of the Vollgarim that followed. It was an all too familiar sound for Alex as her eyes widened and she gripped her short sword tightly.

"Come, let us cross the river and be done with this place," said Alex as they left the forests edge and waded across the river.

Gudrun entered the water holding Reis above his head while the others followed. The water was ice cold. Its frigid touch froze their skin and drew the air from their lungs. Alex and Ødger were submerged up to their necks. They waded through fast-flowing and turbulent parts of the river until they met the other side. They could hear the thrashing and gnawing upriver, and fragments of what once were horses floated in front of them with unmistakable claw and bite marks. Having met the other side, their bones shivered and shook as they moved quickly, forward and upward towards the misty mountains.

The mist seemed to only grow as they moved up higher above the forest. It began to rain, and they saw the light of a fire high above them on the mountain side. Frozen, chilled, and numb, they carried on seeking the warmth and safety it might provide. Lightning and thunder filled the nights sky with brilliant flashes which helped them traverse the steep embankment. They came upon a cave and saw the light of a fire deep inside, and eagerly went in.

"Do you hear that," said Reis as they paused.

Alex stood in front of Reis and listened inside the cave. It sounded like the muffled cries and moans of a man. Gudrun stood with his sword drawn looking down into the valley. The mist had risen as high as the treetops and with every flash of lighting they became more and more frantic.

"We saw the light of the fire from below, the Vollgarim could see it too and come," said Gudrun with his eyes wide open surveying the landscape.

"Maybe someone is here who can help us, and it beats being soaked by the rain," said Ødger as he rushed deeper in the cave.

"Wait!" Alex screamed softly as Ødger vanished into the darkness.

Moments later, they heard him scream and a loud thud which they took for him as falling to the floor. They followed slowly with their hands along the smooth and crumbling wall of that dark cave. Alex drew her sword and pressed on without fear as Gudrun kept his hand around Reis who seemed reluctant but curious as to what they may find in that dark and forbidding place.

Ødger was there lying on the ground. He was crying, wailing, and whimpering like a beaten dog as he crawled and pushed himself back along the ground and up against the wall. Alex rushed to his side and covered his mouth for he was making noise which echoed there into the deep, bouncing and rolling down into the depths of that place.

"Whatever is here will know of our presence. Perhaps they will think it is a frightened woman and pay us no mind!" said Gudrun as he laughed at Ødger who was visibly shaken.

Ødger had tripped over something while running through the dark. There was a man lying down on his side who had an iron helmet with a chain mail cloak. His hauberk covered his torso down to his legs. He had leather pants, gloves, and boots. He carried a Warhammer and a shield; the shield had been battered and broken and bore the crest of a warrior from Stormgarden. He was motionless and as they came closer, Alex knelt near his side. Alex rolled the man over and she could see his helmet had been crushed and caved in; his face was beyond recognition. There was a pool of blood beneath him still dripping out across the cave floor.

"This is recent," said Alex who rubbed her tongue inside the bottom of her lip and pushed her hair away from her face. "Stay here and tend to Ødger," she said while pressing on without fear until Gudrun and the others were mere shapes and shadows in the distance.

Reis moved to Ødger's side and knelt to comfort him as Gudrun kept a watchful eye on the cave entrance as the sound of heavy rain and thunder crashed and echoed all around them.

"She's so brave, she faces danger standing firm and without flinching," said Reis while tending to a small wound Ødger sustained above his brow.

Gudrun looked toward her and then stared down into the dark depths of the cave and thought back to when he and Alex were forced to fight in the far north.

"There's a cost to such bravery and courage, and Alex knows it too well," said Gudrun having felt great sorrow and discontent for Alex.

Gudrun stood watch as the rain and wind grew and the lighting and thunder became more frequent and intense, casting its light out on the sea of trees below them and along the mountainside.

"What was he doing out here alone, and from Stormgarden no less?" said Gudrun quietly under his breath while looking down at the dead warrior, wondering if they would survive the remainder of the night.

The light from the fire was not far now, as Alex kept a hand against the wall which guided her through that passageway which soon revealed a larger room with a fire along one of the walls. The cold, wet and heavy rain pelted the top of her hood and shoulders and as she lifted her eyes up, she could see a large opening above her. She waited there and with each flash of lighting she could see a passageway leading up out of the mountain where dark, slow-moving clouds hid the bright nights sky.

It was not long before she noticed where she was, it was the lair of some wretched beast. The air reeked of rotting flesh and a more sinister stench of death and decay came from the passageway above her.

"What an awful place, what rotten luck," said Alex to herself as she moved across the room, inching towards the fire.

There she found a man on the ground who was injured but alive.

"Help…me," cried the injured man as he gasped for air.

Badly beaten and with a shattered body, he reached out and grabbed Alex with a pale and bruised face.

"We have to get out of here…there's a monster," he moaned in pain.

Alex looked around and saw several large bones scattered around the room and a horde of treasure which contained weapons and armor, gold, and glistening gemstones of various types. Some of the weapons and armors were too large for mere men and she took these to be from the ancient giants who once roamed these lands and further east of the great mountains.

The injured man tried to sit up, but he couldn't and as Alex tried to pick the man up, a dark shadow was cast down from the opening above them. Alex turned to see a figure that resembled a man but much larger; it was crawling on its hands and legs, coming down from the passageway above. Naked and bound with muscle, its voice was low, deep, and roared through the cave.

"Have you come for the spoils yourself or to dine with us tonight?" it said as it walked hunched over towards the fire.

It looked like a giant, but its head was unproportionally large compared to the rest of it. It wore no clothes but had hair like the main of a lion which was grey and silver. Alex could see its silhouette in the light of the fire as it sat down facing away from them and was eating something on the ground in front of the fire.

"I seek to pass, if you'll permit me, nothing more," said Alex as she slowly stood up and began to survey the cave.

There was a passageway leading down, but it was opposite of the fire and there was no way to pass the creature. Gudrun and the others quietly crept into the large hollow part of the cave and as they saw the creature, Gudrun motioned for Alex to run to them as to flee the cave knowing the creature could not fit in that narrow passageway leading out. Alex stared back at Gudrun and without saying a word, slowly opened her cloak to unveil her bow.

She slowly and quietly took out the bow and prepared an arrow when the creature shouted, "Leave if you must," with its deep voice that resonated throughout the cave, "but have a taste of what you shall become!" and upon this it threw something at Alex which sent her flying back and against the wall.

Alex laid stunned on the ground, looking at the half-eaten body of a man that was thrown at her. Not a moment later the creature stood up, turned and with great speed charged Alex on its hands and legs. Crawling in a most terrifying manner, Alex could see the whites in its huge eyes and the dark silhouette given off by the fire.

"I have killed man and beast, demon and giant, and the ancient evils of old. I have survived your predecessor and I will survive you!" it screamed a most horrific scream which was deafening as the sound vibrated throughout the entire cave.

Alex and the company covered their ears as the noise was unbearable. Seeing her time was short and no room to escape its dash, Alex let an arrow loose and struck the creature in its right eye, but it was unphased. It stood up and nearly reached the ceiling and continued to charge. Alex let loose another arrow striking its left eye which sent it into a rage. It began charging wildly as Alex slipped away, dragging the injured man towards the fire and away from the creature.

Gudrun pushed Reis back into the narrow passageway along with Ødger and circled around the back of the creature. With his enormous sword he struck a blow straight through the creature's calf and upon removing his sword, blood gushed out like the opening of a flood gate. It turned to face Gudrun and with a scream it reached out only to be met with a hack and slash from Gudrun, severing some of its fingers.

Unexpectedly the creature fled up and out of the cave through the large opening. Alex and Gudrun were breathing heavily from the battle as it was short and intense. They had never seen or heard of a creature like this before. While watching the creature flee from the battle, Gudrun wiped the sweat from his brow as Alex put her bow and arrows back inside her cloak and went to tend to the injured man on the ground. It was still raining heavily and as the lighting flashed outside and down into the room from above, Gudrun could see the creature crawling and knocking bits of rock and stone down as it moved further away from them.

"That was easier than expected. Mighty words from a mighty foe indeed but no match for the great Gudrun!" said Gudrun in jest as Reis and Ødger walked over to see Alex, paying Gudrun no mind.

Gudrun shrugged his shoulders and wiped some blood out of his hair as he was covered in it from the battle.

"We need to carry him, maybe we should take him back to Grom. It is two more days until the nearest settlement, and I doubt we will live through another two nights like this," said Alex as she propped the injured man's head up and let him drink out of a water pouch made from sheep skin.

"We cannot stay here! What if that thing returns!" shouted Ødger as he was very frightened.

It was all too much for him, and he walked over against the wall and began to shake and vomit. Gudrun laughed at him and pulled out a small wine skin. As he began to drink, he threw insults and taunted Ødger.

"Don't worry boy, you have Gudrun to protect you. The great demon slayer is here to stand by your side!" shouted Gudrun and continued to laugh. "If you're in a hurry, lead the way boy," said Gudrun as he threw his now empty wine skin at Ødger, striking him in his head.

"Leave him be," said Alex as she tried to wake up the injured man. The man drifted in and out of consciousness but managed to say a few words.

"We must leave, for when we arrived there were several of the creatures. My son was with me, a strong youth carrying a Warhammer and a shield, is he here?" he questioned in a worrisome manner.

Alex and Gudrun looked at one another remembering the body they found upon entering the cave a short time ago but remained silent.

"There's a passageway leading down, we can take it back to our encampment," the injured man said as he began to lose consciousness. "In the water…follow it…down to," said the man as his blood-stained head tiled back, and his dark brown eyes closed.

Alex stood up and fashioned a torch from the branches and twigs in the fire. They walked over to the dark passageway which seemed to lead down and peered inside. It was a very steep and slippery path leading downwards along the caves edge and the torch did very little in providing light. It was very cold, pitch black and they felt a light wind rising from below.

"Sounds like the rush of water," said Alex and she threw the torch down below them which revealed some light rapids at the bottom of what seemed to be a long vertical shaft.

"Beware, its slippery here. Let us move down to see if theres a way out, come on one by one," said Alex as the others approached. "Stay along the edge, it's a sheer and sudden drop should you miss your step," said Alex again as she encouraged the party to follow.

Alex went first, followed by Ødger, Reis and Gudrun last carrying the injured man behind them.

"Gudrun, can you hand me a torch? I cannot see a thing," said Alex as she stood there in complete darkness listening to the faint sound of rushing water below, feeling the wind and the cold chill of that dark place.

As Gudrun placed the injured man on the ground and walked out into the dark, putrid room where the battle had commenced, he grabbed some wood from the fire to fashion a torch. It was eerily silent, and he was full of trepidation and dread by the lack of sound. Just at that moment, a creature crawled down out of that large opening in the room, followed by another, and another. Gudrun slowly stepped back and away with a torch in his hand and drawing his sword, he saw the figures of five large creatures in the same likeness of the others they had fought.

"What's taking him so long?" said Ødger to Reis and Alex. "Gudrun are you there!" he shouted.

Gudrun turned toward the shouting and when he turned around towards those towering, menacing, fearsome creatures, they turned to him. They were as tall as the room which was quite large. Some with dark eyes and some with bright eyes that seemed to glow there in the dark. They let out a howl and roar and threw their arms in the air and stamped the cold earthen dirt beneath them. They charged Gudrun and before he could take another step, he was slammed against the ground and slid back down into that small passageway.

As he slid in, he collided with Reis, and she lost her footing on the narrow, slippery ledge. She let out a panicked scream as she plunged down below, into the dark. Her scream echoed and soon became faint, followed by a large splash.

"No choice, jump!" shouted Alex as she quickly leapt off the narrow ledge into the water below.

Ødger was frozen with fear as Gudrun climbed to his feet and raised his great sword. The passageway leading in from the creature's den was not large enough for the creatures to follow but they reached in and clawed toward Gudrun. Those monstrous fists slammed against the smooth, porous side of the cave knocking stone and rubble loose as they reached out to grasp Gudrun. He raised his sword above his head and with a downward slash he struck blow after blow against those rock-hard monstrous fists.

He laughed, shouting, "Back for more! One against five are good odds. Come, let us finish what we started!" as he laughed hysterically.

He glanced toward Ødger who was shaking with fear looking at the injured man who was resting motionless on the narrow ledge. One of the creatures stuck its head inside and Gudrun dashed to the side to avoid being devoured by its bite. He navigated that narrow ledge and some of the earthen stone gave away beneath his feat, crumbling down into the water.

The creature's head was as tall as Gudrun. It chomped and tried to bite at him with every breath. It had dark red, piercing eyes which glowed like embers in a night's fire. Its hair wild and untamed like a feral beast. It was fierce and full of rage, and when it cried out, it had the voice of a child. Gudrun stood face to face with it, just out of reach of its jagged, serrated fangs.

"You come seeking treasures and fame, but all you have found is doom and ruin! It comes with an unquenchable thirst, driven by the madness from within, it will consume you all! It has already begun, you only hasten its plan! The blood you have shed brings its return! For it is in the mist that men's heart will fail them, and we will rise again to devour this world. Three of seven are free and soon it will return!" the creatures exclaimed with crazed eyes that locked onto Gudrun's.

Gudrun raised his great sword and with several blows he removed the creature's head. Its head rolled off the ledge into the deep, dark, watery depths below. The blood from the creature's body poured out like a cascading waterfall and its very blood gave off a bright glow as it gushed and flowed over the ledge and down into the water beneath them.

Gudrun picked up the injured man and carefully looked down. He could hear the giant splash from the creature's head entering the water, and at this, he pushed the frozen stiff Ødger over the ledge and jumped down to the icy waters below to seek out the fate of Alex and Reis.

4   DREAMS OF SHADOWS AND MIST

The water was ice cold, and it pulled the air from her lungs as it thrashed her around in the darkness. Alex could not see anything; it was pitch black and the only light seemed to come from far above her as she drifted further and further down through the cave. The frigid water turned into faster moving rapids and Alex was helpless against the current. The water flung her into the side of the cave and as she desperately tried to cling to its walls, the water lifted and slammed her against the jagged, sharp rocks and pierced her side. Alex bellowed in agony as the current pulled her head under the water and she struggled to keep above the fast, swift current.

The current swept her down deeper under the water, and in that moment, she was blinded by a bright flash of light that pulsated. She gasped for air but reached the water's surface only to find herself on a great plain overlooking a great, charred chasm.

"What is this place?" she questioned aloud as she turned around to see the sun rise and fall in the distance in quick succession.

Day turned to night instantly, giving rise to a magnificent moon which glowed white in the nights sky. Alex could see the stars brighter than she ever has, and the horizon went on endlessly in every direction. The wind roared and howled, and the nights sky was filled with lighting and thunder. The moon turned red, and the lighting intensified as Alex looked around in astonishment as she began to walk to the chasms edge. In the distance, far across the chasm, several lights appeared.

"Am I dreaming?" she wondered aloud as she looked across the great, charred chasm.

She knelt at the chasms edge as she peered out into the darkness. This place was devoid of all light, save from the bright glow of the moon, the twinkling sparkle of the stars above and the thunderous flashes of lighting which lit the sky in all directions endlessly.

There in the pitch black, seven figures appeared, all cloaked in shadow and mist. They were larger than any man and a terrifying sight. Alex soon began to hear whispers and she was reminded of the dreadful place some years ago that haunted her day and night. At each whisper, the mist and shadow around each figure gave way and revealed them, only for them to be shrouded in mist and shadow when they went silent.

A whisper came from one of them as it turned and gazed at Alex. It stood taller than any man, had the body of a man but the face of a lion and the horns of a ram. Its face was scared, and its fur was wild and white as snow. It had several arms, each large and powerful. It continued to whisper and as its deep sunken black eyes gazed at Alex, it turned to the figure next to it. As it went silent, it was cloaked with shadow and mist, and another began to speak.

This figure was greater in stature and appeared to be floating in the air. It had two large wings, but one had been severed near its shoulder. Its remaining wing had several layers of feathers with different shades of blue, black, purple, red, and grey. It stretched its wing out and spoke with the figure next to it. Its whisper echoed throughout the dark plain and Alex was in awe but fearful as she clutched her sword. Its face was that of a skeleton and as it continued to whisper, its whole body was revealed to be that of a skeleton. It wore a crown of glistening gemstones that were pleasant to the eye and soothing to the soul.

As this figure ceased to whisper and was engulfed by shadows and mist, another figure began to whisper. As the mist drifted from its body, it resembled a large bear with wings. Its wings were burned and charred, covered in ash and soot. It stood up on its hind legs and let out a terrifying and deafening roar towards Alex. Unlike a bear, it had no fur and was muscle bound with large dark eyes and ferocious fangs.

The fourth figure began to whisper, and immediately all the others fixed their gaze on it. It was shrouded in mist and shadow and as it began to whisper, what was revealed was a beautiful woman. Flawless and unblemished, she was the most beautiful woman Alex had ever laid eyes on. She was dressed in a fine robe with a hooded cloak. She held a great sword of magnificent design; the blade glowed and changed colors as she pointed it towards Alex, and the hilt was decorated with gemstones of the color she has never seen before.

Now there was a fifth figure which whispered, yet its shadow and mist remained. Alex could not see its face, nor its body. As it whispered, the shadow and mist hid a body which glowed of different colors, and it flashed and pulsated like bright lightning in a dark sky. Upon this, the sixth figure receded into the distance and the remaining figures followed suit. Each of them moved further away, into the distance until Alex lost sight of them.

The seventh figure remained however and when it whispered, the mist and shadow revealed a figure of a man who laid on the ground injured. Its whisper gave way to words and with a shout it called to Alex, but she could not understand it. The seventh figure said no more, and it was slowly concealed in the shadows and mist. It began to recede toward the horizon until its light could no longer been seen.

Alex had never seen anything like this before, yet the great chasm seemed familiar. She stood there, staring into the distance for quite some time pondering the mystery of what had taken place. She thought back to that horrible day, the day Chieftain Grom was injured and her journey into that dark abyss full of woe and despair.

"Why can't I remember what happened? Where is my father!" she lamented as she gazed up at the stars. "Better to fight and fall than to live without hope," she repeated to herself over and over. "What did my father mean? Why can't I remember?" said Alex to herself in frustration as the night slowly turned back into day and she began to recognize a familiar voice.

5   THE EXILES

"Alex!" someone cried from out across the chasm.

Alex moaned in pain and clutched her side. Gudrun stood over her as she was lying in bed. Reis and Ødger rose from the fire and knelt next to Alex. Gudrun leaned over Alex and removed her hand from her wound to see that it was still bleeding but the stitches were still intact.

"Finally, your awake. It's a nasty wound, but you've had worse," said Gudrun with a laugh and a smile. "Rest now, were safe here," he said as he knelt by her side.

He held her hand and brushed her hair away from her face. Alex tried to sit up but screamed sharply while examining her side. She was battered and bruised but otherwise in good health. She put her other hand on her head as she had a severe headache.

"I'll go call for some water, I'll be right back," said Reis as she stood up and removed the animal hide hatch and exited the large tent.

Ødger was sitting next to a young man who had a few odd supplies and was washing his hands in a bowl of water. The young man came closer to Alex and examined her wound.

"It will heal nicely, I'll check on you a bit later. You must be hungry, I will send for some food," the young man said and exited the tent.

Alex rubbed her eyes and stretched out, watching Gudrun stand and drink some mead from a cup across the room and warm himself by the fire. Alex, now awake and aware, looked around to find herself in some type of makeshift yurt.

It was a structure that consisted of several pieces of wood which were crossed and fastened together which supported a large animal skin roof. There was a small hatch which was made of wool felt on the side which allowed entry in and out. In the center, there was a hole in the roof which ventilated the room, along with a stove that Gudrun was standing next to. The stove was ablaze with a fire, but it was cold here. Much colder than expected given they were approaching the winter but not yet in it.

"Where are we, and what happened?" asked Alex as she rubbed her eyes and nursed her wound.

Gudrun was warming his hands in front of the fire and eating a few pieces of cheese with fruit and bread. There was an animal caraccas hung next to him and he used a small knife to cut a piece of meat off and eat it.

"Hard to say, but we seemed to wash up along the river leading out of the mouth of the mountain. It seems these people found Reis pulling you onto the river's edge. I saw them when I swam down with Ødger and they brought us here to mend your wound. Some here say it's an ancient fortress while others say it was an ancient city when giants roamed these lands, but it looks like an ancient ruin to me. Carved straight out of the mountains face, they have been hiding here," replied Gudrun while letting out a large burp.

Gudrun walked away from the fire and sat on a small wooden chair, but it broke and shattered as he sat in it. Seemingly unphased, he sat on the ground which was covered in various animal furs as he ate some of the food that had been brought for Alex some time ago. Alex stared at Gudrun, and Gudrun could tell that something had been bothering her.

"Having bad dreams again? You have been yelling out in your sleep. Something about your father and seven figures in the dark," said Gudrun as he ate food, picking out pieces that were stuck in his beard.

Alex turned away and didn't reply. Her dream seemed too real, more like a memory than a dream.

"How long have I been out for?" asked Alex as she stretched and rolled to her side with slight pain.

She examined her wound; it was a deep and above her hip.

"It has been a few days, and you have that young man to thank. Did not leave your side that one, a fine healer I'd say," said Gudrun as he picked his teeth with the small knife.

"Theres another issue, one of a more pressing matter," said Gudrun as he stood up and folded his arms.

"Since our arrival, people have gone missing or found dead and they suspect one of us is responsible. Reis pulled you from the river's edge and you were at deaths door. The injured man we saved inside the cave came from their encampment. For saving his life, they agreed to grant us safe passage and a place for you to rest while your injury healed," said Gudrun while licking his lips and cutting another piece of meat from the hanging animal carcass.

"These killings though, they have aroused suspicion and we are not welcome here anymore. I fought and killed one of those foul beasts from within the cave and they are worried our actions will bring more of those creatures out to destroy them," said Gudrun as he handed Alex her clothes from the edge of the bed along with her weapons and armor.

"Where is Reis and Ødger?" asked Alex as she slowly stood up with the help of Gudrun.

Gudrun told Alex to get dressed and meet him outside. He exited the tent through the small animal hide hatch, pondering the cryptic last words of the creature he killed as Alex in turn wondered about the dream she had.

There was shouting and screaming as Alex exited the tent. She looked up and saw the creatures head, whom Gudrun had slain, stuck on top of several large pikes for all to see. It was a frightening sight and several people stood in awe at the size of it. Reis and Ødger were there as Gudrun motioned for Alex to join them as a large crowd gathered around them. They came out of their yurts and tents as they circled Alex and her company.

Among the crowd was a fierce man in solid black armor. He wore a black chest plate which covered his torso. His arms were exposed, tattooed, and looked powerful. In his left hand he carried a bearded axe and a small black shield in the other. He had a black battle skirt made of leather which covered his thighs, and his greaves were solid black as well. He had short hair, a long beard and he wore a dark red cloak which hung around his neck. He was an intimidating sight and as he walked through the crowd, people gave way to him.

"I'm called Zain, leader of these brave men!" the man exclaimed as the crowd cheered and roared in excitement.

"We are grateful to you for bringing our man back to us, but we know one of you is not what they seem. For each night you have been here, some of our men have been slain and we have hidden here for quite some time living in peace and without drawing attention to ourselves. We pulled your woman from the river when she was at deaths door. This is the thanks you give us?" shouted Zain and he glared at Alex.

He stood before the four of them, walking up to each of them before moving on to the next.

"These are troubling times, but perhaps we can come to an agreement," said Zain as he walked back towards the crowd as they cheered again and shouted.

Alex grabbed Gudrun as she lost balance and was in pain from her wound. She looked around and indeed it was an ancient ruin from times unknown. The entire city was carved right into the very mountain. The shapes and figures of giants were carved into the rock, with many large passageways leading into the mountain but none dared to enter. The encampment itself was on a large ledge that jutted out away from the ancient city and it was there that they raised a great many yurts and tents as an encampment.

There were numerous tents scattered around, in a similar fashion to the one she had been resting in with small fires here and there along with several animal hides which were tanning alongside the tents and yurts. There were several horses tied up throughout the encampment but very little grass for them to feed on, for it was a large rocky overlook.

"These killings are lowering moral and raising fear in the hearts of these brave men. You see, we do not get much in the ways of entertainment up here apart from raiding the southern kingdoms and hunting the beasts in the forbidden forest. Tomorrow you four will fight and should you survive, your free to go," said Zain which brought on more cheering and shouting from the crowd.

Alex took in the cool evening air as the crowd dispersed back into their tents while several people remained to observe the creature's head.

"Take rest, for tomorrow we will see if you are brave warriors of renowned or spies from the southern kingdoms!" shouted Ziad as he glared at Ødger.

Alex, Gudrun, Reis and Ødger all went inside their tent as some men from the encampment brought more animal furs for them to rest on. Gudrun was in good spirits but Ødger looked nervous and fearful for he was no warrior. There were eight men, heavily armed carrying sword and spears, who would remain outside to make sure they did not attempt to escape. Alex went inside and slowly sat down, knowing she was in no shape for a duel in the morning.

"You look surprisingly cheerful given our circumstances," said Alex to Gudrun as he sat down in a corner and sharpened his sword.

Ødger was talking with Reis on the other side of the room as Gudrun glanced at them and then answered Alex.

"Demon slayer, giant slayer, and now I'll be known as the Exile slayer. My fame grows with each passing day!"

said Gudrun as he chuckled and continued to sharpen his sword.

"Exile slayer?" asked Alex as she laid down in bed and examined her stitches.

She had slept the better part of a week and was still tired, fatigued, and weak. She glanced at Reis and Ødger to see them sitting and talking, no doubt about what peril they would find themselves at dawns first light.

"These men, they are a part of the Exile Legion from the last war. The war and the drought that followed, with crops destroyed and the kingdoms in financial ruin from a war that raged longer than it should, there was no money to pay most of the soldiers who fought. Refugees started turning up in neighboring kingdoms which made matters worse. It was then that the Exile Legion was born, mostly peasant soldiers but some renowned warriors among them like Zain. They oppose the kingdoms and especially the nobility, for they have lost their trust in them and seek to cause a rebellion," said Gudrun while sharpening his sword and gliding his finger along the side of the blade.

"Nothing more than bandits, thieves, and thugs now though. They survive by attacking trading and supply caravans, kidnappings, and extortion. That Zain though, he was the leader of Stormgarden's military," said Gudrun as he put his sword down and put more twigs and logs in the stove which would give off heat for several hours into that dark, cold night.

Reis and Ødger came closer and sat on the edge of the bed Alex was resting in. They called Gudrun over and began to whisper, not to alert the guards who were right outside their tent.

"I think it would be wise we try to escape during the night," said Reis. "We could take our chances in the forbidden forest below or take the river to the west to the seaside settlements. Let us not forget why we are here, to reach the northern settlements to seek out with certainty if this great evil has returned. Indeed, with the appearance of the Vollgarim and those foul creatures inside the great mountains, much evil is at work, but we must continue on," said Reis with great authority while looking back and forth between the company and at the hatch of the tent.

"That's more than you've spoken this entire journey," said Gudrun as he leaned in closer to her and smiled. "Spoken like the daughter of a great chieftain," he said as he and Reis began to discuss how they should escape, and which route would be safer to venture further north.

Gudrun suggested they enter the mountains through the ancient city, but Reis protested. Ødger sat quietly but listened carefully for he had no interest in fighting in the morning against their battle-hardened captors.

Alex eyed Reis carefully and thought of her and poor, fearful Ødger. He was far from home and out of place, and she remembered a time before she herself had been tainted and scared with war and its horrors. Her mind drifted back to those times of peace and merriment, but she was a long way from home. She wondered, was it still possible to reach the shore and sail across the sea? Would she find her people there in the great forests and on the gentle rolling plains or had the terror that casted its shadow from the north indeed end her peoples, save those who escaped across the sea like herself.

"Perhaps I can reason with Zain, for he fought side by side with my uncle in the north. Look around you, they live like frightened cattle here upon the mountains face. They are starving here, dying here. I wager the northern settlements are all but destroyed in the likeness of Stormgarden. With the mist and no traders venturing forth across the lands, they will not survive this coming winter and indeed its chill can be felt already," said Alex as she leaned up and took the soup which was handed to her from Gudrun.

The soup was served in a small wooden bowl with ingredients you may find in most of the eastern settlements. It was goat meat, still on the bone in a hearty broth. It had several herbs in it along with carrots, onions, celery, rosemary, black pepper, and lemon juice. It was very refreshing, and Alex ate it hastily as she was famished. Gudrun eyed her with a smile, peering into the bowl as he smiled at the others. His belly growled and he went to cut another piece of meat from the animal carcass hanging near the brick stove.

"They are not hiding here, they are trapped! He only seeks to raise his men's spirits before they themselves try to flee this most barren wasteland," said Alex as she leaned back down with a sigh as her side ached with each breath she took.

"We must push north, but I don't see any way we can escape," said Alex.

Exhausted and weary, Alex slept as the late afternoons sun shined brightly on those towering, snowcapped mountains. They were jagged, sharp, and went on as far as the eye could see from east to west, as the golden sun casted a shadow down on the forbidden forest below them.

Reis was visibly angered at the decision to stay and fight, as was Ødger for he knew he would be no match for a seasoned warrior. Gudrun was in high spirits and seeing them distraught, said "fear not, for Alex is cunning and should her words fail, my sword will fly on your behalf."

They were comforted at this and as they spoke, the young man who tended to Alex's wound entered with a small group of warriors who carried some food and drink. Gudrun took a large, wooden cup of mead from one of the men and Reis and Ødger sat next to one another on a bed with a bowl of fruit, cheese, bread, and lamb meat.

The group of warriors were all heavily armored in blood-stained chainmail and carried spears. They eyed Gudrun warily and carefully. As they left, the young man who was dressed plainly stayed behind and inspected Alex's wound without waking her. He applied some type of green, glossy paste and said, "There, it should heal by sunrise. Is it true you are Gudrun of Grom?" he asked as he turned to face Gudrun.

"You've heard of me?" asked Gudrun as he took the portion of food that was brought for Alex and began to eat.

"We all have, for it was you who saved a great many of us in the battle of Kazulgard some years ago. I remember it, for in those days the land was in perpetual darkness. There in the winter months, the sun shines but for a few hours of the day. A troubling time indeed as those from the Frozen Wastes entered our lands. I tended to your Chieftain Grom when he was ravaged by those beasts," the young man said as he closed his eyes and thought back to a time of war.

"Yes, I remember it well. In truth it was Alex, for I arrived sometime late in the day. You owe your life to her. She was there from the beginning and ventured into the dark abyss with the bravest on that day," said Gudrun as he stood up and paced the room.

"Kazulgard? Near the Frozen Wastes?" asked Ødger as he stood up and walked over to the young man. "My name is Ødger, and I'm from one of the southern kingdoms. They say the battle of Kazulgard took place on the high plains, beyond the raised cliffs of Stromgarden. There where nothing grows, and the land is twisted and corrupted. They say there's a great ruin there and beyond that you can find the Frozen Wastes which no man dares enter," said Ødger as he knelt down near the man while he tended to Alex.

"My name is Katla, and yes, you are correct. In those days we gathered at Stormgarden and marched into the great plain. It was there that Chieftain Grom was injured, and I took care of him and a great company of those who fought and were wounded. Many men here fought in that battle and returned to Stromgarden thereafter. You may even find some men form the southern kingdom as well," said Katla as he pressed too hard into Alex's side and caused her to flinch.

Alex awoke and pushed the wolf skin animal hide off her and rolled over on her side to face them. She rubbed her eyes and pushed her hair away from her face. The guards outside called for Katla to move along and he stood up and bid them farewell and luck in the morning battle. The late afternoons sun now dimmed as it casted a great shadow over the encampment. With dusk approaching, Gudrun and Alex shared stories of battle in the far reaches of the north, Ødger told tales of the southern kingdoms and their great cities, yet Reis remained silent and listened.

They all became weary, and soon they fell asleep. It was not long before the shouts and cries of the encampment woke them, and it was Zain to enter the tent first with a great many of warriors. There, Alex and the company were forced out quickly to see a large gathering around them with torches lit and axe and swords drawn. It was dark outside, and the stars were bright beyond measure. They were clustered in a band across the sky accompanied by brilliant clouds in the heavens. Dark purple and shades of blue highlighted the clouds, and the darkness masked the forest and mountains on the horizon.

"Murderers!" many of the warriors shouted as Zain stood with his axe and shield in front of them in a small clearing.

The guards who had been placed outside their tent all had their throats cut and their blood stained the ground. How could eight heavily armored guards have been slain like this?

Alex wondered as she stood and leaned against Gudrun. The wind was fierce, and the fire of the torches danced and swayed with each passing gust.

"Wait!" shouted Alex at the crowd who was most agitated. "We are not your enemy. We seek to travel to the north, for an ancient evil has returned to these lands. Surely you have noticed the rise of the mist and have no doubt been forced to move by day and shelter here on these high mountains at night. We have come from Grom and have not heard from the northern settlements for some time. We saved your man in the depths of the mountains from an unspeakable terror. Why would we slay you and your men with each passing night?" said Alex as the crowd quieted and calmed down as they began to look at one another.

"The Vollgarim have returned! You are not safe here, join us and travel north," Alex suggested as the gathering now went silent and talked amongst themselves for all knew of the Vollgarim and their plight, yet not all believed in them.

Zain was not convinced and shouted back, his voice pierced the air and echoed within the ancient city's depths.

"Lies! You are spies from the southern kingdoms. That one there, Ødger, some of us know of him. He is the prince of Durga!" shouted Zain as the circle of men around them closed in closer and they pointed their spears towards Alex and his company.

"The king of Durga cared little for the north peoples who fought to protect their lands in the last war. They hunt us now as if we are traitors. Ødger, the Prince of Durga with his fine clothes and his forked tongue, tonight he will reap what his kingdom has sown!" shouted Zain and at this he charged at Ødger with his axe.

Alex, who was in great pain from the wound in her side and struggled against the harsh wind to stand up, lunged toward Ødger knocking him to the side and met Zain's axe with her short sword. The two exchanged blows as some of the crowd charged Gudrun only to be met with a cleave of his sword. Several charged through the circle of spears and Gudrun picked them up with ease and casted them back into the crowd. Ødger crawled on the ground seemingly back into the tent but was met with a line of spears that pushed him back in the center with Alex and Gudrun. Reis was unphased and moved behind Gudrun with each step he made.

"Let us pass, I'm warning you!" said Alex to Zain as they traded blow for blow.

Zain was intent on killing her, but Alex would parry and riposte his attacks, deflecting all that she could without making a move to injure Zain. The nights sky suddenly filled with clouds and the brightness of the moon was dimmed.

"My uncle saved your life, what honor is there in killing his niece?" shouted Alex as she glared at him.

Zain, not being able to land a blow and seeing that Alex would not engage him, attempted to throw his bearded axe and strike Gudrun in the back. Reis cried out in seeing this and in that moment, Alex struck a blow to Zains left hand which severed it. It lied motionless on the floor as Zain let out a cry which startled all the warriors around him. The fighting ceased for a moment as Gudrun came to help Alex stand as she was hunched over, clutching her side which had begun to bleed.

It was at that moment that something happened which they did not expect. A rolling thunder came from deep within the ancient city. It echoed there in the depths of the mountains and out of the great halls which were carved into the mountain side. Mist crept slowly at first and then poured out covering the encampment. In total, there was some three hundred brave warriors, and the mist engulfed them like a wave at sea.

Alex peered into the darkness and waved the mist away from her face. She could barely see a few paces in front of her. The only light was from the stars above and the torches that the warrior held fast to, scattered around her.

At first it was a terrifying scream, and then a painful shout followed by several other moans and groans of despair. Zain was standing a few paces away from Alex, holding his arm below the wrist where Alex had landed a swift blow. Katla rushed to Zains side through the mist and tended to his wound.

"You've brought death and ruin to us all!" said Zain as Katla wrapped and bound his arm at the wrist with some fabric and cloth.

There in the darkness someone cried out, "Flee! It's the Vollgarim," and not a moment later several descended upon Zain and Katla.

Gudrun dashed in and with a swing of his sword he cut the head off one. It rolled along the dusty ground to Alex's feet, and she could see its razor-sharp fangs and large tongue sticking out of its mouth. It's tongue still flickered this way and that and its mouth tried to bite at Alex. Its bright, glowing red eyes slowly turned to black like a coal that had been extinguished.

Several more Vollgarim leapt through the mist as the shouts and screams of the warriors filled the cold nights air. Their torches provided the only glimpse of these creatures, as they casted their shadows in all directions. Gudrun slayed a great many but to no avail, they encircled him. Alex pulled back the strings of her bow and struck several of them that pursued Gudrun. Some arrows would pierce their skin while others would ricochet off, for they had scales strong as iron in some places along their body.

They soon heard a great crackling and rumble along the mountain side. One of the carvings along the mountainside gave way. It was the figure of a giant and it broke away from the mountains face and shattered on the ground below. Out came a monstrous creature of the likes that Gudrun had slain inside the mountain. One followed by several others as they poured out and the monstrous horde was seen by all as they fought the Vollgarim and feared for their lives.

"What evil is this! Flee men! Run for your lives!" cried Zain as he and Katla turned to face Alex and the company.

Alex called out for Gudrun to join them, and Gudrun slashed and hacked his way back towards Alex, but his sword and Alex's bow would prove too little for the enormous horde of the Vollgarim. They fell upon them, and Gudrun and Alex were pinned down on the ground and helpless against the myriad of Vollgarim.

Reis removed the ribbon from her hair as she stood and looked upon the encroaching horde of Vollgarim, followed by the monstrous creatures from within the mountain. Her hair flowed and swayed in the violent wind and in her eyes, a raging tempest formed. The necklace which hung from her neck began to shine and pulsate magnificent shades of blue, red, and orange. The light pushed back the mist which revealed the battle which had waged on under the concealment of the mist. Reis raised her hands in the air and flashes of lighting filled the sky.

She called down lighting that struck the Vollgarim. The lightning bolts crashed and burned them as they screeched and wailed. Alex and Gudrun were able to stand and rushed to her side. They were amazed as nothing like this had been seen or heard of. She turned to them, and with a storm in her eyes, she continued to rain bolts of lightning down onto the battlefield.

"Hurry, we must flee! Get the horses!" said Zain as Katla had already begun to gather a few, although they jumped and neighed at the flashes and sound of the lighting and thunder.

Katla and Zain mounted one horse together while Alex and Gudrun began to mount their own.

"Where is Ødger?" said Alex as the horses began rearing on their hindlegs in excitement and fright.

They were so frightful they nearly broke away from Alex and the other riders. Ødger could not be found anywhere as they shouted out his name and looked for him.

"Reis, what are you doing! What sorcery is this!" shouted Gudrun as Zain and Katla cried out to the warriors to flee and escape into the dense forest below.

The Vollgarim continued to pour out of the great hallways that were caved and etched into the mountainside, all the while Reis held them at bay as their jagged, scaled bodies had begun to pile high on top of one another.

"I will find Ødger, follow the river from whence we came. Meet us where the river breaks to the east and west," she exclaimed with bolts of lightning in her eyes.

Zain and Katla told the others there are a few concealed passageways leading down away from the encampment to the river, should they be able to reach them.

"We shall meet you there, don't delay!" said Alex and she and the others began to push their horses through the Vollgarim.

They reached out to claw and bite them as they passed, but Reis smote the Vollgarim with bolts of lightning which fell from the dark sky.

"Here! Follow me," said Zain as he and Katla led Alex and Gudrun down away from the encampment and through the mist until they met the river's edge.

The river had many curves, bends, and turns and they travelled alongside it for a rather lengthy time. Soon its edge was rocky with large stones, and they turned and followed it through the tree line. The forest was thick here, and their pace slowed. After some time, they came to a point where the river broadens and flattens at the base of the mountains, and they rested awhile.

Zain moaned in agony as the cloth and fabric which bound his wounded hand had turned from a dark red to a light brown. Zain dismounted his horse as Katla tied it to a large tree so he could tend to his wounded hand. Gudrun walked his horse alongside Alex as they looked out across the river. The water reflected the bright stars in the cool nights sky and the reflection of the trees was casted along the shore.

"What do you make of it?" said Gudrun as his horse neighed and steam rose from its mouth.

The air was frigid, and Gudrun shivered against the cold. The river was calm here, and in its shallow depths he could see stones of various colors. Some shades of white, red, blue, orange, green, teal, and grey. Gudrun plunged his sword into the soft, earthy floor in front of them, and while holding onto his horse, he grabbed a small stone and skipped it across the river. The stone hit the calm, slow flowing water and bounced across its surface several times in quick, rapid succession before it sank under the surface. Gudrun rubbed and stroked his horse along its neck, ears and head and it calmed down here in the silent, darkness of the forests edge. It drank from the water's edge and neighed softly, and Gudrun patted it along the side to raise its spirits.

"I think I can do better, what do you wager I can skip my stone further than yours?" said Alex with a straight face as she looked at Gudrun.

"No, what I meant was," said Gudrun as Alex interrupted him.

"I know what you meant," said Alex with a smile.

She examined her horse to find that it had several pouches and drinking horns which hung from its saddle. She tossed one of the drinking horns to Gudrun and he began to drink.

It was the horn from some type of cattle, measuring the length from elbow to wrist and was curved, polished and smooth.

"The Vollgarim and the creatures which poured out of the mountain like a demon horde, the forbidden forest which is fabled to have creatures that appear out of thin air and claim men's souls, or Reis whom we've known as a child who conjured lightning from the very heavens," said Alex as she shook her head back and forth with tight lips.

"Few eyes have seen and less ears have heard of such mystery and terror," said Alex as she looked on to Zain and Katla.

"I will get a fire going. There is no mist here, we should be safe. Keep an eye out for Reis and Ødger," said Katla as he tied up their horses to a large tree and began to search for branches and twigs.

He took the axe which belonged to Zain and set off into the forest. They could hear the rustle of leaves and twigs snap underneath him as Katla walked briskly through the darkness until he disappeared from their sight. His eyes were wide open and darted this way and that as he ventured forth.

Zain sat on the moss-covered ground and leaned against a large oak tree. He took several heavy breaths, then leaned his head back and closed his eyes as it began to rain. The sky was bright with slow moving clouds that uncovered a bright, glowing crescent moon and a sparkling sky.

Alex loved to gaze up at the stars and enjoyed her time in the far reaches of the north where the sky would glow magnificent shades of green. Like a great serpent that slowly slithered and squirmed across the sky, she would lay on the frozen ground covered in animal furs with the warmth of a fire nearby and fix her gaze up towards the heavens at this sight. Indeed, the starlight north of Stormgarden was a sight to be seen and traders and caravans from the south would marvel at the nights sky.

Gudrun and Alex laid down across from Zain, for they were tired from the midnights battle. Alex checked her wound and she winced in pain as she tried to get comfortable along the mossy ground. Gudrun leaned against a fallen tree as he eyed Zain who was fast asleep.

First it drizzled, then the rain seemed to all but empty from the clouds in a fast and abrupt torrent. They sat there quietly, resting as the pitter-patter of the rain relaxed their mind and calmed their nerves. The large, dense raindrops pelted and battered the river, and they were comforted by the pitter-patter that each drop made on the river and on the tree canopy above them.

They were chilled by the rain and the cold nights air. A gentle breeze came from across the river, and they began to wonder when Katla would return, but he didn't. Nor did Reis and Ødger come down from the mountains, down through the mist.

"He has been gone far too long. He will not survive out here, not here in the forbidden forest, alone in the engulfing darkness," said Gudrun as he took another drink from the drinking horn that Alex had given him.

"Neither will we," said Alex and she looked at Zain sleeping motionless against a large, old oak tree. "None of us are in any shape for any more surprises out here tonight," said Alex as she exhaled with a long sigh.

Gudrun stopped drinking and sat up for a moment.

"What do you propose," said Gudrun as he took another drink, this time the ale ran down his beard and onto his armor.

"Why don't we rest here for a little while, and let's see what happens," said Alex as she looked up along the curved river towards the towering, dark, snowcapped mountains in the distance.

The dense, white mist slowly crept down along the river, then into the tree line towards them. They laid there fearful and exhausted, wondering the fate of Reis, Ødger, and Katla. Gudrun and Alex fell fast asleep as the rain intensified and soon the forest was filled with the chirps of crickets and the croaks of frogs.

6   ANCIENT BEAST

Alex slowly awoke as the warm, bright sun shined on her face. She could hear the crackling and snapping of branches and twigs as they gasped for their last breath in the blazing fire behind her. In its warmth, she laid there still and motionless, gazing out at the gentle flow of the river. The colored stones resting at the bottom were even more vibrant, in various shades and hues.

She had nearly forgotten where she was or the great peril she had faced the night before. It was the first night in a long time that she did not dream of dreadful, fearful things. The gentle, soothing chirps and tweets of birds filled the air and a small black bird landed on the ground in front of her.

With a gentle gaze and a turn of its head, the bird chirped quietly towards her. With gleaming feathers, its scaled and rough legs hopped on the mossy ground, and it picked with its sharp beak against the earth. Without warning, it flew to the east and out of sight. As she turned her head, she saw Gudrun standing with Zain who seemed to be in good spirits.

"Always sleeping!" joked Gudrun as he laughed heartily.

He and Zain were drinking from the smooth, curved drinking horns that Alex had found attached to her horse's saddle. They were standing near the fire which raged with fervent heat. Its flickering flames danced and cooked a piece of meat which was hanging above the flames. Gudrun and

Zain were exchanging tales of battle and were discussing some of the events which had taken place after the last war, where Zain had left his position as the military leader of Stormgarden and ventured south with a company of men.

"Always drinking," replied Alex with a grin as she slowly clambered out of the mossy ditch that she had slept in.

To her astonishment, her wound had all but healed as it was sealed shut and the stitches removed. Katla was kneeling over the ground a few paces away tending to Ødger.

"How is he?" asked Alex as she peered over Katla's shoulder.

Ødger was unconscious with some small cuts and bruises but otherwise unharmed.

"Where is Reis? asked Alex as she looked around and through the forest.

In the daylight she could see a vast and deep forest with a great many trees which rose high into the sky and created a canopy where very little light found its way through. The ground was moderately flat and completely covered in soft, green moss. There were large stones scattered here and there and some fallen trees which had all but been smothered by the growing, creeping moss which crawled and consumed the forest floor in all directions. It clung to the ground and climbed the very trees which were all very tall but not wide. A gentle breeze passed through their camp, and they could hear and feel the tiny, wet rain droplets which fell from the canopy above them.

"I saw something out in the forest. Out there in the dark, in the pitchiness of the black," said Katla as he turned away from Ødger to face Alex.

"When I returned from gathering firewood, I found you all asleep. I was too afraid to lite a fire, for it may draw both beasts and demons who would seek to devour us while we slept. I awoke early this morning with a pain in my belly, so I crept back into the forest to hunt whatever I could find. The stag that is cooking on the fire now is enough to fill our stomachs and to raise our spirits. Much to my dismay, I found Ødger here on the ground, cold as ice and stiff as stone," said Katla and then he stood up to cut a piece of meat from the tender stag.

The meat was rich and flavorful in taste and firm to the touch. Katla motioned for Gudrun and Zain that it was ready, and they both cut several pieces of it, continuing to drink and laugh by the fire. They both took their share and ate to their content as they looked around them briefly before returning to their idle chatter.

"They seem to be getting along," said Alex as she felt despair for Zain and the injury he would bear for the remainder of his life.

She took no pleasure in battle, for it was peace and quiet which she longed for. The days of solitude and enjoying the warm sun on her face were beyond her, here in the cold, dark unforgiving north and she wondered what her life would have been had she stayed behind and braved the encroaching darkness that consumed her homeland.

"It's the sword and mead that binds them, as it does with so a great many warriors," said Katla as he passed some meat to Alex who ate it with a nod of gratitude.

"What are you if not warrior," said Alex as the sun shined on her and Katla through the treetops. The rivers current gained strength and she saw small, gentle waves spilling over at the tree line. It was early morning with some frosty dew still along some parts of the ground and a light, misty fog on the opposite side of the river slowly crept down the river.

"I was a healer during the war, although I prefer hunting," said Katla with a nod toward the stag roasting on the fire.

"We come down to hunt here in the forbidden forest, but never this far in. Last night I saw something that looked like a child as I gathered firewood, yet its face was unlike anything I have seen. Its large, bright yellow eyes glowing there in the dark. Several of them appeared, out of the very blackness of night. All in the same likeness, covered in feathers and horns with skin that reflected the moonlight. They are the faceless terrors, the fabled ones from ancient times," said Katla as he began to eat the tender, tasty stag.

Alex looked to Gudrun who was eating and laughing with a drink in hand, but Zain stared at her with threatening eyes. Zain's anger was visibly growing for it was he who marched an army of strong, fierce men who were renowned warriors north of Stormgarden during the war. Their chieftain fell in battle, but it was Alex's uncle who was rewarded as the new Chief, over Zain. Zain left shortly after with a great number of brave men, disheartened and resentful.

"Something you want to say?" asked Alex to Zain who continued to drink with mead spilling down his beard.

His eyes were full of rage, and he glanced at Ødger who was still motionless on the ground.

"You outlanders are not welcome here. Nothing but trouble, you and your peoples from across the sea and that one there, that coward from the south," said Zain who then pointed to Ødger.

"Can't you tell something else is going on here?" replied Alex as she stood up and warmed herself by the fire.

"Do you still suspect it was one of us who killed your men last night, but who also saved your man whom we found battered and injured inside the cave?" said Alex while turning her hands back and forth over the fire.

Sleeping through the night, they were all cold and frozen to their very core. Zain crossed his arms at the rebuke and turned his head away from Alex and the others. Gudrun passed him another drinking horn, which he took and drank hastily. The fire had begun to die down and the once rising flames now turned to a pile of smoldering ash and glowing black and red charred coals.

"It does not matter where we come from. The mist is growing, and something is coming which is beyond any of us. Alone we do not stand a chance Zain, we must stand together against the tide," said Alex as she walked along the soft, green moss towards him.

She picked up his axe which Katla had brought and handed it to Zain. His muscled arm took the axe from her hands and leaned it across his armored chest and over his shoulder.

"What do you propose outlander?" asked Zain, now having a calm demeaner and the fire in his eyes had all but gone out.

The four of them discussed which way to continue and as they did, Ødger woke up screaming loudly and frantically. His body shook and twisted on the ground as Katla rushed to his side. He was confused and disoriented and could not remember what had happened or what had become of Reis. They were all troubled for they knew not what to make of Reis who summoned thunder and lightning to smite the Vollgarim and the monstrous creatures from within the ancient giant's city.

"I don't think we can wait any longer, she should be able to take care of herself," said Alex as they all began to depart.

They picked up their weapons and put on their armor as they untied their horses, some of whom neighed. As Alex untied her horse from around a large tree, it nudged her with its head and leaned in close and breathed on her face. They heard a deep rumbling noise and a loud crack like a distant thunder, but it was coming from underneath them, deep within the earth.

"They don't call this the forbidden forest for nothing," said Gudrun and before any of them could mount their horses, the river turned to rapids and grew to a fierce speed.

The very ground shook and vibrated, and some trees gave way and fell over into the rushing river. The horses were startled and reared into the air. The ground along the shore gave way and one of the horses fell in as the others ran off through the forest, into the unknown.

"The horses!" shouted Alex and Katla as they gave a short chase before returning to the others.

"The mead!" shouted Gudrun as he spat on the ground and gripped his great sword as he was most annoyed.

"The river flows to both the west and to the east. Following it east and along the great mountains, it bends and curves southwards to the southern kingdoms. To the west is a seaside settlement, nearly a day's travel to reach. We hunt trolls, goblins, and ogres along the mountain path for them and in exchange they give us provisions, food, and mead," said Zain as he passed his axe to Katla and pushed his fingers through his bear.

"What are we waiting for, to the west with haste!" shouted Gudrun, but without warning the ground gave way and they were all sucked into the river.

Standing there now separated at length by the raging river, fighting the swift current and the frigid water, they gathered themselves to see the ground give way with waves, rock and stone that were sent flying into the air.

Something emerged from underneath the water's surface. A large jagged and spikey shell, similar to that of a turtle's shell, appeared which rose slowly as water flowed over top of it. The enormous shell was made up of layer upon layer of jagged dark spikes which were rough and broken with sharp and pointy spikes on the outer rim. The shell was solid black with some places giving hints of green which seemed to glow as it rose out of the water. A rumble and roar gave way to the beast's head which stretched back and forth, side to side, as it let out a high-pitched howl. Water flowed out of its iron jaws which revealed a small dark red tongue surrounded by layers of jagged teeth. Its jaws looked formidable and could swallow several men whole.

It stood on its back legs with its head reaching high above the trees as Alex, Gudrun, Zain, Katla and Ødger gazed upon the beast in awe and at the sheer size of it. Its skin was rough and wrinkly, and its underbelly was smooth and armored. As its roaring and howling subsided it peered down at them, standing there in the water fighting to keep their balance they were frozen in fear and wonder.

Its bright, sparkling red eyes which were set back in that darkened and charred face, glared at them as it flared its tiny nostrils with water and air spurting out. It had a pointy, scaly nose with a series of small, jagged spikes leading from it to the back of its head and neck.

It raised its right arm and reached towards Gudrun who was some ways away from Alex and the others. Covered in scales with giant white claws, its arm stretched out as Gudrun stood against the rivers current as he raised his sword. Screaming a battle cry that his ancestors would be proud of against the insurmountable beast, he cried out to Alex.

"Shoulder to shoulder, shield to shield, it's been an honor, Alex!" shouted Gudrun as he lowered his sword and nodded to Alex with a smile knowing of his impending demise.

Alex waded through the now raging river towards him. Gudrun stood helpless against the indomitable, ancient beast which sought to smite him and send him into eternity.

7   SCATTERED PARTY

The air was filled with the high-pitched sound of a war horn. There on the other side of the great river, deep in the forest and far beyond the tree line it sang its tune. Shortly after, another war horn bellowed a long, deep, loud roar and the beast turned its head, as did Alex and the company to the large trees which bent and wobbled in the heavy wind along the river's edge.

Stone, rock, and boulder came soaring through the bright blue sky, high above those ancient trees and smote the beast in a furious tempo. The boulders crashed and pummeled against the beasts armored shell and many of them crumbled to ruin. Alex, Gudrun, Zain, Katla and Ødger themselves had to take care not to be crushed by the falling debris which showered the raging river all around them like a torrent of hail.

Gudrun dived under the water as stone and rock came crashing towards him. The beast tucked its head away inside its dark, jagged shell and turned its fortified back against the bombardment as Alex and the others swam with the current and were swept away from the beast. Alex cried out to Gudrun, but she could not see him, nor could she see the others as the once calm and tranquil river now rushed and surged and was most ghastly.

Alex was plunged under the water, gasping for air as she drifted down through whitewater which crashed against rock and the swirling vortex's which sought to drown her. It was as if the very river had turned against her to halt her in her quest and she began to think of her father in that dire moment.

Alex wondered candidly if this journey was in vain, for she had never heard or seen of such fright. They had not traveled far from Grom, yet the danger they had faced was unimaginable. Further still from the icy, desolate north which she was tasked to travel to from Chieftain Grom. How could they last against this evil and peril? she thought to herself. Surely something more wicked, fouler and loathsome has befallen the land since the last war, she thought as she scanned the river for Gudrun and the others.

Alex looked back above the turbulent waters and saw the terrifying head of the beast emerge from within its giant shell and with a mouth full of dark fire it spewed out against the forest. An incredible light pulsated from the jaws of the beast and Alex was forced to turn her head and raise her hand to cover her eyes as the bright, glowing light had temporarily blinded her.

When the bright flash of light subsided, a good portion of the forest had turned to stone! The trees ceased to move and sway in the wind. They turned from dark and light shades of green to now appearing like a great many statues, white as pearls, against the large green trees and the towering, dark mountains in the background. As the river turned and bended, the last thing Alex could see was the beast rear up out of the water and charge towards the forest, shattering all the trees which were turned to stone by the beasts mighty and fiery breath.

Alex wondered whom had sounded the war horn, and who launched the mighty rocks of stone and boulders against the foul creature, but it wasn't long before she could hear the unmistakable sound of a roaring waterfall. As the water turned to a foaming, raging white, she saw its end and did not have much time before she would be plunged over and to the depths below.

"Mind your head!" shouted Katla from a small area along the river's edge which was made up of large, smooth stones and jutted out a short way from the trees.

Katla hurled Zains axe with both of his hands out into the river towards Alex. The axe was fastened to a twisted, braided rough rope. It sailed over Alex, and she swam and gripped it with all her might as Katla and Zain pulled her to the shore. They were covered with water themselves and it dripped off their bodies and out of their hair as they pulled Alex toward them and helped her out of the cold, frigid water.

"What luck," said Zain and he and Katla stood shivering as Alex twisted the water out of her hair.

The three of them moved away from the river and stood under trees along the cliffs edge which overlooked the waterfall.

"The gods favor you, for if what you say is true, you've escaped the Vollgarim, the giant creatures under the mountain and now this beast that rose from the depths of the river!" laughed Zain as he stood kneeling with his hand on his axe.

They unbound the rope and tossed it aside as Katla tended to his wounded hand, but Zain paid him no mind and pushed him away.

"Did you see Gudrun and Ødger?" asked Alex as she composed herself.

She had been bashed and dragged along the bottom of the river, against rock and stone and she was still coughing up water. With the great, dark mountains to their back, they looked out across from them beyond the waterfall to a great forest below which stretched towards the horizon. The waterfall fell to a great length over the edge and as she peered over it, Katla began to speak.

"Gudrun, I saw him as we swam and fought the current. He was hanging onto a great tree which had fallen into the river and was carried over the edge," said Katla as Zain peered over the waterfall and into the river below which was calm and serene, flowing towards the west.

"A long way down from here, let us make way along the cliffs edge until we can climb down. We still have enough daylight to reach the seaside settlement, if we just follow the river and," said Zain as Alex interrupted him.

"I will not abandon him! I am going over, he could still be alive," shouted Alex as she glared at both Zain and Katla who were still drenched with water.

"The beast is still out there in the forest, along with whatever or whoever attacked it. The river is the fastest way to the seaside settlement. We can fashion a raft once below and search for Gudrun," said Alex as they stood with the sound of the raging river near them and the crashing waves below.

The water was a frothy white which tumbled over the cliff and pounded the rocks below. Its ice-cold breeze and gentle mist rose from the bottom of the waterfall, back up into the air which sprayed and drizzled onto their skin.

"As you like, but I will not risk my life. You and your lot have been far more trouble than expected. Should you survive the fall and find your friend, meet us at the seaside settlement," said Zain with a raised eyebrow.

Zain lifted his axe and rested it across his chest and over his shoulder, and motioned for Katla to join him, walking along the cliffs edge and deeper into the forest as he sought to find an area which fell towards the river below. Katla nodded at Zain and glanced at Alex. As Zain walked away into the depths of the forest, Katla looked saddened and distressed. His eyes met Alex's bright gaze and he shook his head and let out a sigh.

"His wound, its infected," said Katla as he knelt down and fiddled with some of the green, yellowish grass and small, smooth, rounded rocks along the ground. He picked up one of the rocks and inspected it as if it were something of importance, and then tossed it out over the waterfall.

"I will have to remove his arm if the infection grows. I was rather hoping to stay and explore the forbidden forest and brave the dangers that are within it, for they say there are plants here that have magical properties, much like the one I used on your side," said Katla as he pointed to Alex's wound on her hip.

Alex moved her cloak to check it and indeed her wound had sealed and healed with a slight scar that ran from her hip to ribcage.

"Pay him no mind, he has suffered a lot. He has lost all those whom he sought to protect up on the face of the mountain, there in the ancient city which was overrun by evil and death. He lost more than his sword hand which you severed, for he knows in truth you could have removed his head from his shoulders but in your mercy, you spared him. He was once the mighty leader of a great and fierce army in the north and now he has nothing, and his fighting days will be a distant past. Unless his hand grows anew, I fear he may seek solitude to the east or across the great sea, save the Leviathan takes him under the waves to be lost forever," said

Katla as he rose to his feet and casted some more of the small, tiny pebbles out over the calming waterfall.

"What of Ødger?" asked Alex as she stood with her eyes closed.

She felt the gentle breeze from below rise up and flow through her hair and the gentle, cold mist spray her face and skin. It was moments like this which she had forgotten but longed for, for she loved nature, and it was a reminder of home, however distant it may be.

"The snake of Durga, I hope he is there on the bottom of the river with thrashed skin, bones broken, and lungs filled. However it may have happened that he crossed your path Alex, he can't be trusted. You will remember my words before your end," said Katla as he picked some wet leaves which were wet and stuck to his arms and threw them to the ground.

"He seems harmless," said Alex as she opened her eyes and looked to the sky and felt the warmth of the sun on her face.

She fastened her cloak and prepared herself as she was still chilled from the river with broken nerves and a restless spirit.

"As do all who seek to deceive," said Katla as he walked closer to Alex and looked up the river towards the darkened mountains in the distance.

He stretched out his hand and in turn, Alex grabbed him by the forearm, and they nodded to one another as friends would.

"I hope you find your friend. Meet us at the seaside keep, we will be waiting for you there," said Katla as he let go of Alex's arm and they parted with a nod and a smile.

Katla didn't take many steps away before they heard it. First a roar, then a rolling crash through the forest. They looked down and a good distance away from them they saw something along the cliff leading into the gentle, calm river below. The earth there gave way with loose dirt, brown mud and dark green tress falling over into the depths below. A massive land slide, no doubt caused by the menacing beast they had escaped from previously, for the trees that fell and continued to fall, were of solid white and crashed and broke into pieces as they shattered against the dark, jagged rocks below.

Alex wondered what became of Zain, for he was alone, injured and was moving slowly along the cliffs edge. Katla took a few steps back, stunned and frightened with fear as he walked into Alex who stood firm but was weary. They both looked up to the bright, blue sky and saw stones and boulders of fire, flying through the air. As the boulders of fire came crashing down into the forest around them it ignited a great blaze and they saw many fragments of trees, rocks and earth lifted into the sky, high above the treetops where the boulders of fire had landed.

"What is that. Do you hear it?" asked Alex as she grabbed and nudged Katla who was trembling.

A familiar roar and piercing noise filled the forest around them, and they saw the turtle-like beast emerge. This time, it crawled with great speed towards them, breaking down trees and carving out the earth as it lurched through the forest. Its jagged, aged shell and armored head tore through the forest and dirt. Its dark, black shell was now ablaze by the falling fiery boulders that lashed down from the sky.

"We have to jump!" shouted Alex as she looked over the waterfalls ledge as the water flowed over and down with great fury.

She could not see the bottom, only the rising mist and great spray of the falling water below which concealed its depths. Katla was frozen in fear and slowly looked up at the raging beast. With its sharp jaws open, its bright red eyes and head stretched out toward them, Alex grabbed Katla and leapt into the water below.

They fell along with the icy, cascading water into the unknown depths. With a large splash they hit the water at great speed, and it sucked the air out of Alex's lungs as she was plunged down, deep under the water. Alex struggled to swim as the water had a fierce current and it sucked her down and along the bottom of the rocky river. She could see the cascading water above her with the suns light that flickered along the surface as she was surrounded by rising bubbles.

The small, rising bubbles gave way to dark waters where she could see Katla and a reddish tint of water around him. Grabbing him, she swam up along with the small, rising bubbles and gasped for air. The spray and mist of the waterfall showered her face, and she met the grassy, rivers edge with the wounded Katla. His head battered and bleeding, he spoke a few words which were impossible to understand.

"Hang on!" said Alex and she pulled him out of the water and up on dry land.

She looked up and saw the monstrous beast, still standing and roaring at the top of the waterfall. In an instant, it disappeared and some of the cliff's edge gave way underneath it and fell down near them. Alex covered her eyes and turned her head as dirt and earth came crashing down into the water and the rising, cold mist all but consumed her and Katla in its white, drizzling spray.

Alex bandaged Katla the best she could, for he had a small but deep gash on the side of his head and was visibly bruised and battered by the rocks deep under the water. She dressed and bound his wound with a bandage he had in his sheep skin bag. Wrapping it around his head and covering one of his swollen and closed eyes, she pulled him up and against a large tree to rest.

The trees here below the waterfall was absurdly large, for they were now deeper in the forbidden forest where only the very brave dare to enter. The trees here were all very tall, dark and twisted. Some of them were as tall as two hundred paces and twenty paces wide, and still some were even larger! The trees were ancient, and their bark was rough and uneven. Some trees were brown, and others had a reddish color and they rose high up and towered over the waterfall above them. Very little sunlight penetrated through the treetops and the air was much cooler and smelled fresher than the forest above them.

Indeed, with the temperature plummeting and being drenched in water, Alex sought to build a fire but was mindful of the time, for the middays sun had now fallen and the perils of the night would be upon them. They were still several hours away from the seaside keep and Alex was distressed, and her countenance fell when she realized she would spend another night outside and endure the mystery of the encroaching mist.

Tending to the wounded Katla, she remembered his desire to explore the forbidden forest, for in its depths were plants which carried magical healing properties. In remembering this, she ventured close by and gathered various plants which were different shapes and sizes, the likes she had never seen before. Some stood only but a foot off the cold, forest floor and had three or four petals of various hues of green, white, black, red, purple, orange, and yellow while others where as tall as she was in the same likeness.

There were mushrooms, some small and of typical nature while others rose to great heights and were spotted red, white, and black. There was a great number of plants and small trees which she had never seen before, many of them dark and twisting around and along the earthen floor. Unlike the mossy, green covered forest above them, this ancient forest was covered in dirt, rock, and stone with various small pools of water and tiny streams which led deeper into the forest.

Some time had passed, and Alex went back and forth between Katla and the forest, gathering and brining plant samples to their small camp. The fire she had lit for Katla had already warmed his clothes and comforted him. He could speak now and was in good spirits, save the itching and burning wound on his head which ached at each heartbeat. He was astonished at the plants that Alex had gathered and understood her intention to bring some plants hoping they possessed magical properties.

Alex had tried to help Katla to his feet, but he stumbled and fell. With a moan and a scream, he reached towards his ankle which was bent and twisted. He could not stand, nor could he walk, and he sat back down and breathed heavy as he tiled his head low and then high up to the tree canopy letting out a long sigh. Exhaling and in pain, Katla sat there next to Alex for some time, enjoying the warmth and comfort of the fire despite the gash to his head and pain in his ankle.

They were accompanied by the warm late afternoons breeze as the flames from the fire flickered and capered up towards the sky. The branches and twigs bent, snapped, and crackled as blue clear skies turned to grey clouds until it was all but overcast and the sun could no longer be seen.

"Great, now it's going to rain," said Katla as he inspected some of the odd, colorful plants that Alex had brought back from just inside the tree line from where they were resting.

The spray and mist from the waterfall had coated some of the plants along the earthy, green floor and Katla discovered something of interest. It was a yellow plant with several petals which extended from hand to elbow. They were slim, slender, and long and had spikes running up the sides of each petal. Katla peeled it from the side, along the spikes and the petals oozed a glowing substance. He applied it to his wound, and it instantly healed!

"How about that, leave it to you to tend to my wounds," said Katla with a grin as Alex leaned back against a large, brown tree with her bow and arrows in hand.

They rested there, along the river's edge under the vast and giant trees until late afternoon as they were exhausted but alert. The chirping of birds and gentle, rolling waves from the waterfall gave way to the chirps of crickets and the croaks of frogs. Alex's stomach growled and she and Katla looked at one another.

"I saw a fluffle of rabbits not far from here. Several hopping, some sleeping and others hiding in their warren. Barley any meat on them but they will do for one night. Can you manage here while I am away?" asked Alex while looking at Katla and then up to the rolling grey clouds above.

Alex stood up and removed her cloak and pulled her dark hood over her head. Her bright eyes seemed to glow as Katla nodded without giving much attention to her while he inspected some of the plant specimens that Alex had brought from the forest. With her sturdy bow and a few black, obsidian arrows in hand, Alex set off into the forest to hunt rabbits. She glanced back at Katla briefly before moving into the tree line, knowing they were still in terrible danger despite the peace and calm of the forest.

Some time had passed, and Alex had not returned. The clouds receded and gave way to a bright yellow sun which turned to a golden orange. When the sun had finally set, it revealed a radiant silver moon. Its glow was casted down along the deep, dark forest and flowing river. The waterfall was a beautiful sight as the falling water glistening and shimmered in the moonlight. The stars above flickered and twinkled, as the clouds slowly rolled on and it began to gently rain.

Katla was relaxed and the pain in his ankle, which was throbbing and painful at each beat of his heart, had all but disappeared. It was only with a bright, white flash of lighting which zigzagged across the nights sky and the sudden, sharp snap of thunder that followed was he reminded of Reis and what he had witnessed up on the mountain's ledge just in one nights passing. Where is Alex? He wondered as his belly grumbled and growled. He peered deep into the dark forest and that is when it happened.

The lengthy howls of wolves in the distance seemed to all but stop in an instance. The calls and hoots of owls, which were quite boisterous and lively had ceased. A faint glow in the distance out in the dark, a snap of a branch and twigs followed by heavy footsteps. Katla who was now full of fear, stood to his feet and turned to run but he ran into a towering, stalwart figure and fell on his back. He turned to crawl along the ground only to see his fire stamped out and was surrounded by shadowy figures. His screams and cries for help were masked by the crashing waterfall which battered the water and thrashed the hard rocks at the base of the flowing river.

8   MIRVI AND THE BARGAIN

A short time had passed, and Alex could no longer recognize the path that she followed deep into the forest. With two rabbits in hand, she carried them by their large, fluffy, grey paws as she searched for the way back to Katla and their small campsite. The forest was now dark, and the endless sea of tress seemed to continue in every direction. Pausing for a moment to gather herself, she felt the cool nights air on her skin as the temperature had dropped significantly since the sun had set.

Alex gazed up through a clearing in the towering canopy above her. The twinkling and flickering heavenly bodies high in the pitch-black sky glowed shades of blue and white and a shooting star soared across the nights sky. She sat down and placed her bow with arrows and the rabbits which she had caught next to her. Resting there on the cold, firm earth, she wondered if she would ever find her way out in the dark.

Alex rested her eyes and leaned against a large tree which had been wrapped with numerous vines. The vines were dark green, brown and were made up of many fibers as they twisted around the base of the tree and along the cold, hard earth. Alex struggled to keep her eyes open as she slowly seemed to succumb to exhaustion. As she slowly opened her eyes, she saw a bright, yellow glow in the distance between some trees. She took it to be the eyes of an animal which glowed and reflected the moonlight in the dark, but soon there was another set of glowing yellow eyes next to it.

It wasn't long before there were several sets of the glowing, yellow lights which seemed to all but surround her. She slowly picked up her bow and loaded an obsidian arrow when the creatures rushed forward through the trees, vines, and leaves until the closest one was some twenty paces away from her. The glowing moon casted a beam down through the high tree canopy above and casted its light on the ground. The creature moved slowly towards Alex and as it passed through the moonlight, she could see it clearly.

It stood the height of a small child and was covered in a feathery garment. Its skin was covered in small horns and its face looked more like a mask. It had glowing yellow eyes which were unproportionally large compared to the rest of its face. Alex could not see any ears, nose, or mouth on the creature but its face glowed various colors and had small, sharp, white horns above its head and along the sides of its cheeks. Steam and vapor seemed to radiate off its body constantly in soft hues of blue, dark red and orange. Alex wondered if this was what Katla described as the fabled creatures of the forbidden forest, and not wishing a fight she casted her bow down to the ground. At this, all but one creature vanished from her sight, as it slowly approached her seemingly gliding across the ground until it stood in front of her.

The forest then came alive! Glowing green plants along the ground at first and then the vines which crawled along the earth and around the trees gave way to enormous plants, all wild and strange for nothing like them grow in other parts of the world. They all glowed magnificent shades of light and bright blue, green, red, orange, purple, and white. Some glowed steadily while others pulsated or changed colors periodically. There were bugs which glowed, and their lights flickered in the cool air as they flew and floated past Alex and the large yellow eyed creature.

Alex stood in awe as she looked around, almost forgetting about the appearance of the fabled creatures or Katla who remained by the warm campfire near the base of the misty waterfall. She was at peace and for the first time, in a long time, she felt as if she was back home. She strolled and meandered through the now illuminated forest enamored at the wild and wonderful plants, trees, and wildlife. She was charmed by its beauty and saw the very streams and rivers flowing through the forest now glowed with ethereal fish.

There was a school of fish, but they were very large, silver and shining through the crystal-clear water accompanied by red and blue frogs which hopped, flopped, and leapt into the water along with other strange tiny creatures which crawled and crept along the bottom of the stream. A large, fearsome wolf appeared, followed by several others as their silver fur reflected the moonlight. They were ethereal and Alex could see right through them as they growled and howled with jaws that revealed a menacing set of jagged fangs. Indeed, all the animals were strange and many much larger than their normal counterparts outside of the forest.

The wolves passed by Alex and rubbed their ethereal, see-through bodies against her as they proceeded into the forest alongside the glowing, blue and white luminescent stream. She reached out and felt their fluffy, soft fur. It was long, wild, and unkempt and the wolves reminded her of Flux, Gudrun's dog back at Grom. Then and only then did she remember Gudrun and Chieftain Grom and the task she was on as the wonder of the arcane forest broke, and her mind was thrusted back to the task at hand.

She turned to leave, yet the fabled creature appeared out of thin air and took her by the hand. It all but disappeared with only its glowing eyes and face which was most grotesque up close, as she could feel its tight grip around her hand as it led her deeper into the forbidden forest. Its bright eyes and hideous, gruesome face glared at her and then set its eyes towards the distance. They walked what seemed like an eternity to her, together through the mystical forest until a large opening appeared. An ancient, crumbling ruin stood before them with strange symbols carved into the stone.

Alex could see what appeared to be the remnants of an ancient tower of some sort which had long decayed and crumbled as bits and pieces of stone were scattered here and there around her in the small clearing. The earth was devoid of grass, and it seemed that a fire had raged and scorched this patch of earth. As they came closer, she could see the figure of a giant, adorned in battle armor with a great war hammer carved into the face of the stone. The giant sat on a throne and the opening or doorway, as it seemed, was directly underneath it.

The passageway was open, and Alex could see a set of spiraling stairs leading down into the darkness. She was hesitant and familiar feelings of dread and trepidation took hold of her. She was exhausted as quite some time had passed since she had entered the forbidden forest and she longed to see the sun rise and find out what became of Gudrun.

Her mind was flooded with memories of her childhood. Sitting along the river with her feet dipped into the cold, refreshing water, and staring at the fish swim underneath her feet. Those bulging eyes and bright pink gills with shimmering bodies and golden scales. Their fins and tail moved back and forth as they swam around her. The wind gusts in her hair and the warmth of the sun as she could hear children form the village laughing and playing, seeing hunters return from the forest carrying a butchered dear with them for the evening feast.

She tried to remember the face of her father, yet she could not. With frustration she realized she could not remember much of him at all. Not his face or the color of his eyes, nor the length of his hair. Alex bit her lip gently and knitted her eyebrows. Why couldn't she remember? She wondered.

It was then the fabled creature appeared, complete in body and form and motioned for her to enter the darkened stairway leading into the depths of the earth. Alex glared at the creature, and it returned her look with a grimace as its body began to glow different shades of color. To her dismay, Alex entered the passageway underneath the carving of the ancient giant and she moved slowly and unhindered by fear. Deeper and deeper, she moved until the last bit of moonlight could be seen from above her and she was now in total darkness.

The passageway leading down was hollow and she took care to hug the rough, stony, and broken wall of the staircase as to not fall into the middle opening which no doubt fell to a great depth. A great rumbling could be heard from up above and she took this to be the sound of thunder. After a time, a soft blue light appeared from a small opening along the stairwell. The light was comforting as she had been traveling in complete darkness and it was an all too familiar experience for her. Not wanting to be haunted of the memories and terrors of her past any further, she gladly entered the small opening alongside the endless stairwell and saw a great river which flowed slowly through a great dark void there under the earth.

The river could be seen traveling far into the horizon across the void and while otherwise pitch black, its gentle shades of blue and green illuminated the area enough around her where she could see her own self again. A figure appeared far off which glided down and across the water to the river's edge. It approached Alex without delay and that is when she heard it. A voice that was calm, gentle, and seductive began to sing.

Forget your peace inside
You've given way to the lords of destruction
Full of fear and anger
Your surrounded yet alone
Naught but misery and grief
You longed for battle, now seeking again the past
Was it worth it?
Unknown to be your last
Now you seek to find
That which is already lost
Nowhere to hide
Would you continue whatever the cost?
Return to the depths
Avoid the final destruction
Down the forgotten steps
Where you bled and believed their seduction
Where will you go now?
Seeking he who knew his fate
To watch you succumb to corruption

The gentle voice echoed in the dark as the figure stood in front of Alex who looked on in awe. It had the voice of a woman, yet Alex could not discern her appearance. It was shrouded by a foggy, misty light; like a figure swimming beneath the water's surface that glowed and reflected the sunlight.

"What is this place?" asked Alex as she was truly frightened.

She was exhausted, and her whole body trembled with fear.

"And what are you!" exclaimed Alex in angst as the figure moved around her in a circle.

"Oh, come now, I think you know," it said as it floated, and continued to encircle her high in the air.

"Are you so quick to forget?" it said as Alex looked around herself trying to keep track of its quick, swift movements above her.

"Don't you remember?" it asked as it came down and landed behind Alex.

Alex thought to herself but could not remember. Nay, she could not remember a great many things since that day she entered the dark, haunting abyss and her memory had lapsed and was getting worse by the day. She searched her thoughts again for her father and to her dismay she could not recall details about him or his appearance. Before she could utter a response, and knowing her thoughts, the figure revealed herself and indeed she was a sight.

A beautiful woman on one half of her body while the other half resembled death and decay. She had glowing, bright flowing hair with tips that appeared like dancing flames on a windy, cold night. A deep, bright eye which flickered shades of green, yellow, and orange like a shining star that resembled a jewel. Her skin was fair and without blemish, yet on the opposite half a grisly sight which caused horror to anyone who saw her. Her face on this half was burned flesh with parts revealing solid white bone underneath; her eye on this half was normal but receded deep into her face. She was tall and slender with clouds of fire and mist that concealed her feet. At times, her body was again concealed by the foggy, misty, light which would flicker back and forth to reveal her image.

She stood there, all but seemingly to show herself to Alex as more and more was revealed. She bore no wings, yet a great wind gust always blew from behind her like an approaching hurricane at sea. One of her arms was concealed by a fiery cloud while the other carried an impressive sickle. It was long and the handle glowed a dark orange like the rising sun and the blade was thick and curved with what appeared to be words embedded in the bright blade.

This sickle then changed into a magnificent blade which had a long thin handle which seemed to only be an extension of her hand and a blade that was thick and broad beyond measure; Gudrun's sword which was the largest Alex had ever seen was dwarfed by this mighty blade. It too had unfamiliar words and symbols embedded into the blade and appeared to have droplets of light which dripped from it.

Again, the blade turned into a dark orb which hovered above her hand near her shoulder. Inside it, only what can be described as flashes of lighting and burning embers could be seen and then whispers seemed to come forth from it which were quite menacing and mysterious. These three seemed to rotate, where the figure would be carrying one and then switch to the others repeatedly.

Upon hearing the whispers coming from the mysterious orb, Alex had remembered the same whispers from the deep abyss some time ago. The dread of that place, the memories of the battle that followed and the long journey through the dark haunted her day and night. Alex closed her eyes and turned away from the figure, straining her neck and head this way and that but there was no forgetting the past as she had forgotten many things but could never forget that.

"Whispers in the shadows, a hard thing to endure," it said as the figure shrouded itself in light and muddled itself from Alex's view once more.

Alex was intrigued that it knew of her plight, and while still fearful, she sought to understand the meaning of this place and the nature of this figure. Knowing her thoughts, it spoke once more to Alex. It turned and glided across the flowing river in a random pattern, circling back to Alex now and again. Alex, who was previously tired beyond measure, was now wide awake like someone who had been shaken from a peaceful sleep to the sound of a waging battle. With eyes wide open, she listened earnestly to what this figure had to say.

"I roamed and wandered through the myriad of stars and far beyond the boundaries of what is and what has been. There between the perpetual darkness and light, I laid low the multitudes who gathered to bind me, and their likes have been scattered as far as east is from the west. Eons upon Eon and then in the era of the ancients, and now with the likes of you. I shared wisdom and experience, yet it was not enough to remain immaculate. Tell me, how did you come to this place, may I ask?" the figure asked as Alex looked up at its calm and gentle gaze.

Alex's fear and anxiety abated, and she was beginning to feel very comfortable again. She was warmed by the figures gentle, calm voice as it was roving about in the darkness. Alex told it that one of the fabled creatures of the forbidden forest had led her by the hand to the crumbling, ancient ruin above and motioned for her to traverse the fragmented and deteriorated stairwell down into its depths.

They talked for a while; about Chieftain Grom and her quest to uncover the mystery of the rising mist which had befallen and brought woe and despair to the lands. These events were very similar, with traces and shadows of the previous war that broke the people of the north and south. She told the figure of the Vollgarim and the wild, untamed giant-like creatures in the caves between Grom and the ancient giants city. Then, how Reis had summoned lighting from the heavens to save them, all the while to face the turtle-like monstrosity along the river below which led them deep into the forbidden forest. She explained how she needed to return to find Gudrun and her companions and continue west to the seaside settlements and further still to see what has become of the northern settlements. It was only when she spoke of her father and uncle did the creature stand still and then at once come up to face Alex.

"There is something about you. Something old, but not forgotten. Perhaps you are a means to an end, yet not fully capable. I have guessed their foul intentions long before the first was unbound and unchained," it said in a calm, gentle voice.

Alex could see it was clearly indignant, yet it spoke in a calm, gentle voice that was pleasant to the ears and seductive to the heart. She could not understand what the figure had meant but paid it no mind, as very little made sense of what this being had said.

"We have much to discuss. Rest now, and on the morrow at first light I will tell you what has become of your father. Your dreams, those memories, I can assure you they are more than incoherent thoughts and images," it said as it floated there into the distance slowly disappearing from her sight.

Astonished by this mentioning of her father and her dreams, she called out into the darkness.

"What is your name?" Alex called out as she searched the darkness only to see the soft blue, greenish glow of the river.

There in the silence, she heard a loud whisper which came directly behind her.

"I was called Mirvi, for a short time" the whisper said as Alex sat down there in the dark, looking all around her as the voice echoed into the deep.

The calm flow of the river and the trickling of water which fell from overhead and echoed throughout the darkness calmed her nerves. As she slowly succumbed to exhaustion, she wondered could her father still be alive?

It wasn't long before Alex found herself on the surface and looked up to the risen sun which all but rushed to greet her. She smiled and was grateful for its warm embrace as the sky spread its blue blanket and white clouds high above her. Panting and gasping for breath, it was a long climb back up those dark stairs out and into the pouring light of the sun, as she was not well rested and very hungry. Her belly growled and rumbled, and she felt a great wind coming up from behind her that scattered the leaves along the ground and pushed her hair over her face.

"A tomb," said Mirvi as she appeared behind Alex and slowly walked around the burned, scorched earth.

A bird flew down from one of the branches, high up in the dark green trees and landed on Alex's hand as she looked on as it chirped and hopped around on her finger to fingers.

"A tomb?" asked Alex as the small, brown, and red bird nibbled along her fingernails with its bright yellow beak, singing its morning tune.

"You had asked what is this place, did you not? For it is a vestige, a relic of times lost but not forgotten. For mighty men of old, renowned for their feats, once dwelled here in this forest and much further to the east beyond the great mountains. With them I shared my wisdom, my experience, and my might. I was the exalted ruler of these lands and the master of the beasts on land, the fowl of the air and that which is beneath the sea. There was none to dispute me and yet the hearts of men are depraved and profoundly wicked. As I shared my righteousness and virtue, they too shared their malice, their guile, and their desire for power. My presence among them led to many becoming the giants of old and further still, some Titans whom none compared for my pure and powerful nature bled into them and created a greatness that the world has and never will see again. To my dismay, their wickedness bled into me and with the passing of each sunset, I felt my heart turn and sway for an evil was stirring from within my depths. I vigorously fought to subdue this newfound evil and casted it out only to find it had become the embodiment of raw chaos, evil and madness. Soon after it fled to the Frozen Wastes to the north and out of sight, for I fought with others whose corruption sought to take hold of me. Seven embodiments of evil, bound in chains in the deep, secret parts of the earth now hatch a foul plan. Three have been freed, empowering, and corrupting those who would roam these lands like a lion, ready to devour and destroy. The abyss, you remember the whispers in shadows, do you not?" asked Mirvi before standing in front of Alex, face to face.

Alex, who was listening with great concentration, now turned white as snow and her countenance fell as she was deeply troubled. She remembered very little of that place, and what she remembered she would rather forget.

"I know of that place. The footsteps in the dark, the whispers in the shadows and the long, arduous journey through the pitch black to reach the surface. I remember entering with several brave and able, including my father," said Alex as she faced Mirvi who was circling in the air around her now.

"Ah yes, your father. No memory of the battle fought, nor what became of your companions though. Nay, I'd say you remember very little of what was a great consequence," said Mirvi in a gentle voice as she landed again in front of Alex.

She walked slowly, although her feet were concealed by clouds of fire and mist, and a great wind from behind her rushed through Alex's hair. Alex fought to stand firm without tumbling over and the wind subsided in strength as Mirvi began to smile.

"Alex, I propose that you venture to the far reaches of the north. Far off into the Frozen Wastes beyond the mountains of fire and seek out what lay there. Return to me, divulge what you see and in return I will restore your memory and show you what has become of your father," said Mirvi as she stared into Alex's azure eyes.

"What has become of my father!" exclaimed Alex. "If he's alive, tell me!" shouted Alex in angst as it had tormented her night and day.

While the sun was high and blazing in the sky, a darkness spread through the forest and all the enchanting sounds of nature and creatures within it went silent. A bright light emitted from Mirvi and the darkness which was encircling them was pushed back deeper into the forest, and yet, it continued towards them and several of the fabled creatures appeared in their horrific and terrifying appearance.

"He's alive," replied Mirvi in a calm, soothing voice. "If you wish to see him, do as I ask and venture into the North beyond the Frozen Wastes and tell me what you find. For now, your friends are in danger. You will find them along the river to the west which flows out to sea which leads to the seaside keep. Go now, it is no longer safe for you here," said Mirvi as she began to glow and concealed herself in a blinding light.

The forest was silent and a heavy, dark mist had all but surrounded them. It crept closer but stopped along the tree line in the small clearing they were standing in as if it had a mind of its own.

"Why don't you venture into the north yourself?" asked Alex as she looked around her at the encroaching mist.

"That's no concern of yours," replied Mirvi as she set her sight on something deep within the forest.

"Do as I ask, and I will grant you a request as a promise to my word. You have a fortnight to decide, for the mist is coming and with it an evil of old. You know of what I speak, and it will destroy these lands in a fortnight! Do as I ask and venture into the north. Cry out with your request and it will be honored, for while I may seem far away, I am always within your grasp," said Mirvi as a great wind scattered the leaves and twigs along the ground and rocks and stones tumbled along the scorched earth.

An ethereal, giant elk appeared along the tree line and walked towards Mirvi and Alex. Its antlers were as wide as it was tall and reflected the bright sunlight almost blinding Alex. She ducked her head as it walked over her and up to Mirvi as it lowered and bowed its head toward her. It had six large, powerful legs instead of four and a tail which was long and forked like the tail of a whale. Mirvi instructed Alex to climb on and the elk would take her away to find Gudrun and her friends.

At once and without delay the giant elk dashed into the forest with great speed, leaping over rocky areas of ground and around the ancient, gigantic, and warped trees. They were shrouded in mist and Alex could see very little in what was a once vibrant and magical forest, filled with mythical creatures pleasing to the eye and soothing to the soul. A great echo of a whisper came from behind her in what was now a pitch-black forest which said, "Consider our bargain."

The calm, gentle, and seductive voice of Mirvi permeated the cold, terrifying darkness. Alex looked around while holding onto the colossal, jagged antlers of the great elk, only to see glimpses and flashes of a quick moving army underneath the giant elk charging back towards Mirvi.

The Vollgarim, a silent horde of them charging with serrated fangs and relentless fury. Alex wondered what had become of Gudrun, Katla and Zain or if it was already too late. She shrugged off the horrible and intrusive thoughts and held onto the elk's antlers tighter. Her heart was fluttering and began to race as they continued to move through the darkness, into the unknown to discover the fate of her friends.

9   MADS AND ARVID

"This will be over in a minute, one way or another," said Katla as he tried to stop the bleeding from the man's wound.

Bright red blood spat and spurted out as he moved his finger off the wound to apply pressure and a bandage.

"There, he'll survive but he needs rest, as do you all," said Katla as he finished bandaging the man's wound and wiped his hands on the man's red, rent armor and fabric pants.

The man groaned and moaned as he was in terrible pain. The injured man thanked Katla, although he was in agony as he slowly sat up and looked to his comrades. They were all injured, after an ill-fated brush with death no doubt. Katla rubbed his hands together, cupping them over his mouth and breathed into them deeply. His large, callused hands were warmed as the mist from his breath rose and disappeared into the cool air.

He missed the sun on his face, the sound of the bustling markets and the seagulls flying overheard, soaring and signing their song near the wooden, creaking docks full of fisherman and traders. Here in the far north, he wondered how his life would have fared should he have stayed home, how his family and youngest daughter was doing and if they missed him, but he was a long way from home and further still from childhood dreams. A shadow was cast upon him, and he felt a sensation of chills and tingling run down his spine, out into his arms and down his legs.

Katla looked up as another man stood bearing over him, devoid of compassion for the injured man next to him. The sun was behind him, casting his shadow down causing a sense of fear and dread. Katla, blinded by the sun, could not see his face. The man was injured as well, a deep wound to the shoulder and chest but he was indifferent to the pain. He knelt beside them both with a beautifully crafted dagger in hand and stared at Katla.

His stare was deep, like he was peering into his very soul. Those dark, piercing eyes, smoldering as they were intimidating which made Katla uneasy. Then, after what seemed like an eternity to Katla, he simply took the dagger and plunged it slowly and deeply into the injured man; down through his neck into his chest. The injured man's eyes widened, and he gasped for a short shallow breath of air before succumbing to the darkness. The blood from his wound ran the ground red and into the vast, flowing lake next to them. The water ran a murky red as the intimidating man grabbed the dead man's hair and wiped his dagger with it, cleaning it of the blood.

"It was his fault to be blunt, his choice to be blunter," said the man who stood up, as he turned and walked away.

He wore a garment that is not typical of the peoples of the north or south, and had a rugged, rough accent. He had a complexion darker than those in the north yet lighter than those in the south. He was dressed in tightly fitting black leather armor and bore a hood which covered his head, with a small opening for his eyes which consisted of a mesh fabric, concealing his eyes further.

He carried a dagger which had a beautiful handle and elegant blade. Like his dagger, he carried a sword of the likes Katla had never seen before. It was short, slender, and slightly curved. A blade that was exceedingly honed with a handle that was much longer than can be expected compared to swords of the warriors in the north. The handle was wrapped in silk and leather of a beautiful shade of red; perhaps it was blood stained, it was hard to tell.

"He chose to fight, and the lot that followed are getting only what they have earned for themselves," the man said as he stood up and placed his elegant dagger back into its sheath which was attached to his side.

"Mads!" shouted a heavily armored man in the distance.

A large man walked out from the forest and approached Mads and Katla. The forest was full of pine and spruce trees that ran the length of the mountains from east to west. The mountainside was grey, white and was covered in shades of the green and black spruce and pine trees. A heavy mist was creeping along the mountains and towards the lake which laid at its base and rose a great height up and over the mountain. There were three large, sharp peaks which soared high above the tree line and were caped with snow.

Mads, with a nod of his head, motioned for Katla to stand up. Katla did so, all the while reluctant as he looked on to the other injured men who stood or sat nearby. There was a small encampment with fires here and there burning bright and warming the injured men. A great many of them suffered broken bones, slashed skin, and rent armor. They were a tough lot, tending to themselves and one another as their wounds were fresh but spirits unhindered.

Katla looked across the great lake which was shallow enough to walk across with a greenish hue. Those calm, serene waters were clear and reflected the trees and the mountainside across its smooth, tranquil surface. Large boulders were scattered here and there protruding out of the lake. Some spiked with pine trees and covered with patches of wild grass and green moss. It was an enchanting lake for Katla's tired eyes to rest on, considering his dire state after being captured.

"Arvid, what news?" asked Mads as he stared into the shallow water at the smooth, dark stones embedded into the lake.

Arvid walked closer to them with his hand on his swords hilt, as he breathed deeply trying to catch his breath.

"Horses scattered, spirits broken, and the trail now riddled with corpses," replied Arvid who now hunched over, still struggling to catch his breath. "Trolls, goblins, and ogres. I'd say they lost about half their men up there on the mountain pass and those remaining are maimed or now crippled. All the same, some managed to escape," said Arvid with his hands on his knees, breathing in the fresh, mountain air.

"What do you make of the fire," said Mads as he rose and turned his gaze towards the west, towards the seaside keep and up to the misty mountains.

Arvid stood and shook his head in vexation for these times were dire, even among bounty hunters and hired killers.

"Come on lad, what are you and your friends doing out this way, did you come from Grom?" said Arvid to Katla.

"What are you, that cripple and the big fella doing out here?" said Arvid as Katla looked along the lakes edge to see Gudrun and Zain a way off.

Gudrun was bound in chains; both his legs and arms were bound, and Zain was laying on the ground, seemingly tending to his wound which Katla presumed was now infected and utterly tender to the touch.

Katla said nothing but looked on to his friends a short distance away. They were by the lake, among the cattails that grew at its edge. Some of the men were separating the long, bright green reeds to collect some tinder from their brown seed heads while others were pulling the roots out of the soft, damp earth to eat.

Bad luck, or perhaps an ill-fated destiny led Gudrun, Katla and Zain to be found by these roaming group of hardened, cutthroat men. Some had the look of being from the north, carrying axe, shield, sword, and spear but they were of a different breed. The sun was high above them, casting its tepid smile and its feverish rays in a sky completely devoid of white, puffy clouds. Arvid called again to Katla, but he paid him no mind.

Arvid, now feeling refreshed from his arduous journey down from the mountain pass, combed his hand through his beard and crossed his arms. He was wearing an impressive, shinning plate mail armor which covered his chest along with elaborate, ornate pauldrons which protected his shoulders and neck. His long hair and large, unkempt beard were like a fire, a bright red and orange which contrasted his bright blue eyes. He tried to pick up Gudrun's sword, which was laying on the ground, but could not lift it. After a few attempts, seemingly exhausted with a great exhale, he came closer to Katla who was still staring off into the distance at his friends, wondering the state of Zains arm now being untreated for quite some time.

"Would you let us go back there if we were?" responded Katla as he shivered feeling a light wind come across the lake.

Arvid shook his head and looked to Mads who was staring off, deep in thought but listening.

"Look lad, we were, eh, tasked with going to Grom and upon our arrival we found it in ashes. Fire and ruin, nothing left but dust and smoke! We tracked those who fled up through the mountain pass towards the seaside keep, but were ambushed by a number of trolls, goblins, and ogres. We lost a few of our men, nothing compared to the slaughter of those fleeing Grom though. If your one of their party you can tell us, for we are heading to the seaside keep ourselves," said Arvid as he spoke gently and friendly to Katla.

Mads turned and walked over to them, and Katla could see him clearly now. He was tall with a strong, lean frame. His face was chiseled like that of stone, with a heavy brow, protruding cheekbones and a large defined chin which sat upon a powerful neck. He spoke slowly, with a deep and coarse accent. An eerie fellow indeed, for Katla could not place him or discern his intentions.

"I just saved your man, there was no reason to kill him. What are you going to do, kill me?" asked Katla and while he wanted to run, he was too paralyzed with fear.

"Yes," replied Mads in a calm, deep voice.

Katla was frozen stiff with shock and feared for his life as Mads eyes were fixated on his with a dark, cold stare. Arvid came closer and pleaded once more, for he wondered who else would be out here, along the forbidden forests edge in the middle of cursed lands if not others who came for the bounty in Grom.

"Our purpose in Grom is lost but the one-armed man is an exile, and the seaside keep will surely pay a price for his safe return. We need to salvage this trip! We did not come this far to return home empty handed. It was not our intention to serve every troll, goblin, and ogre on the mountain a buffet of mercenaries! Come lad, what are you and the big man doing out here and in the company of an exile? Tell us and we may very well spare your life," said Arvid while looking at Katla, waiting for his response.

Katla did not respond, perhaps he was thinking of what to say, or was too afraid to say anything but Arvid lost his patience and at this he took him by the arm and dragged him away to Gudrun and Zain. Mads looked out across the grassy plain and stared towards the forbidden forest, into its depths which hid many secrets and wonders.

"Get them up!" shouted Arvid, now seemingly frustrated and annoyed at the inconvenience of finding Gudrun, Zain and Katla here in the depths of the wilderness.

It was their ill fate to be captured and taken by the group of hard-hearted, ruthless men. Arvid and Katla came upon a group of cutthroats, standing around the cattails and high grass all adorned in battle armor with fine weapons which glistened in the sunlight. These men seemed to be in good health and better spirits than most, some with scared faces and rugged faces for men like these are a tough breed.

"Enough rest! Move out, we make our heading to the seaside keep," shouted Arvid as the men began to prepare themselves.

Several men helped Gudrun to his feet who was bound in chains while some others followed behind, prodding him to walk with spears which were long, sharp, and beautifully made. They were tired from their journey to Grom and through the mountain pass, having lost several of their best sellswords during an ambush. Some eaten alive by trolls, while others were smashed with heads crushed by Ogres. Remarkably they weren't shaken and disheartened but seemed to be all too familiar with the horrors of battle and the chaos that followed.

Mads approached them, and without saying a word he casted his gaze towards the tree line of the forbidden forest. The men could see a shadowy figure appear and behind it, a much larger beast of sorts. Was it an apparition? They wondered, as the beast slowly receded into the forest and they could not make anything of it. The shadowy figure walked closer with bow and arrow in hand and at seeing her,

Gudrun's expression turned from grim to cheerfulness and Katla's eyes widened, and he tried to speak but was pulled back by Arvid.

"You there! What are you doing in the forbidden forest?" Arvid called out but Mads walked up quickly from behind them and said "don't you tire from asking the same thing over and over?" and drew his sword.

Before Alex could speak, Mads swung his sword and smote Katla in a single blow, lopping his head clean from his shoulders and it struck the ground with a soft thud and rolled a few feet away from them. Katla's eyes were wide open, perhaps now finding the peace the harsh north never granted him.

Alex quickly placed an arrow on the left side of her bow and pulled it back to a full draw. She let her arrow loose and it whistled and soared as it struck one of the warriors and the arrow passed clean through his forehead. She let loose a second arrow and it struck one of the men next to Gudrun in his thigh where it lodged and was sticking out from both ends of his leg. The man fell to the floor, and without so much of a whimper he broke the arrow off from both ends of his leg and pulled the hard, wooden shaft out of his leg.

Mads dashed quickly behind Gudrun and the men with spears prodded and poked Gudrun to make him kneel; even kneeling Gudrun was taller than all of them. Mads had his dagger at Gudrun's neck and glared back at Alex. Pressing the beautifully crafted dagger against Gudrun's large, thick neck, he had already started to bleed for the dagger was exceptionally sharp.

"You will soon run out of arrows. You and your friends are all out of place, you are not cut out for this. I gave Katla my word, but I will give you a chance. Drop your bow and come here, or I will kill your friend," shouted Mads.

Alex stood firm but she was weeping silently with tears rolling down her cheeks as she regretted leaving Katla alone to succumb to such an ill fate.

"You don't have to do this," cried Alex as she wiped her face and tears with her shoulder and looked hopeless.

Mads remained emotionless and stared back at her. During the whole ordeal, Alex did not see him blink once as his dark eyes glared at her with a sense of calmness.

"People always say the same thing," said Mads as he grinned slightly and lowered his head with a slight shake as he was amused.

He removed his dagger from Gudrun's neck and sighed deeply for a moment.

"Ok, you can pick between him or the one-armed man. That is the best I can do," said Mads as he stood and stared back at Alex.

"Pick one!" said Mads as his eyes widened and he nodded for Alex to encourage her response. "Pick one!" Mads demanded again in eagerness.

Alex thought for a moment and could see they were without horses, as was she. She had seven arrows left and she could see twelve of them, including Mads and Arvid. Alex paused for a second, her eyes darting this way and that before she yelled out, "Kill him then!" much to their disbelief.

Gudrun's eyes widened in disbelief and with a furrowed brow he looked back at Alex. Mads, without delay, raised his dagger to Gudrun's neck. Alex drew her arrow and let it loose, striking Gudrun on the side of his face cutting a portion of his ear as he fell back, nearly crushing Mads behind him.

She let all her arrows fly, each striking different men as Mads fell to the soft, water touched earth and rolled to avoid the falling Gudrun. Arvid dove behind one of the large boulders protruding in the shallow depths of the lake, peering out from its jagged, coarse surface at what was now six men who had just tasted death or may not live another day from their wounds.

Alex ran back into the depths of the dark, dense forbidden forest. Arvid and Mads gathered themselves, both standing slowly to wipe the dust and dirt from their garments. Arvid crept from out behind the boulder and was perplexed but Mads was wondering why Alex would aim to kill her own friend when she could have just tucked tail and fled. Some of the cutthroats laid in the short grass stiff as stone and had been slain. Their dark, red blood stained the soft earth as some of the remaining cutthroats tended to their wounds. No sobs or whines, though their wounds were grievous, and some would not live to see the sun set nor the sun rise should they live through the night.

"Take the big man with us. While she would find value in his death, we will find it in his life. Perhaps he knows something of great importance," said Mads in a slow, calm voice while he drew his awe-inspiring dagger.

The remaining cutthroats collected themselves and began to move out along the calm shores of the lake. Arvid was breathing heavily, both from the weight of his armor and his short sprint to avoid the fearsome and accurate arrows of Alex.

"So, she tried to kill her own friend to conceal something? What an evil witch!" said Arvid as he shook his head and helped some of the cutthroats get Gudrun to his feet. "What of the wounded," said Arvid as he looked on sympathetically.

"Dead weight, and still a long way from the seaside keep," said Mads as he took his dagger and stabbed each of the men swiftly into their necks. "Fodder for hungry ravens, or whatever comes out of that creeping mist," said Mads as he pointed across the lake to where mist and fog seemed to crawl and creep across the water towards them.

Mads knelt by the cold lakes edge on a soft patch of earth that slightly gave way to his knee and cleaned the blood from his dagger. He splashed water on his face and ran his hands through his hair before standing up to walk along the lakes edge behind some of the surviving cutthroats who went ahead. He took some medical supplies from the now headless Katla and tended to the wound in his chest and shoulder. He looked at Arvid with his cold, dark eyes and with a slight pause, he carried on.

Arvid was daunted and afraid of Mads but was too far from home to return empty handed. Mads seemed perfectly capable of the bounty, and yet he hired Arvid and tasked him with finding several sellswords to accompany them to Grom. Mads didn't know the lay of the land, but Arvid was bound by honor to continue, although in his wisdom he thought to turn and flee. He knew he would not make it alone, in the night with the mist. Perhaps that is what Mads wanted company for to begin with, Arvid thought to himself.

"Easier to survive when theres more fodder for the ravens," said Arvid gently under his breath.

He shook his head while grinding his teeth and took pity on the dead cutthroats. Albeit being murders and mercenaries for hire, their fate was fixed the moment they accepted the journey with Mads.

"What of the girl?" said Arvid as he looked ahead to see Mads walking swiftly and carelessly into the distance.

"The kitten with claws? She must be heading to the seaside keep. Grom is destroyed and she has no horse. Nobody survives a night in the mist," said Mads as he did not look back and kept walking while keeping an eye on the mist across the lake. "There's nowhere else to go and daylight is dwindling," said Mads as he carried on.

They continued on their journey as Arvid led them further west through the forest and out towards the open plains leading to the seaside keep. They soon found themselves passing over the trail leading up and over the mountain toward Grom where their comrades, as well as those who fled Grom, would be dinner for hungry trolls, goblins, and ogres.

The wind-swept path was dry and dusty, stamped and kicked by horses and devoid of grass as it winded and twisted up through the open plain. It was a heavily traveled dirt path with bits of stone and rock which lay alongside the green grass and high yellow reeds which twisted and swayed in the wind.

The seaside keep was not much further and they seemed rather relieved they were almost there. Soon they could no doubt rest their blood shot eyes and calm their souls for their lot had been traveling days with very little to eat. Braving the mist at night and the terrors that lay waiting in ambush, their remaining company would take refuge inside the seaside keep, at least that is what they thought.

They moved slowly yet with intent along the swift moving, twisting river that led to the sea. Great white, fluffy clouds created an overcast sky that began to rain tiny droplets of refreshing water. The men looked to the heavens with opens mouths as it was refreshing and nourishing to their bodies and spirits. A great shadow was cast across the yellow and golden trees leading up to the dark mountains, with the ruins and ash of Grom far off on the other side of the mountain range.

Arvid's mind drifted to the heavens and was lulled by the gentle chirping and singing of birds and to the call of a wild moose which was a throaty, airy grunting sound. What could have befallen Grom? And was the girl who rained death and destruction with her arrows lying in wait for them as they journeyed on? He thought to himself. It was then that it happened, something most unexpected.

10   CAMPFIRE AT DEATHS DOOR

"Unshackle the big man, flee for your lives!" shouted Arvid as the cutthroats loosened Gudrun's chains and in a frenzied motion, began to run.

They had reached the sandy shore, along the river that flowed out and into the sea. The ocean waves here were known to be great and fierce, carving the sands and reclaiming the sandstone cliffs along its raised edge.

"Too early in the day for mist, in fact I hear these parts never get mist, why the seaside keep is still standing I wager," said Arvid to Mads as he stood with his eyes squinted, looking back towards the mountains in the distance.

The fog was rolling quickly down and across the plain towards them, as if it had a mind of its own. Too quickly for comfort, it was unnerving and Arvid turned to Gudrun while Mads stood firm and continued to stare at the approaching mist.

"Carry your friend, and with luck we will reach the keep by nightfall!" Arvid exclaimed to Gudrun concerning Zain, as he and the others ran as fast as they could along the cliff tops.

Zain was unable to run, for he was exhausted and in pain from his arm. He was in terrible shape; his arm having turned color as he was now fighting an infection. With a very pale face, drooping eye lids that hung low and a limp in his step, he fell down on the ground as Gudrun approached. Gudrun picked Zain up and threw him over his large shoulders. Gudrun glanced back at the approaching mist which fell like a raging avalanche down over the mountains in the distance before running to catch up to the others.

The ocean waves crashed against the sandy beach, carving out deep depressions in the sand with a mighty blow. With frothy, foamy bubbles, the water ran up along the sand reaching its hand out towards those golden, sun touched cliffs before returning to the depths of the sea. Gudrun, Zain, Mads, Arvid, and the remaining cutthroats breathed in the salt-laden air while making their way up and along the cliff tops.

The rocky earth was covered in fragile grasslands with shades of yellow and green grass. The wind caused the grasslands to sway back and forth. An occasional orchid blossomed here and there. Its bright purple and yellow pedals brightened their spirits as they ran past the occasional tree. There were some trees that were notable for their distinctive blossoms of white and pink, some bearing berries which were very delicious and were used in mead, while other trees had very distinctive bark. It was a pleasant sight as they ran with great speed and intent through the grasslands with the wind in their hair and the sun scorching the side of their faces.

There were some small, grey birds with exceptionally long, tan beaks perched in the trees and more so in the large, sharp bristled bushes. A few small birds, no bigger than a child's hand, flew past them singing their song as the cutthroats were breathing heavily and wheezing as they tried to catch their breath as they continued on in haste. A few large pelicans with their bright white feathers and large orange beaks were soaring above the ocean as a lone falcon sat on a tree branch. Its wings were brown with a jagged white pattern as it looked at them passing by with its bright black, inquisitive eyes and small, sharp yellow beak.

There were some large, grey clouds a great distance from them out at sea, and Gudrun could see a great fountain from the heavens open as heavy rainfall fell on those dark grey ocean waves. The sun peaked through the dark, grey clouds, casting rays of light across the great blue, greyish ocean. It wasn't long before they would see the seaside keep, and its lone, great tower. With the great sea to its back and the forbidden forest to its front, the high stone walls overlooked a great clearing of farmlands. After some time, they could see the lone tower which stretched high behind the seaside keeps stone walls.

"There!" shouted Arvid as he could see the seaside keep across a great plain which stretched out in front of them.

They were mindful to keep a watchful eye on the forbidden forest, for who knows what evils may reach out to find them running along its borders.

"With haste men, for by the nights end we shall drink sweet grog and eat roasted lamb!" shouted Arvid with his words slurred and mangled as he struggled to speak, for they had been running for quite some time. It was then that Gudrun's pace slowed, and they all came to a stop.

"We are approaching from the south," said Gudrun as they all stopped and were breathing heavily.

Some bent over gasping for air while the others were standing tall with their hands on their aching sides.

"Keep moving and keep quiet!" exclaimed Arvid as they saw the mist creeping and crawling a great distance from them towards their direction.

One of the men sat on the ground, or perhaps he fell as they were exhausted from the long journey and the battle on the high pass to Grom a short time ago before they found themselves in this dire place. Gudrun placed Zain on the ground for him to rest, as he was tossed and battered across Gudrun's shoulders as he ran along the rolling plain.

"This is Ang'daban, resting place of a great many. These lands are cursed. We won't reach the seaside keeps gates before nightfall, and should we find ourselves within Ang'daban, then we will have ghouls, wraiths, specters and dark shadows to contest with," said Gudrun as he checked on Zain, for he was pale as a ghost himself and was hot to the touch and drenched in sweat.

Arvid stood up after catching his breath. He was panting and walked along the rocky, earth cracked ground as a soft sea breeze rushed up and over the jagged cliffs edge and a gentle mist sprayed their sun scorched faces.

The seaside keep stood there at the base of a volcanic mountain chain and all the men longed to find themselves behind its stone walls with good food and in good company. Mads and a few of the remaining cutthroats grouped together and began speaking in whispers with slight nods and moving their hands in gestures with one another. Arvid, who was visibly upset and eager to continue towards the keep looked on at Zain. He was in a dire condition and Arvid thought he may not live to see the next sunrise.

"What do you propose? We have the mist gnawing at our feet, and we would find ourselves within its grasps shortly should we rest here. The forbidden forest to the east would see our deaths should we enter it and with the ghouls of Ang'daban waiting for us to the north, how do you prefer to die?" asked Arvid who stood firm but was frightened and becoming hysterical for he had experienced a number of terrors on his journey through the north in the company of Mads and the cutthroats.

"We make camp here, and we arrive on the morrow," said Mads as some of the cutthroats started to journey towards the forbidden forest while others remained to set up a small fire.

They gathered twigs, sticks, and cut some wood from the scattered trees here high up on the great plain which overlooked the ocean. It was late day and with night approaching they were all worried and anxious but none more so than Arvid. What choice did they have? They wondered? At any rate it was an opportunity for a short rest they thought, and after a short time the cutthroats returned from the forbidden forest with a small boar, enough for all to eat.

With the sun setting fast and the twilight approaching, the men found themselves alone in the dark awaiting what unknown horrors may find them. Together they formed a circle around the calming fire as some of the men prepared the boar. A small reward, as soon they would be eating in delight the sweet, savory meat as they cast their restful gaze to the bright stars above. In the north, they found whatever comfort they could, be it the savory meet of an animal they hunted, or the sweet wild berries during their arduous journey along the forests edge.

Gudrun laid down with his side up against a small patch of wild grass. Zain was just one pace away from him, laying down on his back and staring at the stars. It was a small clearing in the wild grass, and they all made themselves as comfortable as they could with the very little supplies and provisions they had. There was not much chatter as the cool, quietness of the night chilled their bones should they move too far away from the fire. They were afraid, the lot of them as nighttime was a time where their imaginations ran wild with the horrors and unpleasantries that could come for them.

A heavy wind all but put the fire out as several of them scrambled to restart it. They first cut several shavings of some wood and bundled it together along with small sticks and twigs. One of the cutthroats pulled out some bark from his brown leather bag. This particular bark was flimsy and light, and it broke into pieces as he grabbed a fistful and placed it on the fire. They had placed several stones, about the size of a fist, around in a circle and the wood pile in the center of it. With flint came a flash and then a spark as the bark quickly went up in flame along with the rest of the tinder and kindling.

With some of the wood from the forest they fashioned the boar on a spin. First the boar was cleaned of its fur, then gutted and then they drove a wooden spear which passed clean through it. They rested the boar on top of two wooden poles which were drove into the hard earth on each side of the fire. These were crossed over one another to create a base for the boar; the spear with the boar rested on top and one of the cutthroats fashioned a handle to spin the boar over the fire as he blew on the fire and watched the bright yellow and red flames dance and the smoldering dark and orange embers glow.

Gudrun could see the men clearly now, as some had come closer to warm themselves by the fire. Removing their battle garments and helmets, some of them leaned in and warmed their rough hands over the burning fire, while others sat next to it. Waiting in hungry anticipation of the boar's savory meat, bellies growled, and the men grinned at one another. Arvid was pacing back and forth by the fire. His elaborate shinning plate mail reflected the moon light as it peaked its head out from behind the rolling clouds.

The men looked rough, with all bearing tattoos and scars. One man was missing a nose, and another an ear, and further still some their fingers or had scars with a slash across their face. All had clearly seen battle and had shown surprising courage being this far out in the wilderness for days on end. Gudrun knew though that while they may put on a good show, they were all frightened, spirits ready to be broken at any moment.

Mads had instructed some of them to march south and build fires every so often until they could no longer see their own campfire, or should they find themselves in danger they were to return at once. Slowly Gudrun and the others could see fire after fire being lit in the distance; Gudrun took this to be a warning that should the mist approach them they would see the fires go out, or perhaps it was a means of navigation should they need to leave quickly and return where hence they came and not run blind over the cliffs edge to crash on the rocks below.

Gudrun was relaxed and spoke with Zain who was also rather cheerful. They spoke of the previous wars they fought in, about the demon horde that poured out of the mountain where Zain and a great number of the exiles had made refuge and about other things for the campfire raised their spirits, if only for a short while. Gudrun peered into the darkness, towards the forbidden forest and he could see Mads eyes reflecting the moonlight.

Sitting by himself, Mads was the only one not eating. He was an eerie fellow indeed. He sat quietly and stiff on the cold earth in the middle of some grassy reeds. He was injured but made no mention of it at all, nor did he show any sign of fear. While the other men talked and looked to the stars and listened to the crash of the waves below the cliffs edge, Mads sat seemingly watching them, and listening to the forbidden forest behind them.

Upon hearing the conversation between Gudrun and Zain, Arvid came over and sat next to them. With a sword in one hand and some boar meat in the other, he passed the meat to Gudrun and then Zain before sitting down next to them. His armor was loud and heavy, it clanked and rattled as he sat down, and he almost fell over backwards before Gudrun caught him from tumbling.

"You call it Ang'daban, resting place of a great many. You say these lands are cursed?" said Arvid as he placed his battle sharpened sword on the ground and let out a sigh. "We have seen many hardships on our journey, I can't imagine this will be any worse than the rest," said Arvid as he leaned back and breathed up into the nights sky, watching his breath and the hot steam come from his mouth.

"You'd be wrong," said Gudrun as his eyes squinted and he grinded his teeth in despair. "For these lands are indeed cursed. Men's souls trapped and left to wander at night, for a great evil resides here. I've seen brave and courageous men reduced to flesh and bones who thought it was no difficulty to travel through Ang'daban," said Gudrun now seemingly staring off into the distance in remembering things he had rather forgotten.

Some of the brute cutthroats gathered around, listening to the tale as Gudrun spoke more of Ang'daban and its horrors.

"After the battle of Kazulgard, we rested at the keep before returning home to Grom. Several of the warriors were injured and had no hope to see the sun rise another day, and a greater number laid injured and needed tending to inside the seaside keep. All enjoyed the sweet grog that night for it had been a long while since anyone took part in merry making for the battle of Kazulgard was not against flesh and iron but against a great evil which has not been seen since old times. We were warned not to pass through, during the blackness of night, and wait for the daylight to continue home to Grom but a few did not heed the warning and were eager to return home to their families. Perhaps too jolly from the victory in the far reaches of the north, or homesick and drunk on the sweet mead, it didn't matter," said Gudrun as he lowered his head and stared into the burning fire.

Now, all the remaining cutthroats formed a circle around Gudrun. They stood with arms crossed or sat around him on the cold, hard earth, seemingly forgetting the cold nights air that rattled their bones as they were full on the savory boar's meat and listened intently. The sky was a dark overcast of clouds which gave way to moonlight which shined bright, silver rays across the plain that gave way to the dark silhouette of the forbidden forest as the trees swayed and creaked as the wind raged around them.

Gudrun still stared into the darkness while recalling the horrors of that night. As he spoke, the men exchanged sulky, depressed looks between themselves as some frowned, shivered and winced as he continued. A few of the brute cutthroats looked back at Mads to find him gazing right back at them with his piercing, glistening eyes as they reflected the bright moonlight on that cold, dark and sorrowful night.

"We heard screaming, one after another as we peered out into the darkness over the stone walls of the seaside keep. I gathered up a small party of uninjured warriors from the battle of Kazulgard and we rode horses out into the darkness to find an awful sight. It was an army of undead, the spirits of men in battle armor roaming this way and that across the plains. Tombs and mounds of dirt open as we watched the unhinged and deranged minds of the dead roaming about, mindless and dreadful. Ghouls as well, for they walked crouched with bodies bent across the ground, moaning and grunting as their disfigured bodies ate upon some of those who didn't heed the warning to wait until daylight. I saw wraiths who were cloaked in burning light feast upon men while they were still alive! Their screams and shouts made no difference as their lifeless bodies were lifted up into the air and torn apart and thrown about. Specters, which had the body of old men with white hair and glowing eyes, approached in white robes gazing at us. A most terrifying sight as they glided across the plain and passed clear through our bodies, and I felt a cold like falling through ice on a frozen lake. There were dark shadows there, indescribable, but I could hear their voices. Piercing our minds and hearts and they screeched and moaned all about us. We were descended upon and only but a few escaped with our lives. As we fled back into the keep, I saw a great white figure which stood taller than the rest. He bore a necklace made of the heads of the dead, all bearing crowns of magnificent splendor," said Gudrun as he broke his gaze out into the darkness and looked most distraught.

There was a moment of fraught silence, no doubt from telling the tale as his face was grim as were the faces of the cutthroats.

"With the gates to the seaside keep closed and Ang'daban behind us, those who had lived in the seaside keep told us more of a great battle that took place and claimed the lives of some three hundred thousand men! It was a battle that took place in ancient times, and much of the tale is lost but what remains is the cursed grounds of Ang'daban," said Gudrun as he composed himself and checked on Zain.

It was at the moment that the hoot of an owl was heard. One great hoot followed by a series of smaller hoots. Its high-pitched screeching song rang out into the cold nights air, a most unnerving and alarming noise as the men in the north associated owls with bad luck and misfortune. It flew right into the middle of the crowd and landed on Zains chest as he laid there staring up at the stars and now at this magnificent creature.

It had a solid black coat with a checkered pattern of white and dark stripes across its body and wings as it stretched out its feathers while landing on Zain. It turned its head in short, quick movements as it seemed to cast its gaze on the fire warmed men, as they pondered the mystery of each other. Its beak was sharp and curved with hints of gray and white, nothing out of the ordinary except for its unusual eyes. They were much larger than a normal owl, and they were glowing red. It seemed to have an entire night's sky in its eyes, with little sparkles of white stars that seemed to move and float about as it reared its head back and forth at the men. It began to hoot violently but not before flying away quickly up into the nights sky as it vanished in the smoke cloud which rose form their fire.

The men went silent, exchanging alarmed looks between one another before Mads rose slowly from the ground and walked towards them. He gave orders to some of the men, and they began to assemble themselves quickly. He spoke in a low, quiet voice and seemed to be the only one not moved by fear at the telling of evils which rested just north of them in Ang'daban. An ambiguous and mysterious man indeed, Gudrun thought to himself as he stared into the fire remembering the revulsions of Ang'daban and the ancient terror that he fought against in the battle of Kazulgard.

"Enough of your fear mongering, gather yourself," said Mads as he picked Zain up off the ground by his arm and shoved him towards Gudrun.

Arvid looked on in confusion and upon reading his expression, Mads motioned for the men to march.

"Nobody wishes to die here in their sleep. Your stomach is full, and your feet are rested. There is danger in the mist, and there is danger in the forbidden forest, and soon we will find out if his tongue speaks the truth," said Mads to Arvid as he turned and slowly walked north towards Ang'daban, disappearing into the darkness for the sky was covered by clouds and the moon was nowhere to be seen.

The cutthroats had quickly gathered their possessions and began to march their tired bodies north, and Gudrun who carried Zain followed suit. Arvid however stayed behind, only for a brief moment as he warmed himself by the fire. One of the cutthroat men had forgotten some of their possessions, for a great bow with arrows along with a bag made of goat leather lay on the ground at the base of the fire. This bow was made of yew for it had the ability to stretch and flex and was greatly valued in battle. It was as long as the height of a large man and was easy to draw.

Arvid peered to the south and saw that the fires had gone out which some of the cutthroats had started. He searched through the rough, goat leather bag and took some of the materials out. He covered an arrowhead with some light-colored cloth and sealed it together with molten pine resin. Lighting the arrowhead aflame, he removed it from the fire and drew back the string before letting it loose to watch as the flaming arrow pierced the nights sky as it soared into the distant darkness.

To his astonishment, it soared some one hundred paces into the sky before abruptly stopping and resting midair! It had struck something there, out in the darkness, out in the black of night that stood the height of a tall pine tree. With great fear, Arvid casted the bow to the ground and fled to the north in great haste to catch up to the rest of his company. Turning back but once, he could see the fire he warmed himself by now shrouded in rolling mist. Shrouded in the mist, something smashed the fire to bits as the glowing embers were scattered up into the nights sky and rained down, falling to the cold dark earth below.

He wondered if fine promises and treasure beyond measure was worth this journey, or if he should even live to see such rewards. He had been travelling days without rest, and with Grom destroyed and his bounty lost, what was left to salvage for all his hardship, he wondered. The mist stalked him and was at his heels as Arvid continued to run in his heavy armor which rattled in the dark. Gudrun yelled out to him; he was only some twenty paces away.

"Where wolf's ears are, wolf's teeth are near!" shouted Gudrun as some of the cutthroat men began to laugh, chuckle, and howl, for it was a known expression among the battle hardened in the north. Arvid saw no humor in the matter and wondered what manner of beast or evil thing sought to devour them, as he could hear a low, deep growl pursue him in the distant mist.

II ANG'DABAN

A terrible thing to be alone in the dark. The mind wanders and every whisper and shadow are an unimaginable, frightening foe which creeps and crawls towards you as your filled with what becomes an ever-growing sense of panic and alarm. A sense of dread filled the men as they wandered through that grassy plain. They found themselves deeper inland and the crashing waves below the cliffs edge were very distant now. The only comfort they found was the brief moment the bright, white moon stretched out and casted its rays across the plain. The dark silhouette of the tall, wavering trees to their east reminded them of the dangers lurking within the forbidden forest and the large mountain chains to their north reminded them that the seaside keep was close, yet still too far for comfort.

Gudrun called out to the frightened men, and they all gathered to him, for he knew these lands better than the lot of them. He took a moment to compose himself, for even Gudrun was shaken and on the edge of becoming hysterical. They spoke in whispers, and he motioned with his hands for all the cutthroats to come close. It was a dark night indeed, for their faces were concealed in the pitch black, and the only indication of a man standing next to you was his soft, panicked voice and the steam vapor that spewed out of his mouth on that cold night.

"I propose, should we wish to pass through Ang'daban unscathed, we do so without armor and weapons. Not a thing which makes noise nor a thing that poses a challenge to the evil that resides here. Perhaps we should pass through unnoticed, and we do so silently and together," whispered Gudrun although he himself was unsure of its success for no man escapes such evil twice.

At this the men began to remove their armor and cast their swords, axes, and spears to the ground. Arvid was reluctant for his armor was impressively ornate, and no doubt the spectacular armor was crafted by a master armor smith and must have come at a heavy price. Grudgingly and with indignation, Arvid removed his armor, and it clanged along the ground as Gudrun and the men looked on with a scowl. They counted their lot but Mads was nowhere to be found. Like a phantom, he had slipped away, vanished into the darkness of night.

"Mads?" Arvid called out and Gudrun quickly placed his hand over his mouth to silence him.

The men listened yet they heard nothing, only the rustling of leaves and twigs rolling across the hard, earth as strong gusts of wind now rolled across the grassy plain.

"No time, we move! Silent and together," exclaimed Gudrun and he led the men who huddled together like frightened sheep northward.

Near naked and defenseless as the day they entered this world, they walked on into the unknown. Poor Zain was half conscious as Gudrun carried him across the plain. They kept the dark silhouette of the forbidden forest to the east in their sights as the wind was gusting through the branches of the trees. A flurry of leaves came swirling out of the forest and the men covered their eyes for small bits and fragments showered their faces. They carried on for some time, following the sound of their footsteps and heavy breathing along with the vapor of mist at each man's exhale.

Soon they saw the tiny, bright flickering fires of the seaside keep. One, then two and then another could be seen in the far distance. They took these to be torches mounted on the high, stone walls of the seaside keep and they knew it wouldn't be long before they reached safety. Arvid began to wonder if this was a ruse, and perhaps Gudrun sought to bide his time and wait for a moment to strike. A scheme and clever trick he thought. Should he choose to take revenge for his capture, he could no doubt take on the lot of them with his bare hands as they were unarmed, and he was exceptionally strong.

"Where is this Ang'daban you speak of?" said Arvid in a slight whisper. "For we have walked silently for the better half of the night, not seeing any of the evils you mentioned," said Arvid who was now peering around in the dark nervously.

"It is because we have walked silently we haven't seen any. I suggest you keep moving and keep quiet!" exclaimed Gudrun angrily back at him.

They began to stumble as the ground here was filled with small mounds and they found themselves bumping into objects and tripping over stones. Gudrun urged them to keep moving but Arvid's courage and fortitude had failed him. He was exhausted, and his panic and fear had turned to frustration and intolerance. He removed a small torch which he had concealed and lit it a blaze. The men stopped and Gudrun's eyes widened, and his jaw dropped. Without hesitation Gudrun began to run while the other men looked around in the dark to find themselves in dire condition.

The small mounds were shallow dirt graves, and several of them had been opened. The stench of death was in the air, and they found themselves in somewhat of a tomb. A graveyard of sorts with all manner of burials. They saw a large, dull, wooden post which stood high above them and on it hung several iron cages. Inside were skeletons and their arms and hands hung free and their legs dangled and swayed in the wind. The skeletons cried out to their astonishment, hurling insults, and angry threats towards the men for disturbing their slumber. There were several of the wooden posts all around them and as they looked on, they saw graves opening and the dead rising. The dead rose and lit several iron braziers which were scattered around. The fire from these braziers were great and the dark grassy plain was now lit, and the men could see clearly.

Gudrun was running with Zain towards the seaside keep and by now was a great distance from them. Gudrun could hear the screams and shouts for help, but they were in vain, for he knew their fate was fixed. Arvid watched on as a skeleton from a small, earthy grave rose up and latched onto one of the men. He wrapped his boney arms around a cutthroat, pulling him down into the grave as he screamed and struggled to break free from its icy, boney grasp. The skeletons jaw opened and rattled as it laughed a most menacing laugh that filled the men with dread. It was not only skeletons for many walked aimlessly through the plains and had the appearance of men in battle armor but were aged beyond measure, walking mindlessly all the while moaning in despair as they continued to light up iron braziers.

The spirits of men wandered about, as several ghouls approached them. The cutthroats were frozen with fear as several ghouls, crawling along the ground, slowly stood up face to face with one of the men. Staring with a grimace, and with ooze pouring and dripping down from its dark and greenish face, it bit into the man's head and lifted him up as his body thrashed around before tossing him to a pack of ghouls who feasted upon his flesh. They made high pitched noises followed by low grumbling grunts as they descended upon him like a pack of hungry lions. One of the ghouls turned and screamed a frightful scream, its mouth full of sharp teeth which were jagged to the touch and were stained a dark red.

Arvid stumbled back and tripped over something, falling face first to the ground. He dropped his torch and upon looking up, he found another cutthroat being feasted upon by a ghoul. Its body was hairless and bound with muscle. Its skin was green, and it appeared to have the face of a man but had two small pointy ears and no nose or hair at all. Its eyes were black as night and its entire body oozed a foul-smelling slime which dripped and bled the ground a greenish hue. Arvid leapt up with his torch and turned to run, only to be face to face with another cutthroat whose body was suspended in the air as the man gasped for life.

A wraith, which had the appearance of a body shrouded in shadow, floated there in the air and flashed a terrible light. It was incredibly bright, Arvid raised his arms to cover his face, as he listened on to hear the cutthroat gasp for breath before being torn to pieces. The wraith was tall and slender, and Arvid could see two legs beneath a dark cape, yet his face was concealed and shrouded by a heavy dark mist. With a heavy flash its body was engulfed in flames, and it screeched across the field, lighting up what Arvid could see now clearly was a horde of undead roaming about.

Arvid ran as fast as he could towards the seaside keep. He looked around frantically, passing all manner of the undead although they seemed to pay him no mind. It was then he was faced with specters, and as he ran, they passed clean through his body. They were ice cold to the touch, their ethereal bodies resembled old men with long white hair and glowing eyes. They wore white robes of magnificent splendor, whiter than the whitest pearls or priestly robes. As Arvid ran, these specters paid him no mind but passed clean through him, one after the other. His body was chilled to its core, his skin was cold as ice, and his beard froze with icicles.

Gudrun glanced back to see the terror-struck Arvid running for his life and soon found himself within shouting distance of the great seaside keep. He could see figures standing along the high ramparts, bearing spears in hand and bows at the ready and cried out. To his dismay, a heavy mist engulfed him and like a great deluge it came forth from the forbidden forest and he was swarmed and consumed so that he could no longer see ten paces in front of him. There in the mist, he cried out but to no avail. It was not long before Arvid joined him, bending over with his hands on his knees as he gasped for air.

Then a great voice called out to them, far and high there beyond the mist. In an instant a great fire bellowed, and it roared and grew to be the length of some one hundred sheep in length and further beyond what they could see. The mist slowly scattered and vanished as if it was banished by the fire, and a familiar figure approached them. It was Alex riding the great ethereal elk. Alex rode out, leading two other horses bound by a hefty, rough rope and rode in a furious temper to reach them. Gudrun looked on in disbelief as Arvid quickly mounted one of the horses and rode off towards the seaside keep.

"The great Gudrun at a loss for words?" said Alex while grinning from ear to ear as she motioned for him to mount the elk as she switched to the horse, knowing he was far too heavy to ride the horses here.

They looked through the dark, cloudy mist and saw a great horde of the undead roaming about towards them. The undead wore battle armor, with sword, spear, axe, and mace at the ready. Their flesh was missing in some places and their bones were exposed as they moved slowly and directly towards them. With ghouls, wraiths, and specters all lurking about, they headed to the keep. Gudrun could see now that the fire was from the moat, and instead of being filled with water it had been filed with tinder, wooden logs and felt trees. Perhaps they did this to keep the mist at bay, to prevent it from breaching the keeps high stone walls, he wondered. Gudrun held onto the elks antlers as they charged across the tough stone, windswept bridge, over the engulfed and burning moat and into the great seaside keep for which they had longed for since leaving Grom.

"What happened to you?" asked Gudrun as he dismounted the elk and walked over to Alex.

"We must speak with Chieftain Grom. Doom and destruction are coming, and we haven't much time to prepare," replied Alex as they both embraced each other in a hug. "Chieftain Grom is here, and some of the survivors," said Alex as some of the men from the keep took the horse from her.

Some of the guards at the gate took Zain for he was in a dire state and rushed him off to a healer, for his wound was severe and his fate would soon be known.

It was a chaotic scene as several men stationed the high, stony ramparts of the keep with bow at the ready while others had sword at hand, guarding the gate. There were shouts and running this way and that, for the seaside keep was well armed and full of men at the ready to do battle with the mist.

"Survivors?" asked Gudrun with a troubled brow.

Alex gave a slight nod and looked out into the darkness.

"Theres much to be told, and it is best told with a drink in your hand and in the company of friends, but I fear our fate is fixed. Come, we should speak with Chieftain Grom, but not after a good night's rest," said Alex as they began to walk side by side.

They both started chatting as they strolled in towards the inner keep but their reunion was short lived. They both heard a loud, deep, and deafening roar out in the distance. Everyone around them went silent, and all eyes were fixed out into the darkness. They turned and looked out to see a large ghostly figure just on the other side of the bridge. A figure which stood taller than Gudrun, breathing heavily and the misty vapor from its breath rose high in the cool nights sky. There was a break in the clouds and the moonlight shined down and upon reaching this figure, it reflected the moonlight in its eyes as it glared at Gudrun and Alex. It wore a necklace made up of the heads of the dead, each bearing a magnificent crown of gold with incrusted gemstones.

With eyes locked on each other, the heavy, dark Iron gates closed behind them as it slammed into the soft ground. They both wondered what manner of evil this figure was, and if the night was indeed over. It began to rain heavily and Alex, Gudrun, and the rest of the folk in the keep sought refuge from the downpour. A great many rested that night and as for Arvid and Gudrun, they were shown to their sleeping quarters and were brought fresh bread, fruit, and a large pail of water.

Alex could not sleep, finding her way to the high ramparts she gazed out across the dark, turbulent, and violent sea. The salty spray of its mist on her face, the warmth from the moats fire which raged for the better half of the night, and the constant thought of her father left her in a state of restlessness. She thought of what was spoken by Mirvi, the mysterious woman in the forbidden forest.

"Do as I ask, and I will grant you a request as a promise to my word. You have a fortnight to decide, for the mist is coming and with it an evil of old," Alex repeated to herself over and over.

Was the evil of old the Vollgarim? Or perhaps the cave dwellers which they fought while escaping the ancient giant's city with the exiles, or perhaps it was the trolls, goblins, and ogres that attacked and killed a great many of those who fled the fires of Grom, and what caused the great fire which laid waste and destroyed the fortified village to begin with? She wondered. Alex stared out across the dark horizon and up to the bright stars as she pondered these things, not before succumbing to exhaustion and falling asleep in the frigid watchtower.

12 THE SEASIDE KEEP

"Nothing beats a warm bath, well, perhaps a thing or two," said Gudrun as he kicked the old, wooden door open and entered the dark room.

He was carrying Alex who was drenched to her bones from the midnights rain.

"You will catch your death sleeping out in the coldness of night," said Gudrun as he carried her over and across the fur draped floors towards a large, wooden tub.

Several women entered the room, servant girls under the authority of Chieftain Grom. A few of them began to undress Alex as she stood wet and shivering while the others emptied their hot, water filled jugs, into the large wooden bathtub. It was lined with a linen cloth to protect her from splinters.

Alex was still half asleep. Her eyes burning when she tried to open them, and with closed, heavy eyelids she leaned against the wall of the tub and breathed out slowly with a relaxed sigh. She was warm, and it had been a long time since she enjoyed a simple luxury in the most unhospitable northlands. The pretty, blond servant girls moved quickly about the room while Alex discovered that she was in one of the noble quarters inside the great keep.

The long, wooden floorboards squeaked and creaked as the servant girls moved about the room. One of them went about lighting a large fire in a magnificently crafted fireplace on the far side of the dark room. It was as wide as a horse, and equally tall and deep. Stacked with chopped and splintered firewood, it quickly went ablaze as it had been doused with some type of oil. The stony mantle of the fireplace was lined with candles and as they lit them one by one, Alex watched the tiny flickering and dance of the flames.

Quite a cozy place she thought to herself while dipping her head under the heated water. With both hands she ran her tiny fingers over her face, brushing her hair back off her face as it dangled and swayed over the edge of the tub. She rubbed her eyes with the palm of her hands and enjoyed another hot pail of water brought by a servant girl. An exceptionally beautiful servant girl brought Alex some soap which she took with a smile of delight.

The soap was made in the traditional fashion in these parts of the north, by cooking some rendered animal fat from a goat, sheep, or cow which they added with fresh spring water and a substance they derived from the ashes of burned wood. While not traditional, this soap was made with added fragrant herbs such as lavender, basil, rosemary, bee balm, catmint, and pineapple sage; a rare find in these parts and Alex gratefully accepted the unexpected gift.

After a short while all but a few of the servant girls remained as they idled in conversation, for they themselves were tired and restless after the previous night's events. They sat on the bed and spoke with Alex about last night as she reassured them, they were safe. The bed was wooden and intricately crafted with a triangle shaped headboard and footboard. At the base of the bed was a wooden chest and a sturdy iron lock on it. There were carvings of dragons, sword and shield, a tree along with some markings that Alex had not seen before. Alex walked across the large bear skin rug, pushing the soft, warm fur in between her toes before drinking from a small, metal golden goblet that had sweet mead in it, no doubt left by Gudrun.

The wooden shutters covering the window were slightly ajar, and the sunlight casted its bright rays into the dark room. Alex opened one and peered out across the courtyard. She was high above the ground; in fact, she could see beyond the stony rampart walls and out across the dark, grey sea and further still out towards the north. Rolling hills and verdant forests covered the countryside and the foothills in the distant north. There were snow covered mountains not a few nights ride into the distance, along with the towering fiery mountains which spouted magma and ash. Those mountains of fire went northward, up into and beyond the great fjords.

Alex dressed herself with the clothes brought by the servant girls and left the room. It was a simple robe, covered by a cloak and she went about roaming the halls of the great keep until greeted by Gudrun and some of the nights guard who accompanied him. Gudrun and Alex spoke of a great gathering and that Chieftain Grom sought them to join the audience in the afternoon. It was still early morning and they decided to roam the city together.

There was a soaring tower which stood in the center of the city. It had but a single door and had been locked and remained sealed since ancient times. It spiraled high up and casted a lengthy shadow. The city was surrounded by a great stone wall and upon its ramparts stood watchtowers filled with guards. Within the seaside keeps walls was the keep itself, a fortified stone structure which housed the nobility in days past when the north was still a great nation. There was a marketplace in town where trade was conducted, a large inn and tavern and several longhouses in the traditional Northman style. The houses were made of timber, stone and turf and beautiful to the eye. The wooden, brown frames with the bright green grassy roofs made a sharp contrast and Alex always found them to be crowded, little cozy homes full of mouthwatering food, and raging fires.

Alex and Gudrun surveyed the surrounding land from the high ramparts and could see the land known as Ang'daban clearly in the bright sun. The earth here was rough, bumpy, and stony. Uneven to travel on, rugged with broken earth as if a great beast has gnawed on it. They could see the large braziers which were now without fire, the shallow mounds and graves along with the skeletons swaying from their raised cages in the wind far off and scattered throughout the land. Indeed, it was a graveyard, a tomb for a great many. Alex looked to Gudrun and asked him about this land, but Gudrun only stared off into the distance towards the mountains which separated them from the now burned and charred village of Grom.

"Just legend and rumor," replied Gudrun as he crossed his arms and leaned over the stony ledge of the ramparts facing the cursed lands of Ang'daban.

"I am sorry old friend, ive reminded you of things you would rather forget. Let us enjoy the remainder of the day, for this afternoon I will share news which only adds to the burden we face and the hardship we have endured," replied Alex as Gudrun looked at her with a troubled brow which he tried to mask with a smile.

They continued along the high, stony ramparts, facing the fields of farmlands. They gazed out across the fertile land here with the wind in their hair. There were farmers working here under the fervent sun. With sunburned necks and blistered hands, they gathered crops at a frightful pace which they loaded onto horse bound carts and ushered quickly back into the fortified city. It was here in the seaside keep they raised pigs, cattle, goats, cows, chickens, and an assortment of animals. A great portion of farmland grew corn and potatoes; much of which is fed to the pigs and chickens. One of the crop laden carts had tipped over as the horses jumped and neighed in fear of being this close to the forbidden forests edge.

Alex and Gudrun found their way down from the ramparts and helped several farmers lift the tipped over cart, although much of the lifting was done by Gudrun. Alex helped pick up some of the spilled corn and was reminded of home. The corn here was colored in various shades and hues. One piece of corn had yellow kernels mixed in with purple, blue, pink, green and white while others were almost entirely blue, purple, with dark shades of green and pink. As she threw them back into the cart, she was reminded of fall feasts as a young girl. A time when corn was bountiful as were the fish in the rivers and buffalo on the great plains.

While daydreaming, Gudrun had picked up a sack of potatoes and placed them on top and across her shoulder to carry. Gudrun and Alex accompanied one of the farmers back inside the town into the cellar of one of the abandoned longhouses. As they went down into the cellar, beneath the earth, they stacked their bag of potatoes among the others. Here they found food which was to be stored for the approaching winter. There were jams, pickles, compote, and honey among other food stocks. When they returned to the cool morning air, they walked along the well-trodden path through the town. The walking paths were devoid of grass for they were worn out by the villagers and horses, but the town had managed to keep several patches of bright, green grass around the longhouses.

It was a pleasant city as they journeyed along towards the great hall which was impressively large and located outside the colossal tower which soared up towards the heavens. Alex and Gudrun stood at the sealed door which had some carvings and symbols not common in these lands or any lands for that matter. They looked up towards its peak but became dizzy due to its massive height. The air was filled with the chatter and laughter of children, guards walking and clanking in their metal armor, an old man walking with his grandchild who skipped along as the old man hobbled along with his walking cane, dogs barking in the distance as a great raven flew down and perched itself atop one of the longhouses, staring at Alex with its eyes following her as they continued towards the great hall.

Alex looked back at the raven whose feathery coat shinned silver in the sun. With its bright yellow iris and dark black pupil, it stretched out its dark black wings and made a loud raspy caw. It flew towards them and then off over the high rampart walls and towards the forbidden forest. As Alex and Gudrun approached the great hall, they were greeted by a number of heavily armed guards out front. Now some of these were guards under the authority of Chieftain

Grom and members of the nights guard led by Gudrun, and yet, some were not.

They walked up a large mound with torches driven into the earth there leading up to the doors to the great hall. It was magnificent and beautiful. High timber posts which had carvings of a great beast at their peak, slanted roofs with dragon carvings at the four corners with a large door that was embedded with gold; it was as tall as three men and it swung open as the guards pulled back on the heavy door handles. There was a large carving above the door that Alex had seen on a runestone somewhere, but she could not recall where. The great hall resembled a long house but was much larger and grandeur.

As they entered, they could see Chieftain Grom slumped over to one side in a large chair at the other end of the great hall as servants attended him. The hall was filled with several long tables that spanned from one end of the hall to the other. There was a great and boisterous chatter for it was full of armored warriors and Alex took it to be a sort of reunion by the manner they conversed. Some of them were from Grom while the others were Northmen she did not recognize. Braziers raged with fire and torches were lit. The tables were full of cups of mead and the servants were busy about preparing for the evening feasts, placing fine silver plates and cutlery on the tables. There was another man sitting next to Chieftain Grom, it was Septimus.

Septimus was a fierce man and a powerful warrior. He was unmatched for he had the strength of a bear and the heart of a lion. He is the only Northman known to have nearly bested Gudrun in a wrestling match. He wore a chainmail skirt with plate mail on top. His arms were exposed, and they were powerful and chiseled. His plate mail bore a picture of a wolf on his chest. Silver and bright, it had two lion heads where the armor would connect the front and back plate mail near his shoulders. His helmet was bright like silver with gold running from his forehead to the back of his skull. His helmet covered his head and had openings for his eyes while leaving his mouth and chin exposed.

Walking through the great hall, Alex passed the large fire pit at its center as the embers from the previous night still glowed and smoldered. She pushed her way through the high-spirited and unruly lot and as Septimus saw her, he stood up with haste and ran to greet her in a warm embrace.

"Loyal and true, brave and courageous, this one knows not death! Who can stand against her!" shouted Septimus as the other men cheered upon seeing it was Alex.

The crowd roared and cheered as praise was made and drinks were spilt.

"Lionhearted!" shouted one man across the hall and there was a great cheering for Alex.

"Unyielding! She who challenged Freyja!" shouted another and the crowd roared and became even more wild and rowdy.

At this Septimus neared her and shouted for the crowd to be silent and he managed to subdue the crowd to whispers.

"Nay, she is simply known as she who greets with fire!" screamed Septimus and at this the entire gathering were on their feet with sword and axe in hand, raising them to the sky.

He hugged Alex and they held onto one another with smiles from ear to ear. Gudrun came closer, simply walking through the crowd as men fell back and were nudged out of his way.

"She who greets with fire?" asked Gudrun, as Alex and Septimus were already reminiscing about the old days of battle and wonder.

Septimus looked to Gudrun and handed him a cup of mead from one of the beautiful, blond servant girls.

"Yes, for on that day all looked on and were astonished. You had arrived later in the day when the sun was setting, and the battle was already won. When the battle of Kazulgard raged and a great fury rained down against us, it was Alex who stood against the tide. For it was at that time an evil of old, an ancient from the depths emerged from the darkness. It smote a great many of our warriors and laid them to rest. I remembered it well, as does your great and honorable chieftain," said Septimus as he looked to Chieftain Grom whom saluted him with a cup of mead.

As Chieftain Grom drank, the mead ran down his aged chin and he was attended to by one of the servant girls.

"Yes, we have all heard the tale, but what does that have to do with," said Gudrun before he was interrupted by Septimus.

Many of the warriors had now gathered around and were listening, for some of them were under the authority of Septimus and had fought on that perilous day.

"This evil, it had the appearance of a man but was twisted and gruesome. It was a hulking figure, bound with muscle and flame. For it scorched the ground with every step it took. Verily I tell you, the frozen earth melted beneath it at every step it took. It bore no armor, nor weapon but its claws could rend armor and flesh alike. It had the body of a man but the face of a lion and the horns of a ram. Its face was scared, and its fur was wild and white as snow. It had several arms, each large and powerful," said Septimus as Gudrun looked on, focused as he was curious.

"Any man who moved too close was burned for their armor smoked and smoldered and their skin and blood boiled. It was Alex who removed her armor and with only her sword, she fought with the beast. As she fought her body ignited into flame, yet she continued to wage battle tirelessly and determined until she wounded the beast. It retreated towards the Frozen Wastes. Alex pursued it, along with a great number of our bravest. What became of it we know not, but we all know of Alex descending into the depths and returning a time later as the sole survivor," said Septimus as the crowed quieted down and most eyes were fixated on Alex.

Gudrun turned to Alex, but she was shaken and her face was as pale as the moon. Her body leaning this way and that, she could hardly stand, and Gudrun had to catch her before she fell to the ground. She had fainted and Gudrun picked her up with both arms and carried her back to her room and stood by her side as she slept.

13   A SHORT REST

Alex awoke to Gudrun combing her hair as she lay on her side, curling up beneath warm animal furs. Her pillow was cold but soft, filled with the feathers of an owl. As she turned and looked at Gudrun, he appeared troubled. He placed the comb, which was made from the antler of a deer, on top of the bedside table and handed Alex a cup of mead. Alex looked back at him with a smile but raised her eyebrows and was not interested in a drink.

"Perhaps you've tasted too much," said Gudrun as he placed the goblet of mead back onto the table. Alex swung her legs out from beneath the warmth that the animal furs provided and sat up. She placed both of her tiny hands against her face, rubbing her eyes and running her tiny fingers through her dark, black as night hair.

"Mead is an acquired taste, and I don't have the desire to become acquainted to it," said Alex as she turned to look at him.

Her eyes were bright azure, piercing, and bold yet warm.

"Not the mead," said Gudrun as he stared back at her and leaned in closer.

He spoke softly and quietly, and Alex shivered slightly from a draft entering the room through the window. Gudrun wrapped a large, dark sable cloak around her. It was soft and silky to the touch and while lightweight, it kept her warm.

"Maybe you have tasted too much battle, too much death. Blood is hard to wash off and you have been doing it for some time now. Women are meant to bear the burden of labor, but not of battle! You once told me that many are haunted by their guilt, unable to live with themselves for the things they did and the things they saw. Perhaps you are at destructions end and need to live out the rest of your days free from the burdens you carry," said Gudrun as he leaned in closer.

Alex looked back at him, but her eyes darted back and forth for she was reminded of something, and Gudrun could see it in her expression. He patted her on the shoulder for he was empathetic towards her plight yet sincerely worried it was worse than she let on.

"My father," said Alex as Gudrun interrupted her.

"Yes, hes gone Alex, no use chasing and holding onto the past. Let us venture forth to new lands, away from war and misery. We could lead a band of companions, start anew in search of lost treasures and ancient mysteries for the lands to the east are untouched and ripe for adventure. We would be a storm like no other and," said Gudrun yet Alex looked away before he could finish speaking and was reminded of Reis at the mention of a storm.

"How long have I been asleep?" asked Alex, and Gudrun replied that it had been two days.

Alex leaped out of bed, for she sought to speak with Chieftain Grom immediately and made haste to the great hall. Her armor and weapons had been placed in the room for her, and as she dressed, Gudrun turned his back and said he would meet her there. He was perplexed for he saw no urgency in the matter, yet worried as his dear friend had been succumbing to a deep sleep more and more often.

As Alex went outside, it was night and the stars in the sky were bright, flickering and sparkling as a shooting star soared across the nights sky. The town was lively, and she surmised that more people had arrived at the seaside keep. Walking past the inn and tavern, she saw a lively crowd drinking under the nights sky. She hurried towards the great hall, greeting guards with spear and shield at the entrance doors. As they pulled back the heavy timber doors, the gathering was feasting and drinking in merriment. Cheerfulness and euphoria filled the great hall as she walked through to find Gudrun standing at the fire in the center of the hall. Gudrun was cutting pieces of meat from the pig which was roasting there. A large savory fat piece of meat fell from his knife onto a silver plate that one of the servant girls carried away to Chieftain Grom.

Chieftain Grom, seeing Alex, stood slowly with the help of some servants around him and cried out but his voice was soft and weak, and nobody could hear him over the roar of the vibrant warriors of the north. Upon seeing this, Septimus cried out for the noise to subside and for ears to be granted to the honorable Chieftain Grom. The chatter and banter died down and with it, all attention went to Chieftain Grom as Alex approached and stood by his side. Chieftain Grom had a maimed leg and the servants helped lower him back into his chair as he sat sunken and almost in a state of complete stupor. The great hall went quiet as Chieftain Grom began to speak.

"We have gathered here to discuss our fate and the fate of the North. As you know, not but a few days have passed since our village was burned to cinder and ash. We fled here to the great seaside keep but not before sending out ravens to the other settlements, seeking out what has become and what is still remaining as we all have felt the sting and lash from this unspeakable foe. I see Septimus and his beloved have arrived, no doubt facing a fierce and relentless foe that stalks us during the light and falls upon us like the ravenous fiend who devours victims under the moon lit sky. You all know what I speak of. Now we are fortunate as luck smiles upon us, for this land does not fall prey to the mist and we are safe behind these formidable stone walls and yet, we will not last," said Chieftain Grom as the gathering of warriors was silent, save for the snap, pop and crackling of the fires in the many braziers spread around the great hall.

"Alex, tell them of what you know," said Chieftain Grom as some of the servant girls had ministered to him, bringing fresh mead and wiping his mouth for he drooled uncontrollably from one side of his mouth.

"Our worthy chieftain had sent me on an errand, to venture into the north to seek out what has befallen us. The evil that was sleeping has awoken and seeks to destroy us all. With luck, the ravens will summon whatever settlements still stand, but in truth we have not heard any news for quite some time. We seek to gather ourselves here to make a stand. A grueling journey from Grom to here, for I saw goblin, troll, ogre, bandits, undead, ghouls, wraiths, and specters. It does not end there for there are those who dwell in the hollow parts of the earth, deep down the ancient evils have risen and further still, giant beasts who roam the forbidden forests borders," said Alex as the crowd looked on.

Chieftain Grom nodded for her to continue; it was evident that he understood their plight better than the lot of them.

"The Vollgarim have returned," said Alex with lament and sorrow.

It was dead silent for all Northmen have heard of the Vollgarim yet many were in disbelief. Fearful and nervous, none of them showed it for it would have been viewed as cowardice and they prize courage and bravery on the battlefield.

"I saw them, verily a great number of them for I escaped the forbidden forest to see a legion whose number was a myriad upon myriad. They have not been seen in a great many of generation, yet they stand now and come for us. We have less than a fortnight before we will be overrun!" exclaimed Alex as there was now much commotion and chatter within the great hall.

"Sit down and be silent! What is this ruckus?" shouted Chieftain Grom.

A number of the men tried to leave the great hall as one of them cried out.

"We cannot defeat the Vollgarim!" one of the warriors cried.

"We can! And we will!" shouted back Gudrun.

He stood up and towered over the other warriors, wielding his ornate, great axe as he walked up and stood next to Alex and Chieftain Grom.

"I fought and killed an evil of old, underneath the mountain in the dark places beneath the earth. Alex wounded the great evil which brought fire and flame as it ravaged the far reaches of our lands in the north. Together we will drive back the Vollgarim and perhaps it is us men whom they will tell tales of to be remembered through the generations!" shouted Gudrun as the hysterical and raving warriors now were much like their own self again.

"Send more ravens at once!" shouted Septimus as several of his own guards left the great hall to prepare letters and at once the ravens were dispatched to warn the northern settlements of their impending doom and to join the great gathering here at the seaside keep.

Chieftain Grom leaned closer to Alex and clutched her arm. Alex knelt and Chieftain Grom whispered into her ear.

"You spoke nothing of the lady in the woods, this Mirvi whom warned you," said Chieftain Grom, and his mouth hung open and drool dripped out onto Alex's arm.

"I thought the Vollgarim would be hard enough to accept, no one will believe I met this mysterious figure, and I thought it not worth mentioning," said Alex as she took one of the linen clothes from a servant girl to wipe Chieftain Grom's mouth.

Chieftain Grom patted her on the arm and leaned back in his chair and slumped over to the side.

"Thank you for believing me," said Alex as she smiled at Chieftain Grom who looked back at her.

The light from the fires made his silver hair shine and his braided beard swayed gently as he hunched over to one side, resting up against the wooden chair. He drank a cup of mead and handed it to a servant girl. The mead rolled down his aged chin and spilt onto the armrest as he looked up to Alex.

"I believe you, and I believe this Mirvi that we will be overrun in a fortnight. The mist is coming and with it an evil of old, what can that be if not the Vollgarim. What vexes me is can we trust her to venture north beyond the Frozen Wastes? From what you described she seemed rather capable, this Mirvi. Could she be using us to her own advantage?" asked Chieftain Grom earnestly as Alex looked on to the crowd, wondering how many would be left standing after the onslaught of whatever they may face in the days to come.

"We will need more men. Even if all the settlements came, we would not be enough for what is coming. Someone saved me in the forest, someone who hurled stone and fire against a giant beast along the river. Allow me to seek them out, the Strange Ones," said Alex as Chieftain Grom looked at her with eyes wide full of curiosity.

"Very well, take whom you wish and seek them out. Little is known of them, rumor and myth surrounded by fog as thick as the very mist which seeks to destroy us," said Chieftain Grom as servant girls tended to him as it was very late.

"This old man needs to rest. I hope to see you again Alex, and I hope your right about them," said Chieftain Grom as he was helped to his feet and led away.

Alex watched Chieftain Grom leave the great hall. He had become like a father to her and while she gave some thought to what Gudrun had said, to flee and start anew in lands far off, she would never abandon Chieftain Grom or the people she had fought beside.

Alex walked to the entrance of the great hall and the guards closed the great, timber door behind her. She breathed in the cold nights air and saw Gudrun some distance away with Flux. As she approached, to her and Gudrun's surprise, Flux began to growl and snarl. Flux was fixated on Alex and Gudrun was unable to pull her away. His magnificent coat of solid black shimmered against the moonlight as he barked and growled at Alex. Gudrun called for some of the nights guard to come and pull Flux away. It took five men, strong and able to drag Flux away as Alex approached Gudrun who already suspected the night was not over.

"So old friend, where are we heading, to deaths door I presume?" asked Gudrun in a jovial, affable manner.

Alex looked up to the stars and closed her eyes, her thoughts were on her father and of the offer Mirvi had made. She remembered her father and a great number of warriors entered the abyss to pursue the ancient evil but to her dismay, not much else. The journey beyond the northern borders, beyond the Frozen Wastes to seek out what Mirvi had desired for the promise of her memories restored and to be reunited with her father was all that mattered but she knew it was a moot point should they not survive the coming battle.

"Rest well friend, for tomorrow we cross Ang'daban and seek out the Strange Ones. The ones who dwell under the mountain and in the forests. Perhaps they will come to our aid for they too will suffer in this war," said Alex as she looked to Gudrun.

Her azure eyes reflected the moonlight and glowed like embers, twinkling there as a gust of wind tore through the city. As they walked back to the keep, Gudrun said he would see her in the morning as he veered off towards the tavern. Alex slept in her room but awoke in the twilight, that time between the darkness and sunrise where the stars started to fade away and the day started anew. She wandered through the city before finding herself up along the ramparts overlooking the sea.

She surveyed the town and wondered what it was like in the past and at full strength. It had grown fat on the land for the farms were fertile and it was the last port city before reaching the northern fjords. Exotic food and trade goods would have lined the city shops for the wealth of the city was great and trade was abundant as were the travelers to and from the city. The ancient tower overlooked the forbidden forest and she thought of the catastrophe that was looming. She went forth and said farewell to Chieftain Grom in those early hours of the day and upon seeing Gudrun, she only motioned for him to follow as they strolled out towards the same dark, iron gates they had entered from to seek out the Strange Ones.

14   AN UNEXPECTED ALLY

"A good day to challenge death, a good day for high adventure!" said a man as he approached Alex and Gudrun who were standing at the large, iron gates of the city.

It was Zain and he was without an arm but in good spirits. He walked over to them with a smile on his face and greeted Gudrun with a handshake. They had cut his arm off to prevent the infection, but nonetheless he had survived his ordeal.

The nature of it was thus: Zain, laying on his back, was laid to rest on the grassy ground with his arms stretched out to his side. Two axes were heated in the blistering fire until the blades turned a fiery red. Now they placed a wooden plank underneath his arm and several warriors held him down. A warrior took one axe and pushed the heated blade into his arm near the shoulder and hammered the butt of the axe so it would pass through his arm like a knife might through warm butter. When the blade of the axe had severed his arm, they used the other heated axe and pressed it up against the wound to cauterize it. Rather painful yet it was said Zain did not make a noise, no cries, or tears for he was tough beyond measure.

The three had been reunited and travelled together out through the dark, iron gates. Zain carried a short axe with him and was adorned in his battle armor. They travelled by foot for the better part of the morning, passing through Ang'daban. Now it came to pass as they traversed a bumpy, broken up patch of earth they heard wailing and moaning from beneath them. Gudrun paid it no mind for he knew that the peril was in the darkness of night and if the sun shines, they were in no danger.

They were chatting, shooting the breeze and talking nineteen to the dozen when it happened. To their surprise, there stood a hulking figure, for if the cursed here had a king, this figure wore its crown. It stood taller than Gudrun and was bright white, bearing a necklace made of the heads of the dead, all bearing crowns of magnificent splendor.

"The dead here cry out, they long to embrace the restful sleep of the long night. For too long have we thirsted, too long have we hungered and not perished. We feel not the blade of a sword or the hack of the axe. Nor the wind on our face or the rain on our skin," said the Undead King as he walked directly in front of Gudrun.

Alex and Zain moved a few paces back, yet Gudrun remained still in place and looked up to the Undead King as they stood face to face.

"A proposal, for you show no fear as you pass through these cursed lands and perhaps you can free us. The unknown one who dwells in his castle far to the north cursed us, for we were once mighty men who lived in these lands. There was a great war here, and many fought and died by the sword. Our lord banished us for refusing to fight in his war and in return he cursed our broken bones and rent our flesh. The restless souls here are blinded, driven to madness for they cannot tell friend from foe and attack all who pass on these unholy grounds. We wait for another, stronger than I who can lift the curse," said the Undead King as he glared at Gudrun with sunken eyes, hunched over and indeed he was a ghastly sight.

"Should you defeat me, you shall reign king of these lands and break the curse and we shall rest forever," said the Undead King as Gudrun listened on intently.

Now Gudrun was prideful just as he was brave and while Alex and Zain pleaded with him, he was not persuaded. Gudrun dropped his axe and removed his armor and Alex and Zain had asked him what he was doing. Gudrun accepted the challenge of the Undead King, and they were to fight as equals. Gudrun fought bravely and was confident but after a time his countenance fell. He had bested the Undead King, but it was a rouse for the Undead King acted weak and unbalanced for he let Gudrun toss him about and smash him to the earth for a while but began to laugh and toss Gudrun this way and that until he was blooded and bruised. Alex could see that Gudrun, who fought valiantly and bravely, was about to die very quickly.

"A ruse, and a deceptive one for you beguiled Gudrun, for he seeks fortune and fame and will shed blood to receive it, much like yourself. Spare him and on my honor or payment of death I will lift your curse. Fight for us in the coming battle and I will kill this unknown one who casted a curse on you," said Alex as the Undead King froze and listened.

He held Gudrun's arm behind his back with one hand while the other clutched his head, turning his head nearly snapping it clean off. The Undead King released Gudrun and walked over to Alex who stood but a fraction of his height. The Undead King leaned in slowly to Alex, who could see his face clearly now. His body, a hulking white mass, formless and large now shrunk down to the size of a man and had the appearance of such. He was an old man whose hair was white as snow. His skin was fair and wrinkly, with bulging, sold white eyes with no pupils. His nose and lips were missing, only the empty cavity where a nose had once been along with broken, white teeth. He wore a crown of gold which covered his head and the sides of his face. He wore a torn purple cloak, and his ribcage was exposed. A frightful sight yet here he stood listening and considering what Alex has said.

Every ghoul, wraith, specter, and manner of undead emerged from the earth and stood without expression as the Undead King looked out upon the masses. Indeed, there were myriad upon myriad of the undead standing before them. The Undead King, now face to face with Alex, simply said "Agreed," before they all vanished as Zain, Alex and the bruised and battered Gudrun looked at each other, pondering the mystery of what had taken place.

15   THE STRANGE ONES WHO DWELL UNDER THE MOUNTAIN

"Sometimes you win, sometimes you lose," said Gudrun as he rubbed his large and rough hand across his bleeding lip.

They paused for a few moments as Gudrun was injured and needed to catch his breath. Bruised and beaten, he moved slowly as he brushed away dirt and rock from his skin.

"What were you thinking?" asked Alex as she crossed her arms and kicked a small stone across the ground.

"I suppose he flattered your vanity with the prospect of becoming king of these lands," said Alex as Gudrun looked at her with a grin, spitting blood and wiping his mouth with his hands.

One of his fingers had been dislocated and he pushed it back into place with a small snap.

"Well then, we march on," said Gudrun in good spirits as they continued to walk along the sun scorched plain.

The river was in sight and they soon crossed it, for the current was not strong and they welcomed the cool, refreshing water on their sunburned bodies. As they crossed to the other side, their water drenched bodies dripped droplets along the ground as they looked up towards the misty mountains which separated them from their burned and charred village of Grom. Nobody said it but they were all thinking it, would they encounter the Strange Ones or is this journey an act of sheer folly? They knew what dwelled in the mountains, what Gudrun had slain and that they would not be able to return before nightfall to find safety inside the seaside keep.

As they set out and entered the dark, thick forest at the base of the mountains, they came across a large object, unbeknown to them. It appeared to be a trebuchet but was much larger and carried a stone that only the giants could carry which had been carved with strange markings. Alex looked to Gudrun, and they recounted the events of fleeing the exiles camp as the Vollgarim and giant cave dwellers pursued them. Down the mountain and out along the river bend, they were reminded that it is not just the Vollgarim they need to be mindful of. For in these lands strange and dangerous beasts prowled, ready to devour any unsuspecting travelers.

They journeyed on through the dense, dark green forest and Alex spoke of the great stones of fire which soared through the air striking the great river beast in the valley to the east. If the Northmen did not build this trebuchet, then who? She wondered. She had hoped they were constructed by the Strange Ones who dwell under the mountain, and should they have a common enemy then perhaps their meeting will be a fruitful one.

It was not long before the mountainside met with the forests edge, and they went onward and upward through the mountains for the better part of the afternoon. They reached a peak that was devoid of all trees and grass, and they rested a short while. Alex opened a small bag and handed Zain and Gudrun a piece of bread. The bag was made of woolen cloth and was fastened at the top with a drawstring. The lid was made of leather, and she placed the bag along the ground and handed Zain and Gudrun a water pouch made from sheep skin. They drank and ate until they were content and watched the golden sun as it started to set over the horizon.

"How did Chieftain Grom take hearing about his daughter," asked Zain as he walked over and sat down next to Alex along the cold, hard earth.

Zain sat and drank and passed the sheep skin water pouch back to Alex. Gudrun joined them and picked up small, jagged rocks and tossed them over a ledge to the dark green forest below.

"As well as can be expected I suppose. Although theres was no explanation as to why he sent her with us nor did he say anything about her power over storm and lighting," said Alex as she leaned back against the cold, hard earth and looked out towards the beautiful, orange sun.

The temperature was dropping, and they soon found themselves underneath rolling, grey clouds and could hear a storm brewing from the heavens.

"Rain is coming, let us find shelter, perhaps a cave," said Gudrun and they began to search and scout the mountainside.

It was not long before Zain found a small cave where they could rest for the night. Alex made a small fire and as they sat inside next to the warmth of the flame, it began to pour rain down upon the mountainside. They sat there, watching the rain cascade down from the cave opening and listened to the sound of the water pelt against the hard, rocky mountain. With it came the rumbling of thunder and the shattering, crack and snapping of lighting across the heavens like a great whip which struck the very sky.

They slept and Zain offered to take the first watch. The evening sky was orange with clouds highlighted with shades of purple and pink, which gave way to the darkness of night and the heavy rain offered them some comfort for it was relaxing and soothing after their long journey from the seaside keep. It did not last, as Zain roused them from their sleep, and they awakened to large footsteps roaming just outside the cave.

Looking out they saw a large creature. It had the appearance of a man but much larger, for its legs were like the trunk of a tree and its arms were equally large. Its forearms and shoulders were unproportionally large compared to the rest of its arms and it walked hunched over with its head merging with its large, rounded back. Its skin looked leathery, and its body was covered with moss and vines from head to toe. It stood the height of four of five men, and it carried a large, spiked club as long as two men. It walked slowly and they could see it was searching for something. It paused and breathed in through its nostrils, and then continued on like it was tracking something, perhaps them.

"Never seen that," said Gudrun softly.

Zain and Alex looked at one another before looking back at the fearsome creature.

"Nor I," said Alex as she leaned back against Gudrun.

She looked to Gudrun and jokingly said, "maybe you should challenge him to a wrestling match, you know, you could reign as king over these lands," and she smiled and nudged him.

"I won't risk the good favor that I have garnered thus far," replied Gudrun with a grin. "That reminds me, I never thanked you for saving my life when I was held captive by Arvid, Mads and the cutthroats in the valley below," said Gudrun with sincerity.

"Ah, so that's why you struck him with your arrow?" said Zain as he poked at Gudrun's ear, what remained of it anyways as Gudrun pushed his hand away for it tickled him.

"It was all I could think of to save his life," replied Alex as they all sat and watched the creature continue out of sight.

They talked among themselves and said it was no troll or ogre, yet they have never seen or heard of any creature like this before. Indeed, they thought, the land is full of magical and hostile creatures, and they wondered what they may find in the depths of the cave. They decided to sleep there, listening to the cold, wet rain pelt the side of the mountain as the thunder echoed down into the depths and the bright flashes of lighting lit up the nights sky.

At twilight, right before the bright sun rose and casted its warmth across the land, Alex fashioned torches from the forest below and they went forth into the depths of the cave. Not knowing what or whom they should find, they travelled what seemed like an eternity before they were met with a soft yet deep voice. They froze in their tracks, and Alex waved the torch back and forth to see what stood in front of them, for the flames and light of the torch casted a shadow of a figure standing some ten paces ahead of them.

"Your far from the realm of men, and further still from the realm of my kind," it spoke as they tried to discern if it was friend or foe.

"What is it that you seek, may I ask?" it said as they could see its eyes glowing like that of an animal at night.

Those bright yellow eyes glowed in the dark, in the depths of that place. Alex stood firm but took a few steps before the creature told her to move no closer. She could not see it any clearer, only those bright yellow eyes hidden within a dark and large silhouette.

"We seek the Strange Ones, the ones of myth and legend. Those who dwell under the mountain, master craftsman of old, who shroud themselves in furs," said Alex as she stretched out her torch forward with squinted eyes that looked keenly into the darkness.

"Is that what we are, myth and legend?" it replied in a gentle but deep and echoing voice as the narrow passageway was slightly illuminated with more bright, glowing yellow

eyes as Gudrun and Zain waved their torches back and forth
to get a glimpse of them in that dark, narrow passageway.

"Truth be told, we know not, just stories from the distant
past. When I was a girl, my father told me of those who dwell
in the earth, in the secret parts where its warm and that those
passageways run deep and throughout the earth. He said they
have dwelled there since ancient times when the earth was
young, and the age of man had yet to come. Our ancestors
had told us that in those ancient times, when a great
cataclysm fell from the sky and all hope was lost, they
emerged and saved our peoples for we numbered as many as
the stars in the sky and yet those who dwell under the earth
were a far greater number like the sand on the shore," said
Alex as Gudrun and Zain listened on for they were without
knowledge of this.

More bright, yellow eyes surrounded them as they could
hear the breathing of a great many creatures. The room
glowed like fireflies floating and dancing in the tall grassy
plains on a cool summer's night. Alex casted her torch to the
ground and it fell at the feet of the creature. The light of the
torch was scattered, and she could see a beast of some sorts,
standing tall covered in hair.

Its entire body was covered in fur, and it stood as tall as
a man plus half of another. Its body was wide, large, and
impressive as it was bound with muscle. Its hair was all
black, save the grey from its eyebrows and beard. It braided
the hair on the sides of its head as the Northmen might braid
their beards, for its hair was long and thick. It wore no armor,
nor did it bear any weapon and it walked closer and stood
over the burning torch on the ground so that Alex and her
companions could see it clearly. It had the appearance of a
man and yet, it was different. Its nose was like that of a dog,
round and solid black and its teeth were white as bone and it
had four, sharp curved canine teeth sitting among them.

"You are wise, a credit to your father. I was there and
indeed that which fell from the sky scorched the earth and

stripped it raw. The rivers and lakes ran dry, and barren was the land as far as the east is from west. Not a single thing remained, the land devoid of tree, grass and flower for in those times it was a prelude to her arrival and a hint of what shall pass. Soon after the titans emerged and with them, peace and prosperity and yet nothing lasts forever. The earth there regrew, and the rivers ran deep yet men remained the same," it said as the other creatures came near and surrounded them.

"Tell me, she who greets with fire, why have you come?" it said in a soft, inviting manner.

Alex was intrigued for it spoke of the ancient past along with some history of her people and the story that even she did not truly believe until now about an ancient foe that fell from the sky.

"I ask for your help. That which prowls the night is coming to destroy us, the Vollgarim," said Alex as she breathed heavily with sorrow, for she suspected her plea would be rejected.

"Did it go on two legs or four," the Strange One asked with a solemn and serious expression on its hairy face.

"It seemed it did both," replied Alex as she tried to recall what she saw at the crossing of Grom through the mountains and of the myriad of Vollgarim as she left the forbidden forest.

"Its face was formless, with pieces missing. Sometimes appearing with one head and sometimes with two. I remember their fangs, jagged and menacing along with their bodies bound with scales as they tore our horses to pieces. We would find our men shredded and eviscerated, none more so than two poor visitors who camped outside the walled village of Grom," said Alex as she looked to Gudrun and Zain, both who stood unwavering, but Alex could tell they were slightly unhinged.

"A grotesque sight that impales the hearts of men and strikes terror into their minds. Favor should have it, that they are still changing into what they shall become and will in fact be weaker when they attack than they are now for their minds are without thought and their skin is like iron but soon it will become like the flesh of a man," said the Strange One as it turned to walk away as did the others in the cave as their glowing eyes retreated into the darkness.

"Will you not help us, please!" pleaded Alex as the figure paused for a moment before turning its head towards her.

"You are not what you seem, she who greets with fire. What you are, I do not know. Perhaps your farther was right about you," it said as it began to walk away down the long, dark corridor until Alex could only hear its footsteps receding away from them.

"Leave this place and make haste for daybreak is upon us and the days are against you. Your father was a great man who stood against evil. In time, we will see if you will do the same. I will take your plea to the elders who reside in the depths below, they will decide the manner of your aid," said the Strange One as the room went silent without the bright, yellow glowing eyes of the Strange Ones and Alex and her companions were left there alone and cold in the darkness.

Alex picked up her torch and they left the darkness of that silent place and returned to the surface to find that indeed the entire day had passed and much of the night for they were disoriented deep in the darkness, underneath the mountains. They moved quickly as the sun was rising, hoping to reach the seaside keep before they were overtaken by the odd creature that roams the mountainside or the ogres and trolls who live not far off near the snowcapped mountain tops above them.

"It knew of your people across the sea, and of your father?" asked Gudrun softly as he was deep in thought and speaking aloud more than asking a question to Alex.

Alex also wondered the meaning of the Strange One's words, for it had great knowledge, even calling her by her nickname that the Northmen had given her with great admiration. Zain was in good spirits, moving slightly slower than Alex and Gudrun for his wound was fresh and albeit having some pain, he made no sign of it.

"I hoped today might be a good day. Returning with news of help but instead we have lost another day and time is fleeting," said Alex as they ventured forth and soon, they reached the great river which empties into the sea.

Before they could cross, they heard a great commotion upriver where it bends and twists like a serpent, through the forest and out of their sight. It was an ogre, a rather large one which stood over the height of the trees there.

"Odd for an ogre to be this far down from the mountain, and alone," said Zain as he and the others hid behind a tree and peeked their curious heads out to watch the ogre.

They watched as it walked slowly, swinging its bulky, grey legs and arms as it entered the river. It walked heavy and clumsy as it splashed large amounts of water that spat out of the river and coated the leaves of the trees. The frothy water and bubbles dripped off the tree's leaves, and Zain motioned that they should leave this place for their feet were tired and their stomachs rumbled and growled.

Alex seemed distraught and Gudrun asked her what was troubling her. She walked staring into the distance as they began to cross the cursed unholy lands of Ang'daban. They walked quickly for they longed to be back, and it was hunger and thirst that drove them. There was a large flock of crows, or perhaps they were ravens, who circled above the treetops in the forbidden forest, and they heard their loud, raspy caw as they walked along the sun scorched earth.

"It has been more seasons than I can remember, and many moons have passed since I left my lands across the sea as a young girl. I left my people behind me, not knowing their fate or mine. Fate would have it I arrived here among you, having washed up on the shores along with my father and uncle after all our ships were sunk and dragged to the depths of the sea by the Leviathan. I am grateful to Chieftain Grom for accepting us and I owe him a debt I can't repay," said Alex as she continued to stare into the distance, up towards the ancient tower which was now visible near the horizon.

"The abyss, my father, why can't I remember?" asked Alex as she and Gudrun locked eyes and breathed in the salt laden air.

Their pace slowed as Zain stopped to rest for a moment. Alex picked at some of the yellow, short reeds which were scattered along the ground. She placed one of the reeds between her palms, up against her thumbs and tried to blow making a whistle before casting the reed to the ground.

"I have tried to forget the horrors that I beheld, there in the cold depths of the earth beneath the Frozen Wastes. Nothing but warped and wicked nightmares every night since then. Haunting my every moment, both asleep and awake. Things have felt different since then, I have felt different," said Alex as she looked on at Gudrun and Zain.

Gudrun shook his head back and forth with closed eyes and sealed lips. He motioned for Zain to join them as he and Alex started to walk again, side by side towards the keep. Gudrun thought to his own dreams. As menacing as they were, he could remember the battles fought and friends lost in great detail. He knew that many warriors have heavy hearts and disturbing thoughts after war, for it was common among those who face such chaos. Many warriors suffered with sleep and irrational thoughts, some could not control their emotions and burst into a rage at the slightest thing, while others relied heavy on a cup of mead or in the company of women. Alex was different though and he started to worry that his poor old friend was suffering in silence as she had become worse since that horrid day.

With boots covered in dirt, cloaks weathered and dusty and sun-dried hair, the three of them arrived in the late afternoon and upon entering the keep they noticed that more Northmen had come. The ravens had worked and some of the closer settlements had survived the perils of the lands to reach the keep. There would be others, and they hoped all would reach them before the Vollgarim attacked.

Alex, Gudrun, and Zain parted ways, each preparing themselves for the evening feast that Chieftain Grom would hold in the great hall that evening. Septimus stood there upon the high ramparts, speaking with some of the other chieftains who had arrived as they prepared a defense for the upcoming battle. Much to their dismay, another visitor would arrive that night, one that they did not expect, nor did they welcome.

16   THE VISITOR

That night a visitor came to the seaside keep and with him, a blistering cold as if the Frozen Wastes themselves fell upon them. The air was calm and quiet, and you could hear a whisper some fifty paces away. Braziers had been scattered about the city as some of the previous days, newly arrived warriors stood around them while turning their hands over, hovering them above the warmth of the flames. A great feast was held that night and people rambled the streets while making their way up to the mead hall to fill their bellies and warm themselves.

Alex, Gudrun, and Zain sat side by side in the great hall, sitting underneath one of the many beautifully crafted, golden sconces which held a might torch. The hall was made with stone and brick with several timber posts holding up an arched roof. Several candles were lit which sat in the chandeliers high above them, crafted of iron while several consisted of the brownish antlers of deer and elk. Indeed, the great hall was beautifully decorated for there was an assortment of round shields and spears along the stony, grey walls along with red and black banners which hung from the wooden rafters above. The tables were lined with a long white cloth and cup and plate were found with an assortment of food. The cups and plates were made from wood while some were made from silver. Wooden and animal bone crafted spoons sat in their small, carved out bowls as each warrior had no fork but a long sharp and pointed knife which served as both.

Gudrun was very excited, to the dismay of the servants, for they knew he would keep them busy as he had a ravenous appetite. It was said that Gudrun could drink one hundred and fifty cups of mead at such gatherings! A great number of servants continued to bring forth food, for there was goat, beef, mutton, pork, lamb, chicken, duck and even horsemeat. Gudrun sat eating the eggs of chickens and wild seabirds as Alex and Zain were laughing at a joke told from across the wooden table. Chieftain Grom was eating a bowl of blueberries. His teeth were stained with a blueish tint, for he ate so many over the years.

The table was nearly full of plates and bowls of food, for they brought out more onions, peas, cabbage, potatoes, corn, and bread. The crowd cheered as two men carried out a deer and wild boar which they placed to roast over the great fire pit in the center of the hall. Chieftain Grom sat in a large throne like chair at the end of the hall and next to him was Septimus.

Septimus was known to be quite fierce in battle, but a very kind man and we was loved by his people. He was the youngest of his brothers, but it came to pass that as his father was ripe with age, the second eldest brother plotted to kill the oldest to become chieftain. He succeeded, but he himself was betrayed by the younger brothers who followed suit in killing one another to claim the role of chieftain.

Septimus was but a young boy and so his faithful mother sent him away. Chieftain Grom raised him for a short time. He was far too young to know what had taken place but upon becoming a brave and cunning man, Chieftain Grom escorted him back to his homeland where he challenged his remaining brother to a duel. He cleft his brother in two,

SHE WHO GREETS WITH FIRE

146

striking a blow so great that his sword slashed him from in between his neck and shoulder down to his waist.

Septimus as the new chieftain served as a man of might and was deeply loved by his people. His kingdom surveyed the forests and the towering mountains that sat upon them. Those eastern mountains spanned along the great eastern ridge which had never been crossed, for the mountain peaks reach out and touch the very sky with spiky granite spires that line the mountain ridge high above where snow falls and rests upon its brow.

A great bell from one of the watchtowers which faced the sea began to sing is tune. A mighty bell, for it stood the height of a man and was struck by several man who swung a large metal bar into it repeatedly. The metal bar had handles and the men swung it like they might swing a mighty battling ram to break down a castle's door. A loud and piercing clanging came forth and the bell reverberated its noise through the air.

"Who approaches from the sea?" asked Gudrun with great astonishment, for the Leviathan roamed like a lion, ready to devour any who set sail.

There was a loud and panicked commotion in the great hall as some heavily armed warriors rushed through the great timber doors; accompanying them was the bitter cold and gusts of wind which lashed their faces and burned their skin. One warrior made haste and reached the side of Chieftain Grom. His silver plate mail armor clanged as his knee struck the floor. Kneeling beside the great chieftain, his hand trembled and shook as he cupped it and whispered. The chieftain's eyes went wide, and he sent the warrior away along with all the servants in the great hall.

Alex rushed to his side and Chieftain Grom only mouthed "bone ship," as he leaned back and seemed to talk incoherently to himself before Septimus approached them both. Alex looked about the great hall and wondered, what could frighten these brave and courageous men. She had never seen anything like it, for even Gudrun was unnerved and stumbled about, staggering, and knocking warriors over as his face was white as snow.

"Welcome him with hospitality and conviviality. Invite him into the great hall but know he will not partake in food nor drink. By no means offend or provoke him for none can stand against him and with luck, he will pass on by the mornings light," said Chieftain Grom as he ordered the guards to prepare another chair besides himself and Septimus.

"I'll accompany you," said Septimus as he and Alex departed from the great hall and walked quickly with intent along the well-trodden foot path towards the cliffs overlooking the sea.

There on the other side of the high stony walls was a narrow path leading down and along the cliffs edge to the rocky shore below. The path snaked and twisted back and forth. Those stairs were forged long ago under the searing sun but now crumbled and decayed as Alex and Septimus walked with haste. The stone stairs had bricks upon brick to their sides as tall as their waists, so that anyone who showed no caution or prudence could not fall to their death.

They reached the beach far below the seaside keep and continued along the causeway which jutted out across the rocky shore. They looked up towards the towering crag, seeing now that the steep rock face was rugged, and they could see the tiny flickering of torches from the watchtowers high above. The sand here was black and covered with tiny, sharp rocks; not pleasant for walking should you be barefoot.

The sea was dark with a heavy fog which rested upon it. With the constant roar of the ocean and the crash of waves around them, they stood there waiting. It was cold, both Alex and Septimus shivered as the sea brought forth a gale that was strong and they were forced to stand fast against it. There was a heavy, unnatural fog and a terrifying ship emerged as it breached the shore with a loud crash.

Formidable in size, it appeared to be made entirely of bone. Alex and Septimus perused the great ship with curiosity, yet Alex was on guard as Septimus seemed to be eager to greet their visitor. The nature of the ship was thus: it was made entirely of bone for the greater part of the keel and hull were made up of entire skeletons. They were animated for the jaws opened and shut as did their arms and legs wiggle and kick about. The skeletons along the keel and hull stretched their arms upwards as if they were supporting the weight of the ship. Some skeletons were larger than others and they appeared to be those of giants.

White and without blemish, the ship was bright, for the bones glistened in the moonlight. The foremast, main mast and mizzen were tall and in similar fashion, comprised of bones. The sails and shrouds were made up of human skin, flayed, stretched, and stitched. The figure head jutted out and away from the ship but ran along the hull and keel. It was a skeleton but the skull hard two large horns. It was menacing, for the jaw hung open and within it, large and sharp teeth which clattered against the cold, ocean waves.

Now this ship had no gunports, nor did it have a crew, and yet three figures appeared along with a tall, slender figure who leapt from the ship as it crashed against the rocky, stony shore.

The fog seemed to envelope the ship and with a gentle spray of the sea, Alex wiped her face as the four figures approached. It was dark and with the clouds concealing the moon she could not see their faces. Three of them wore helmets that covered their face, and the tall, slender figure appeared to be standing behind them.

Septimus greeted them in the old fashion, using an old tongue that Alex could not understand clearly. She could understand bits and pieces, hearing the words "come happy, blessed, welcome, health and friend." The three armored men nodded to Septimus, who turned and lead them back up the steep, stony steps along the rock face. Alex led with

Septimus in toe, and the visitors behind them. Alex did not turn back, yet she felt an intense cold as she walked on. The guards stationed at the watchtowers looked on as they all walked along the torch lit ground, up to the guards who opened the doors to the great hall.

There was no merrymaking or laughter, but silence and apprehension as the visitors entered the great hall. Without a pause they nudged past Alex and walked slowly to where Chieftain Grom had been seated. He was now standing, with the aid of two warriors and his seat was vacant. The tall, slender figure sat in the grandiose throne like chair of Chieftain Grom as his three companions stood behind and to the sides of him. Chieftain Grom took the smaller, less ornate chair beside him as Septimus returned to take his own chair.

"What have they come for?" asked Alex in a soft, quiet manner as Septimus walked by. Septimus paused and whispered in her ear.

"Perhaps for a bride," said Septimus as he looked up at her to see her with a squinted brow and upset expression.

"Don't worry, he shows favor to blonds and red heads," whispered Septimus with a smile as he returned to his chair, walking quickly across the quiet great hall.

The warriors sat silent, and none drank from the cup or ate. The fires in the braziers made crackling, snapping, and popping sounds as the wind whistled as the large, heavy entrance doors to the great hall were closed.

The tall slender figure sat upon his throne wearing a white linen shirt and a dark red robe. He appeared to be very old, for his hair was white as snow, pinned up upon his head and fell to his lower back. His skin was as pale as the moon, old and wrinkly, and he sat with his hands resting upon the arm rests of the chair. His hands were abnormally large with long slender fingers with sharp nails that seemed to be filed to fang.

The three who accompanied him removed their dark, spiked helmets and to the warrior's surprise, they were women. One with red hair like fire while the others were blond with hair that shined like the golden sun touching the top of the sea. They stood in impressively crafted, solid black armor that had been stained with blood and fit them tightly as if their very skin had turned to iron. They each carried a sword of magnificent splendor, not typically found here or elsewhere. Their swords were the same, with a golden pommel and grip made of tightly bound fibers which sparkled like the stars in the sky. The cross-guard shined and radiated the color of gold and with an exceedingly sharp edge and a raised fuller with engravings. The last third of the swords blade came to an extended, sharp point.

The hall sat silent for the visitor said nothing, seemingly waiting for Chieftain Grom to speak. A wolf howled in the distance as Chieftain Grom licked his lips and cleared his throat before straightening himself the best he could, leaning against the wall of his chair.

"We welcome you, and we hope your stay will be a long one," said Chieftain Grom as he was at a loss for words, for he knew he must be careful not to provoke him, yet he was also in danger and didn't wish to patronize.

"Thank you for your invitation, noble and wise king," said the visitor with a scornful smile.

He looked at Chieftain Grom and out to the great gathering of strong and brave warriors with disdain and condescension. Chieftain Grom had seen him before, once when he was a young boy still under the care of his father. He came for men, women, and children, always taking away as many as he desired, back to his castle in the far north which bordered the mountains of fire and the Frozen Wastes.

"Your presence here, as pleasant as it is, is a mystery to me. For I did not expect to see you until another generation had passed," said Chieftain Grom as he sought not to look the visitor in the eyes too long.

Alex locked eyes with one of the women who accompanied him, and as she did, she felt an uncontrollable urge, a thirst like she had not felt before. Parched as she was, she took a drink of mead from the table to the surprise of Gudrun and the others who sat motionless.

"Do not be afraid, nor should you worry, for I came not to spill blood or to take away your beloved peoples. I came ahead of whats to come, that which creeps in the night. You call them the Vollgarim," said the visitor as heads tilted up and the crowd listened more intently.

"My scouts tell me they now spread across the land like a plague, moving without fear and unhindered. They are still but children, for they will grow and morph into a plight which you cannot bear. For in the old times, they were a menace which united the north and the south. Even I and my army engaged them, for at that time they approached my very door and were fully mature, not the mindless horrors which you have seen this season, roaming about in the dark preying on the passersby. The arrogance, the insolence!" shouted the old, strange visitor as he looked to Chieftain Grom with a smile.

Chieftain Grom dismissed the gathering and all the warriors in the great hall left with haste for, they were full on meat and wine and took no pleasure to be in the company of the visitor, for his presence brought dread and angst, and while none admitted it, they were very afraid. Septimus, Alex, Gudrun, and Zain stayed behind and as they gathered, the old visitor stood up and began to meander through the great hall.

He walked slowly yet intently with his three beautiful guards staying near him, and as he approached the great fire in the center of the great hall, he reached in and clasped a smoldering brimstone with his large, boney hand. He squeezed and refined the brimstone as it glowed and smoked before being crushed to ash. He made no sign of pain and his hand remained without blemish as he turned to speak with Chieftain Grom.

"It has been two thousand years since ive seen them. I remember their faces, they call to me to join them for I was not always what I am now," said the old visitor as he shed a tear as the flicker of flames casted shadows upon his face.

He stared into the fire, not before turning to Alex as he stared at her as if he peered into her soul. Alex wondered the meaning of his words for she felt a tension deep within herself.

"I was not always as I am now, she who greets with fire. You and I are not so different, for we both stood against the tide and survived the crash of the waves. Your father understood his choice, as did I. What will you do when your time comes?" the visitor questioned with sincerity as all eyes were on Alex.

She didn't understand the meaning of his words, for he continued to speak in riddles, for his words were clever and wrapped in an enigma. Alex did not answer, and the visitor seemed just as confused as her at her lack of response.

"You are not what you seem. Perhaps in time my conviction will come to light, just as you came to darkness," said the visitor as he motioned with his hand and the flames of the fire grew.

The old visitor turned to Chieftain Grom and his face turned to a blank gaze.

"Well then, are we agreed? You know what you ask, and it may very well force their hand. Are you confident she will come?" asked the old visitor as his beautiful guards circled around Alex.

They appeared to loathe her with a growing repugnance, but she did not understand why, for they had never met before.

"I am sure, she is no longer my daughter. It must be done before the Vollgarim attack," said Chieftain Grom as he took a horn of mead and drank it and Alex could see now that

Chieftain Grom had intended for this strange visitor to come but hid his intensions from all the warriors, including her.

The mead spilled down his braided beard and he wiped his mouth with the back of his arm.

"Very well, I will return before you are besieged and we will see if your convictions are true," said the old visitor, and at this, he and his beautiful guards left without another word and returned to their bone ship and set sail across the foggy sea.

Alex could see there was more to the evening than meets the eye and that the visitor had come at Chieftain Grom's request, no doubt after receiving a raven which was sent to call for aid. She was perplexed, for the old visitor spoke of her father. Chieftain Grom looked upon Alex as she sat down with a troubled brow. She was confused, restless and fought something deep within herself. Alex and Gudrun spoke for a while, long after Chieftain Grom and Zain had left the great hall. They spoke of her dreams, along with Gudrun's and of the things that they have passed through along their journey and of Chieftain Grom's daughter.

"Do you know what's going on?" asked Alex but Gudrun looked away and would not match her gaze with his own.

Gudrun took a drink of mead from a wooden cup and placed it down gently and let out a sigh. He clasped his hands together and leaned towards Alex before speaking.

"I cannot tell you. Chieftain Grom said it isn't safe for you to know. Please do not be angry with me, I am sure he has his reasons," said Gudrun as he took another drink.

Gudrun was visibly disturbed for he cared for Alex and saw the inner turmoil she fought with day after day. He knew her thoughts were on her father, her uncle, and her people across the sea. She had endured much and while she was respected and adored by Chieftain Grom and cherished by the north peoples, she only sought peace and serenity.

"We have a few days left, let us hope some of the other settlements still stand and that they find their way here," said Gudrun before taking another drink and rising to his feet.

Alex seemed distraught and Gudrun could see her holding back tears in her eyes.

"When the visitor returns, he and I will fight to the death," said Gudrun as he took another drink before casting his wooden cup into the fire.

It rolled across the cinders before catching a flame and turning a brownish black hue as it smoked and warped in shape.

"What!" exclaimed Alex as she stood up and grabbed Gudrun by the wrist with both hands as he started to leave the great hall.

"He will kill you!" cried Alex as she began to beat her tiny hands across his wide chest.

Gudrun hugged her and told her not to interfere and to say nothing to anyone. Gudrun pushed Alex away and left the great hall. When he pushed the doors open with great force, the guards outside were nudged back and lost their footing. Alex felt the ice-cold air enter the room and it stung her lungs. She stood there by the fire, wiping her tears away and the blistering cold gave her goosebumps as she wondered how the visitor knew of her father and the riddles he spoke of.

It began to rain gently, but soon poured as if the heavens above broke and a mighty fountain sought to wash away the seaside keep. Alex ran to find Gudrun as he exited the great hall with haste. Her search was unfruitful, and upon entering one of the abandoned wooden houses, she found a small group of warriors there who were drinking good mead and eating loaves of bread. They paid her no mind as she laid down near the small but hot fire and played with two of the wild dogs there, who also sought shelter from the rain no doubt. Alex was soaked and took off a few garments as the dogs cuddled up next to her. As her eyes grew heavy, one of the warriors casted a bear skin fur over her and she slept to the sounds of rain and thunder, pondering the mystery of the visitor and the fate of her father.

17 NEW HOPE

Now the sun was shining and the ground which was previously drenched from the rain was hard and firm, dry like the blistered and broken desert for the sun that day was intense as is the ferocity of the brave Northmen who fought dragons and monsters, beasts, and evils. Their spirits were high as the birds which soared above, for more warriors had arrived in the early hours of that blessed day. Alex awoke to a large, mangy dog licking and nudging her from underneath the bear skin and as she pushed away the playful dog and opened the wooden, creaky door she saw a great number of warriors walking through the streets.

Two settlements, what was left of them, had arrived and she knew both well. She looked forward to the evening feast for it would be a time of joy, merrymaking and reuniting with old friends. There was very little that the men of the north did not enjoy more than mead, feasting, battle and being around good company. Indeed, for whatever hardship lay ahead of them, all worries, fears, and troubles drifted away like the morning dew as they came together for what may be their last few nights alive.

During the day everyone was busy with preparations for the upcoming battle. Septimus was high on the stony ramparts, overlooking the lands to the north. Rolling hills and verdant forests covered the countryside and the foothills further north towards the fjords and the mountains of fire beyond. Pockets of bright, white mist lay in the valleys. Thick as a heavy fog at sea, they could not see what lies underneath. A heard of deer were grazing along one of the hill tops and a gentle breeze came from the forbidden forest which scattered leaves and twigs along the ground.

Septimus had carried out an order from Chieftain Grom that the moat be filled with wood and a great number of men had been chopping down trees on the edge of the forbidden forest. The moat was stacked and a great number of fallen trees filled its depths. Cedar and spruce, and a great number of other trees, for the fires would need to be great to repel the encroaching mist should it engulf the keep. To his dismay, there was not much else to be done, for the high walls surrounding the city provided great protection and he knew they would be huddled inside, for an offensive on the open plain would be folly.

Warriors in town were sharpening swords and axes, crafting arrows and reminiscing of old days of battle and glory. They were encouraged by Alex's presence, for she bolstered their courage and gave them hope. Bundles of arrows were stacked high up along the rampart walls, for it would be lined with archers come the day of battle. Alex joined Septimus and enjoyed the breeze in her hair and listened to the chirping of birds that flew overhead.

A little, fat bird flew down and landed along the rough, stony edge of the rampart. Its gentle, soothing chirps filled the air. Its feathers were brown and grey with a bright orange belly. Its scaled and rough legs hopped along the stony rampart wall before hopping up Alex's arm. It turned its head sharply and quickly back and forth, as if Alex had said something interesting and it was listening. When Septimus reached out his hand, the bird flew to the east and out of sight.

"I've heard you have a way with animals," said Septimus as he leaned against the side of the rampart wall that overlooked the moat below.

Alex looked at him and smiled as Septimus began to recount his journey here to the seaside keep. They lost a great number of men to Fangore, an ancient beast who roamed the lands to the east along the great eastern mountains. It was like a wolf but much larger and ate the better portion of the men who traveled with Septimus.

"Verily I tell you, it swallowed several men whole along with their horses. Spear and axe struck its side to no avail, as did the arrow. It charged and crashed through the trees, running down alongside the mountain before laying waste to a great many. Bones like iron, hide like stone, who can approach him? Who can raise the sword against such a beast? As quick as it came, it disappeared, perhaps having eaten his fill, and being sated on human flesh. We lost at least two thousand men before fleeing. There are legends and myth but there is no dispute, Fangore roams and is beyond approach. Much like the Leviathan," said Septimus as he took a deep breath and licked his lips.

Septimus was a brave man, and even after such perils he was not shaken.

"Do you think more will come?" asked Alex as she looked up to the bright sun and closed her eyes.

She welcomed the blinding light and looked out at the forbidden forest which stretched into the horizon.

"The ravens have returned, and all are accounted for. If none come by tonight, then they have been slayed long ago or succumbed to the mist. Perhaps some tested their fate against whatever evils lurk out in the darkness as they braved it to reach us to no avail. Tonight we celebrate, for Zurn and Osric have come. We will need them in the battle ahead, we will need their swords," said Septimus with a smile as he slapped Alex gently on the shoulder before heading off to speak to some of the men at the nearby watchtower.

Alex returned to find Gudrun and Flux standing by a small, but very deep well. There was a number of men filling up sheep and goat waterskins and servant girls went to and fro as they began preparing the great hall for the evening feast. Flux charged and jumped on Alex, and to her and Gudrun's surprise, Flux attacked Alex with great ferocity. Snarling and gnawing on her, Alex was pinned and fought off Flux sustaining a soon to be bruise and several scratches. Gudrun pulled Flux off with a loud shout, lest Alex be shred to bits.

"Never seen her like that, a bit odd don't you think?" asked Gudrun as he patted Flux on the side of the neck, trying to calm the now growling and snarling animal that was more beast than dog.

"Maybe she smells the other dogs," replied Alex as she stood to her feet, brushing away the dust and dirt and examining small scratches along her arms.

They stood there for a while and spoke with one another, discussing Gudrun's encounter with the giant monstrosity whose head he cleft with his mighty sword and was mounted in the exiles camp along the high mountain ledge far across and above the forbidden forest.

"You come seeking treasures and fame, but all you have found is doom and ruin! It comes with an unquenchable thirst, driven by the madness from within, it will consume you all! It has already begun, you only hasten its plan! The blood you have shed brings its return! For it is in the mist that men's hearts will fail them, and we will rise again to devour this world. Three of seven are free and soon it will return!" the creatures exclaimed as Gudrun recalled his encounter with the mysterious foe.

They could not make heads or tails of what it spoke. Perhaps it spoke of the Vollgarim, perhaps it spoke of this battle to come but they were deeply troubled for Alex recalled her dream of the figures shrouded in mist and while Gudrun tried to comfort her and make sense of it, they were both distraught.

A group of women who were not servants to any chieftain, nor were they bound in marriage to any man, strolled the streets past Gudrun and Alex towards the eastern gate. The spoke a gentle greeting and Gudrun exchanged a few looks from these beauties as one of them handed him and Alex a flower. Their long, colored skirts swayed in the gentle wind as they snickered and whispered softly but not so softly that Alex and Gudrun could not hear them. Giggling and laughing, they continued towards the east gate as Gudrun exchanged smiles to Alex, who tossed her flower to the bottom of the deep, dark well. She could faintly see the ripples of water at the bottom as some warriors dropped a bucket and hauled up fresh spring water.

Flux broke free of Gudrun's grasp and ran free towards the great tower which stood there in the center of the city. It blotted out the sun, for it rose exceedingly high into the crystal-clear sky. Shades of blue and gentle white clouds rolled from west to east. A group of small children were playing with a kite, running down and in between Alex and Gudrun. One of the small boys stumbled along the dirt and rock ridden path, tripping and landing on his stomach but was unscathed. The young boy stood up and kept running as he giggled in excitement, for the kite was twisting and turning, carving its way through the wind above them. Childhood exuberances, the innocence of a child does not last in these harsh lands for the day would come when they would trade their kites and gadgets for the spear and shield or the sword and axe.

The day grew cold and the last remaining men who were cutting trees at the forbidden forests edge came back into the city, for the mist was forming, and although away from the city it was still an uncomfortable sight. The night grew closer, and everyone found themselves inside one of the many longhouses to warm themselves by the fire or inside the marvelous great hall as the feast would soon begin.

Alex walked through the dark, quiet city and passed by the great tower which stretched and reached towards the heavens. Indeed, she became dizzy while looking straight up at it, wondering if it touched the clouds. A sense of dread filled her, the same feelings of when she recalled the abyss. Gudrun saw her from the great halls entrance and called out to her. He waved and motioned for her to follow, and as he swung open the grandeur doors, the great hall was filled with great merriment and laughter.

Alex walked in past several heavily armored guards who stood at the entrance with mighty spears and heavy chainmail to see a great number gathered, for the warriors in the city grew and aside Chieftain Grom there sat Septimus, and the newly arrived Zurn and Osric. Both were mighty men who commanded respect and fear on the battlefield. Alex was happy to see them, for it had been long since they fought in the far reaches of the north and longer still since they shared good food and merriment that accompanies such occasions.

Alex greeted Zurn with a hug and he wrapped his arms around her and rocked her side to side. He raised her up in the air and shook her with a hearty laugh and a shout. He was a wild man from the fjords to the north where he led a great many men who lived off the fat of the land and raided the southern kingdoms continuously despite the peace agreement. They were known for being very tall and broad, having exceptional beards and a battle cry that would make the Valkyrie tuck tail and run. Their embrace was long and warm for he owed her a life debt, for on that day of great woe and despair, Alex had saved his young son who was lost deep beyond the Frozen Wastes.

"What have you been eating! This is a feast is it not!?" joked Zurn, for he had always teased Alex for being tiny and petite compared to the robust and stout women of the fjords.

Zurn was tall and fat, a powerful man who wore chainmail and swung a two-handed battle axe. There was bits and pieces of food still stuck in his dark, wild beard and he pushed his long dirty blond hair back over his head. He sat back down next to Chieftain Grom and slapped the buttocks of a servant girl who passed by as he took a drink of mead from her, then slapped her buttocks again as she left without complaint.

Zurn turned to the crowd who was rowdy and unruly beyond measure. There was a group of inebriated and intoxicated men who were each pulling on the ends of a rope. The men stood on each side of the fire pit until one group lost their footing and were pulled over the fire. The crowd roared and cheered for the winners as they, with hands raised, acknowledged their tiny victory before grabbing servant girls and kissing them as they tried to fight them off in a jovial manner. The few men pulled into the fire jumped and leapt for one's buttocks had caught fire while the others spun and jumped as some servant girls threw pitchers of water on them to douse the flames.

There was another group where one man would stand and the other sat upon his shoulders, fighting another group facing him as each would test their strength. As one man tried to hold onto the man who sat upon his shoulders, the other would push and grab at the other man across from him and the crowd cheered and rooted for their friends. This behavior was typical among them, for Zurn was a cheerful and humorous man himself. He was infamous for leaping over the side of a ship and walking on the oars from one end of the ship to the other. Zurn and Gudrun were naturally great friends, for they loved mead, to laugh, and above all the glory of battle.

Gudrun greeted him with a loud shout and they shook hands, not before each drew their weapons and gave a battle cry in jest and pretended to do battle. All the men of Zurn cheered for him with raised cups of mead and began to sing a song in the old tongue. Alex asked him about his journey from the fjords to the seaside keep, for the land is rather mountainous with difficult terrain to traverse and if he encountered the Vollgarim or any other manner of wild beasts or foul demons along the way.

To her surprise, Zurn told her that they travelled by sea, staying close to the shore for there was an unnatural fog that rolled over the dark waters, and the waves were calm and they saw no sign of the Leviathan. Luck would have it, they arrived without incident, for their own lands had recently been engulfed by the mist and with it, death each and every night as most of their lands were unwalled.

Now while Zurn and his peoples were wild barbarians who had a blood lust like no other, Osric was mild tempered, calm, and wise. He was the chieftain of a peoples from across the sea on a tiny island covered in forests with a sleeping volcano that sat at its center. They received the raven and a call for aid, leaving their black, sandy shores with great haste. A great number of their ships were lost at sea, for the Leviathan was like a lion who pursued a gazelle, devouring their ships as the men could only hope its rage would be subdued for its temper was beyond measure and it roamed the deep sea unhindered without ever being idle.

Osric greeted Alex with a hug and a smile. His high cheek bones rubbed into her soft cheeks. He was tall and slender with sharp, edgy features. His eyes were blue as sapphire and his long blond hair fell below his shoulders, and while he had many great qualitied, he was very vain. So vain of his beauty, he shaved his beard so it would not hide his face. He never married but had many sons and daughters and was constantly on guard, for he had sons who came and tried to slay him for his crown. Alex thought it was sad a father should have to slay his own son, but men are wicked and the greed and desire for wealth and riches will push a man to do unspeakable things, she thought.

The evening passed on and it was only when some of the warriors who stood guard reported an issue with the southern gate facing Ang'daban, were they reminded of the peril they found themselves in and that as each day passed, they were closer to an inevitable battle. Each night, Chieftain Grom would brief the new arrivals of the danger they faced. Osric stood firm and with his great sword strapped across his back, he exited to rest as the midnight hour approached.

It was then, something happened that they could not fathom. The bells of the watchtower rang, and a shout of battle was called. All those in the great hall rushed for their weapons and ran to the ramparts. A great numbers of men lined the streets with bows and arrows at the ready while many more lined the walls of the high, stony ramparts. Braziers were lit a flame throughout the city and formations were made; each chieftain leading their men to one of the cities three gates.

Alex joined Chieftain Grom and Gudrun above the east gate, standing along the ramparts they looked out into the darkness towards the forbidden forest. A large shadow approached, large and wide which shook the ground as it walked. Earth trembled beneath its feet as did the hearts of many inside the keep.

"Lay waste to this fiend! Arrows of fire!" shouted Zurn and without hesitation, his warriors on the ramparts and within the city fired a volley of arrows towards the fiend.

The flame of the arrows lit up the night as if the stars had fallen and hung themselves within the clouds. The arrows of flame struck this fiend, and a great many of other smaller fiends which prowled along the earth beneath it. Their bodies covered in tiny, flickering flames, scattered across the dark landscape. Septimus cried out for the moat to be lit and some warriors from the watchtowers tipped cauldrons over so that a liquid poured out of them and onto the chopped-up trees within the moat. Flaming arrows were fired into the moat and at once, the liquid caught fire and it spread quickly throughout the moat. The moat went ablaze, and the fire reached up to great heights for the men along the ramparts were warmed by the flame and their courage was strengthen by the splendid light.

Now with the great moat of fire ablaze, and the creatures nearing the city walls, they could see these night terrors clearly. They were ogres, trolls, and goblins, small and large, for their numbers filled the farmlands to the east of the city.

More arrows were fired yet the ogres did not attack but stood their ground. Chieftain Grom, seeing something was amiss, called out for all men to cease their volley and it went quiet. The great fiend who was now covered in arrows of flame, took its great mace and shattered all the arrows as it rubbed its mace along the front of its tall, iron hide body. It gave a great roar with its mace raised in the air.

"Peace noble king! For we were once mighty allies in battle against the darkness. Now too has the darkness returned and with it the evil from the depths which rise out of the mountains, for we are also subject to its relentless attack," said the great ogre as its voice was loud and deep, and filled the nights air.

It stood firm beyond the moat of fire and walked closer to the flames as it stood the height of the ramparts and spoke face to face with Chieftain Grom.

"What do you propose, that we should fight together against the mist and those who dwell in it?" asked Chieftain Grom who stood with the help of some warriors as he looked out at this army before him, face to face with the great ogre.

The other chieftains never knew a time of peace between man and ogres, nor did they know of a time where they were under the perils of such mist.

"We once stood together, side by side, for the Vollgarim do not know man from ogre nor do they show restraint against woman and child. We defend ourselves against the brazen attacks of your kind, but have we ever raided your camps and villages or hunted you for sport? The oaths sworn were broken long ago by men and it is we, those that you would call monsters and tyrants that seek peace," said the great ogre as the men along with the chieftains took its words to heart and wondered if men were indeed the real monsters.

"We honor the oath of the ancient kings. None of our kind shall ever attack yours for as long as the sun shines and the stars hang upon the nights sky. Join us in the coming battle, and together we shall live in peace," exclaimed Chieftain

Grom as the other chieftains looked to him with a nod or a face of support, for they knew that they needed arms for battle.

The great ogre leaned in closer, for it was a hulking mass of muscle with a hideous face. Its dark eyes were sunken into its head which had a pronounced brow with tiny, pointy ears. Its dark, grey body stood firm in front of Chieftain Grom and as it leaned in closer, they could smell its putrid breath and see row upon row of jagged teeth hidden behind a powerful and wide jaw. Its skull had a bone which ran from its forehead to the back of its skull like the fin of a shark.

"Honor your oath, just as the ancient kings honored theirs. We will stand together!" said the great ogre in a deep voice, and the men of the keep cheered and shouted praise to Chieftain Grom.

Gudrun was unsure of this alliance as well as some of the other brave warriors, but they knew it was necessary, for they could not fight against the great mountain ogres and the battle to come in a few days' time. Alex looked angry and upon hearing of this alliance she glared at the ogre. Its colored eyes sat deep within its skull. Those dark eyes glared back at Alex and Chieftain Grom called off the warriors and they returned to the great hall and walked about through the city as the cause for alarm had been quelled.

The night pressed on and all rested next to the warmth of a fire, for a great skin blistering coldness came that night along with a wind from the north. Some slept softly while others tossed and turned, for with the ogres came a feeling of insecurity, apprehension, and hesitation, for these were troubling times indeed with uncertainty ahead. Alex knew they had but a few days till the impending attack and she wondered if the north would indeed fall as she thought about how many sons and daughters would never return home.

18 THE DUEL

That day the sun showed them no favor nor was the flame warm to the touch, for a dreaded cold had crept down from the rolling hills and verdant forests to the north. Puffy grey clouds blotched out the sun and flashes of blue and white lighting scattered throughout the heavens as Alex and Gudrun walked the perimeter of the city walls. Septimus had ordered more men to cut trees from the forbidden forest and line them in the depths of the charred moat. The embers of its fire were still glowing, and dusty smoke rose into the dark, cloudy sky.

As Alex and Gudrun walked, each city gate was guarded by two hulking grey and greenish ogres which stood in front of the great iron gates. These ogres were not ordinary, for they stood the height of the rampart walls and carried a great black iron mace which was forged in the crucible of war. The spikes of the mace were exceedingly pointy and sharp. Alex and Gudrun peered out into the soon to be battlefield, and they could see a number of trolls, goblins, and ogres all encamped out in what once were lush and bountiful farmlands.

These were the trolls, goblins, and ogres that Zain spoke of as he hid his face within the city walls, not to show offense, for the exiles had hunted them in exchange for food, provisions, and mead. It was there that Arvid accompanied them, along with Septimus, Zurn and Osric. A lovely gathering, for they forgot about the woe and despair of the battle ahead and took comfort in the company of one another. They had all fought side by side further north and they recounted that day, for it was a great victory, yet they lost many men. Zain joined them, yet he walked nervously through the great number of trolls, goblins, and ogres who roamed about the land.

"Where is Mads?" questioned Alex as she looked back through the city's rusted, iron gate and fixed her gaze upon Arvid.

He slipped out into the darkness on the night of their arrival and yet, they wondered how anyone could survive a night, save several, out in the wilderness and so close to the forbidden forest.

"Truth be told, hes a shady fellow. Eerie and unnerving, I should have never accompanied him," said Arvid as he sat down next to a brazier, as they all did, for they huddled around its warmth on that frigid day.

"You say he came for a bounty, but for whom?" asked Gudrun as he leaned in closer to the fire, warming his hands as did the others.

They all looked around them, eyes darting this way and that as a group of green goblins and trolls lurched and staggered by them.

"Reis, the chieftain's daughter, though I did not know it was her at the time I accepted his proposal," replied Arvid as he kept his hand on his sword.

"Killing the chieftain daughter would provoke a war, all of the north would seek revenge," said Septimus as the others nodded in agreement.

It was then they heard the heavy footsteps and the trot of a horse. It was Chieftain Grom, sitting high upon the black and shimmering horse. It neighed gently as Chieftain Grom held the reins in his left hand for his right arm had been severed long ago. Gudrun helped him down and they all sat upon the soft earth. Chieftain Grom warmed himself by the fire as they gathered around him. Alex sat and leaned against him as a daughter might to her father, for she loved and cared for him like no other.

"It was I who placed the bounty on my daughters head, for she is evil beyond measure and had been corrupted long ago," said Chieftain Grom as the others looked on in shock and disbelief.

As some of them began to speak, he interrupted them with a motion of his hand as he began to whisper; perhaps he struggled to speak for he was old, tired, and run down by life.

"If anyone close to us tried to strike her down and failed, I feared her retribution would be our end and it is why I enlisted aid from another, someone far from us. When we returned from the north, I was maimed and clung to life. Luck be that Alex was with us, for she fought the demon of fire and brimstone and saved me and a great many of us that day. Now there was a great evil which dwelled there on the borders of what is known and what is unknown. There in the Frozen Wastes, we captured an evil and bound it with chains. Gudrun, you remember it well," said Chieftain Grom as Gudrun nodded and stood up with his arms crossed.

"Yes, bounded in chains it spoke in a strange tongue. We struck it with the axe and with the sword but to no avail. It bled not nor did it cease in its murmuring and whispers. Dragged it back to Grom we did and flung it to the flame but to no avail, it burned and glowed like a sword forged in the fire but died not," said Gudrun as he paced back and forth with his hand on his sword.

"Yes, you remember it well. We buried it deep under the village of Grom in a chamber of iron, behind a door that was behind a door, for we kept it secret. No food or water yet it remained and thrived, for in the depths of that place its eyes glowed in the dark and it stayed a secret, save for me and Gudrun knowing its resting place," said Chieftain Grom as he looked on to Gudrun.

Alex had the face of betrayal and bewilderment on her face, and guessing her thoughts, Grom spoke to her with a sad face.

"I am sorry girl, but you returned sometime after from the far frozen north, from your encounter in the deep, dark abyss and we sought not to trouble you further. You were not yourself and the evil was buried and forgotten, but something happened recently, something we did not expect. My beloved daughter began to speak in her sleep once we captured that evil and locked it away, even more so as time passed on, murmuring and whispering in the likeness of that evil," said Chieftain Grom as he shed a tear and his voice began to tremble.

"Soon before you were tasked to venture north, I checked that tomb, deep under the village of Grom. I found its chains opened and shattered yet it I could find no trace of that evil. It had broken free of its bonds and escaped, but it left no trade for it roams free," said Chieftain Grom as he looked to the other chieftains around him.

They were all disturbed for they fought the evils in the far north and felt the pain and sorrow of Chieftain Grom.

"Soon after I was visited by a woman, the Mirvi you spoke of. She warned me that this evil corrupts the hearts of men and urged me to leave that place or send my daughter to the bottom of the sea, but I didn't heed her warning and for it, I believe my daughter has fallen prey to it. That evil, its gaze is like the salt in the sea to the eyes and its murmuring like a poison, for the night you and Gudrun, my daughter and Ødger left for the north, we found a stone that Reis bears in her necklace deep in the evils prison. We suspect she was called to it, like a moth to the flame but the rest is unknown. At first a laugh, then sinister whispering and by the hour of the moon, the village of Grom went a flame and we were forced to flee to the north, here to the seaside keep," said Chieftain Grom as he regained his composure as the others listened on.

"Tonight, he who resides in his castle on the mountains of flame high above the fjords will return. He who is not a man, who cannot be subdued or conquered will come and fight against Gudrun, and none shall intervene on Gudrun's behalf for reasons I cannot speak off. Honor my command for Gudrun and I alone know the reasoning for this, and it will be shared when the time calls for it," said Chieftain

Grom with a solemn face and all made a motion of agreement.

Alex was defiant, and as she stood up to make a truculent and quarrelsome response, Gudrun placed his hand on her tiny shoulder and reassured her that he would survive tonight's duel and that she should remain calm, for all warriors derive a great sense of courage and bravery from her which would be needed against the Vollgarim.

While Alex was tense and wounded from the secret kept from her, her mood changed like a wind at sea, for newly arrived warriors rode in from the forbidden forests edge. It was Odd-eye and his company of warriors which were a welcomed sight. His journey near the forbidden forests edge had unnerved him along with an encounter with Fangore whom consumed a great number of his warriors. Even more so after seeing a band of trolls, goblins, and ogres roaming in between the city gates and the forbidden forest.

They bid him welcome along with a herald from the seaside keep which rode a magnificent black steed. He bore a long spear in one hand and with his other hand he held the reins of the horse. Odd-eye and his company rode in through the city gates as did Chieftain Grom while the other chieftains walked back inside. Gudrun, Zain, and Arvid stayed behind with Alex and with a friendly hail and smile did they greet Odd-eye.

Odd-eye was born blind at birth yet gained his sight as a young man. Strong with the bow and even more so with spear and shield, he was renowned for duels, and it is said he fought over two hundred which were all to the death. Despite his prowess on the battlefield, he was wounded by a jealous lover who slashed and gouged his eye, hence his name. He wore no patch but while one eye was blue, the other had turned white for he was blinded in one eye as if it were his destiny to return to his former self.

He was an impressive youth, beautiful and kind. Tall and slender, his hair was golden like the summer's wheat harvest, with a golden mustache that fed into his golden beard. The youngest of his brothers but they were all slain in the north on that day of great battle. He ascended to chieftain, much to his dismay, for he favored mead and woman, not the sword and shield despite his natural talent. As he passed by, he thanked them wholeheartedly and made a crude joke to which the men laughed but Alex paid him no mind. As he rode in, he leapt from his horse and greeted Zurn heartily with laughs and praise.

The day grew dark and with it, the coldness of night, for the winters cold came early that year. A heavy, white fog rolled in from the expansive sea and while the sun found its way occasionally through the overcast clouds, it began to snow ever so gently. Small snowflakes fell here and there as people went quickly about lighting the remaining braziers spread throughout the town. A bell was rung as the bone ship had returned and with it the mysterious man from the north who was accompanied by his three powerful, beautiful guards.

Once again, Septimus and Alex were asked to greet them and accompany them to the great hall. As they walked down the cliffs edge to the rocky shore below, they could see the ship more clearly in the dwindling daylight. Indeed, the ship was a sight of terror for it was made of bone and the bones themselves were animated and full of life. There were no rowers nor were there a crew to row the ship, instead the skeletons which made up the keel of the ship stretched out their boney arms and rowed through the unfriendly sea. The bones snickered and laughed menacingly towards them, and the mysterious visitor along with his three guards leapt from the ship and pushed past them as Septimus tried to greet them.

Alex and Septimus looked at one another with raised eyes and tucked in lips before following them back up the stony walkway, back up the twisting tower of stairs which were brittle and broke apart under the scorching sun from ages of exposure. As they looked out to sea, they could see a heavy, white fog which stretched up along the jagged, northern coast and beyond toward the great fjords. To their surprise, Chieftain Grom and the other chieftains were standing in the city at the base of the ancient tower. Gudrun had three shields before him, and some warriors were sharpening his sword.

A crowd had gathered, and it began to snow with great speed. The visitor stood there in his dark red robe, unarmed as the crowd gathered around them. This duel was not in the normal fashion of being fought upon the hide of an animal like the ox, nor were there boundaries to the duel, for the crowd served as the limits as they surrounded Gudrun and the visitor along with his three guards.

The visitors three beautiful guards removed their dark, spikey helmets and stood with their magnificent swords to make a triangle instead of the traditional square in such duels. Zurn and Odd-eye smiled warmly and provocatively at the three beautiful guards. They smiled back, only to expose a set of fangs to which Zurn and Odd-eye stopped smiling and looked at one another in disbelief. Gudrun carried a shield in one hand and his sword in the other and walked towards the center of the gathering.

"We stand her to settle a dispute, for Gudrun had made insults and has been challenged. Let the duel settle the dispute so that peace be restored," said Chieftain Grom as he stood in the crowd with the aid of some warriors.

Gudrun looked to Alex with a nod, and she took it as him reminding her not to get involved and his promise he would survive. She stood there with arms crossed as Gudrun braved this fearsome thing, for he was more thing than man. His skin was as pale as the moon, old and wrinkly. His hands were abnormally large with long slender fingers with sharp nails that seemed to be filed to fang, and while Gudrun was armed with sword and shield, the old, strange visitor carried no weapon.

Chieftain Grom began the duel with a shout and Gudrun charged forward. He swung his sword mightily in the air and as it came crashing down like a great wave at sea, the visitor caught it in his hand and tossed Gudrun to the side with the other. His long boney fingers wrapped around the sharp sword and yet, he was unharmed. He exposed his teeth and laughed like an old man would, opening his mouth to laugh a deep drawn-out laugh while applauding his hands together at the abashed and disconcerted Gudrun.

"I expected more from the man who claimed to kill beast, demon, giant, and the ancient evils of old," said the visitor as his red robe danced and seemingly floated off the very ground behind him.

"Do you think you can kill me, the one who has been drunk on the blood of men since ancient times? The one who has survived her, and a great many like her?" said the visitor as he smiled and looked to Chieftain Grom who looked solemn yet viewed the visitor as awe-inspiring.

Gudrun recomposed himself and charged forward again, yet the visitor moved like lighting. He moved at a speed that could not be seen, and his razor-sharp claws struck Gudrun's shield which shattered to pieces. Gudrun grunted as he swung his mighty sword but missed, as the visitor in the red robe moved at a speed like a falling star. His red robe blew in the wind, and he turned his back and walked away, looking up to the clouds which were dark black as a storm was brewing.

His gaze met Alex as he turned back to face Gudrun and with great speed, he struck a blow to Gudrun which rent his armor. His large, red stained cuirass was bent and broken, revealing the chainmail underneath it. A piece of armor guarding his neck was broken into pieces and the iron bits fell to the soft earth as warriors looked on fearfully and thought how Gudrun could overcome such a foe. There were whispers among them that Gudrun could choose to end the duel, but he would be viewed as an outlaw, and casted out from society. Not a fitting end to a noble warrior who claimed the life of many.

It began to snow even greater, and Gudrun picked up his second shield and approached with caution. Gudrun was surrounded by the red robe as it seemed to be more a part of the man than a piece of clothing. He wrapped his arms around Gudrun and began to squeeze, lifting him into the air. Gudrun gasped for breath as his gleaming gauntlets were crushed to pieces. The bracers, forged in fire under the anvil of a blacksmith, were in bits and pieces along the wet ground and Gudrun was released and began to stagger back only to be met by the claws of the red robed visitor who tore his shield to pieces yet again.

Lighting and thunder filled the sky for the dark clouds opened and unleashed a torrent of rain and snow that drenched all who bore witness to the duel. Gudrun picked up his third shield and casted it at the red robed man and charged forward while he was distracted. With both hands, he raised his mighty sword and upon striking him, his sword shattered into pieces; the visitor was unscathed and not a single drop of blood was shed upon it crashing into his head.

"Be patient dear, wait your turn. For after I slay him, I shall come for the one who made a pact with the Undead King to lift his curse," said the red robed visitor as he glared at Alex before laughing a very deep, drawn out laugh which echoed through the seaside keep.

Thunder struck the ground around them as Gudrun was lifted into the air by his throat as the visitor bellowed a most menacing and drawn out, deep laugh. Alex was afraid of losing her friend and as she pulled a throwing axe from underneath her garment, she was seized by someone familiar, it was Mads.

"Little kitten with claws, don't do anything foolish!" exclaimed Mads as he held onto Alex while Gudrun struggled to breath while in the grasps of this unearthly fellow.

At that moment, the dark clouds parted, and Reis descended from the sky bearing lighting down upon the red robed visitor with the sounds of thunder all around them. The three beautiful guards intervened and with their swords, absorbed the lighting that sought to strike down the red robed visitor.

The old, strange visitor casted Gudrun aside and leapt high into the air, sinking his teeth into Reis's throat. They fell to the earth and as lighting fell from the heavens, the three beautiful bodyguards shielded him as he drained the blood from her body. The ground ran red, and the clouds departed and there was once again sunshine. The wet ground was soaked, filled with small pools of blood as it ran down the embankment reaching the very moat outside the city gates.

Alex tended to Gudrun who was unharmed but shaken and sore. She knelt there on the soft earth alongside Gudrun as he nursed his wounds and was slow to stand. The gathering was in awe as the crowded mass spread out and sought the wisdom of Chieftain Grom. Reis was limp and the red robe visitor having drained her of life, stood to his feet and all saw his jagged fangs as his face was covered in blood. The contrast was great for his skin was pale as snow against the bright red blood which was splashed across his mouth.

A great mist rose from her body. A figure shrouded in darkness could be seen within the mist, for it stood in the likeness of a man but was large and powerful. Its body smooth and appeared like water, its face had no shape or form, but its eyes glowed a bright yellow. It moved to smite Gudrun, but one of the beautiful guards of the red robed visitor made haste to intercept it. Her blade pierced it to no avail, and she was flung back several feet. This figure wrapped in mist moved to the ancient tower and began to break apart the great fortified doors which were sealed, and the doors began to give way if only but for a moment.

"It is done! Mirvi, it is done!" shouted Chieftain Grom and then all saw a magnificent light that appeared like a star fall from the heavens and pierce the clouds above.

It fell to the earth, spiraling and sparkling with great haste and landed in their midst. Its light was blinding, and many shielded their eyes. There stood Mirvi, beautiful and splendid, save for the half of her that was death and decay. She was tall and slender with clouds of fire and mist that concealed her feet.

She stood there for all to see, and a great wind emanated from her so that none could stand, and all fell to the ground or knelt to face her. She held a dark orb which hovered above her hand near her shoulder. Inside it, only what can be described as flashes of lighting and burning embers could be seen and then whispers seemed to come from it which were quite menacing and mysterious.

The evil figure who was trying to break open the ancient tower doors worked with great speed, deliberately but desperately as it tried to breach the sealed door. It spoke words which were hostile and unfamiliar to all those around, but Mirvi rebuked the evil thing, and a great light came forth from her glowing, dark orb and the evil was sucked into its depths as it thrashed out violently. Mirvi then sealed the doors before turning to face Chieftain Grom. Her winds calmed to a gentle breeze, and all were amazed and astonished at what was witnessed.

19   THE GREAT FEAST BEFORE THE BATTLE FOR THE NORTH

"Wise king, like your father and their fathers before you. Your line is strong, a great tragedy, for you bear no sons," said Mirvi as her eyes locked onto Alex's and she stared deep within her soul.

Mirvi's eyes glowed and grew wide and Alex was slightly unhinged as she stumbled to keep her footing.

"Zoltar, you've honored your oath and I free you of your curse," said Mirvi in a gentle, soft voice and as she turned to face him, his red robe flew away with the great wind that came forth from Mirvi and he was returned to his former self.

Now what once was a mysteriously old and unearthly figure was now a very young man, barely of age to grow a great beard. Zoltar looked at his hands, turning them over to see his pale white skin returned to the natural sun touched tone. He was happy and cried out in excitement and while he now would show caution to the sword, his gilded life was over.

His three beautiful guards were free as well, for the curses Zoltar placed on them were also broken. A good thing, for Alex would never have been able to slay him as his former self, for he was immune to death and disease and the axe and blade could not pierce his skin. Alex wondered if the Undead King of Ang'daban and their curse would be broken as well. As she looked out beyond the southern gate, she saw a large army riding horses in splendid armor which shined gold against the sun. The army of Ang'daban cheered with raised swords as their horses reared into the air as if a battle had been won.

"A ruse, and a gamble for Gudrun could have been slain and if our plan failed, then we would be subject to that fiend who corrupted my daughter and gave rise to the evils beyond our reach," said Chieftain Grom as he ordered the warriors to return to their posts and continue preparation for the battle to come.

The warriors departed, their soaked chainmail armor rustled against their plate mail and their heavy iron boots sunk into the wet, muddy earth. The ancient towers doors were sealed, and the ground ran a heavy red, for the blood of that evil was greater than an ordinary man. All the chieftain's servants prepared a great feast, for it would be the last before the impending battle. Chieftain Grom looked to

Alex and Gudrun as well to the other chieftains and told them they had much to discuss and that explanations would be made to the events that took place. They all departed and as Zoltar passed by Chieftain Grom, they exchanged words.

"Wise king, my ship is yours to honor your daughter," said Zoltar with heavy eyes as he departed to the great hall with his three beautiful guards.

Chieftain Grom called some warriors who carried Reis's body out of sight as they made preparation for her funeral. And at that, all dispensed and scattered to the wind to find a place of comfort, for it was very cold as the evening grew near. That evening before the sun said its goodbyes and fell beyond the horizon, many gathered below the seaside keep and along its shores was Zoltar's boat which had been fully restored.

Reis's body was placed inside, and the nature of the funeral was thus: Grave goods were delivered to the ship which included weapons and armor, musical instruments like the flute and drum along with a variety of flowers which were delivered by servant girls. An assortment of jewelry, finely crafted and beautiful to the eye were placed near her body along with fine clothes which included a very fine red wool dress and a white linen veil. Several horses, fifteen in all had been slain within the boat along with several dogs, chopped to pieces by some of the nights guard who served under Gudrun. Some everyday items were placed near to her body along with wooden carvings and various tapestries which were made of thick fabric that depicted pictures on beautifully, colored threads.

Zurn had asked Chieftain Grom if they should sacrifice a servant to be killed and buried along with the ship, but Chieftain Grom declined, although it was a normal custom in the northern fjords for Zurn. No Oracle was called for Chieftain Grom did not believe or entertain such beliefs and practices as you might find in the northern fjords near Zurn. The men stood there in the twilight hours with torches in hand before the ship was lit ablaze and verily, it burned bright and quickly on those rocky, black shores below the seaside keep.

Now the evening hour had come and with it, a great feast. All the chieftains gathered there and the formerly Undead King of Ang'daban attended and gave thanks to Chieftain Grom that he was free of the curse. He never looked Zoltar in the eyes for perhaps there was still a grievance between the two.   Regardless, his army made camp outside the southern iron gate, for he had a great number there and would be welcomed in battle.

Zoltar sat at a long, wooden table with his three beautiful guards who were all growing sated on food, for they overindulged on delicious chicken, pork, lamb, and mutton, for they had long been deprived of its savory taste. Breads with a variety of colored and sweet fruits were served and Zoltar and his beauties grew drunk on the mead made form honey. Likewise, the Undead King of Ang'daban and his three commanders sat at a table near Zoltar, enjoying good food and mead for it had been nearly six thousand years and their tongues were parched and their stomachs growled.

Odd-Eye, Septimus, and Zurn all sat with their commanders, each at their own wooden tables which were draped with a red cloth and beautifully made, accompanied with fine cutlery made of silver and wood. They sat with their commanders as the raging braziers warmed their bodies while the dance of its flame calmed their minds. Arvid found Zain and together they joined Alex and Gudrun by a long table that sat at the footsteps of Chieftain Grom who rested in his great throne like chair.

Mads approached Alex from the side and while she had her hand on her sword, he was unamused nor was it cause for his concern. Gudrun and Zain were laughing in great merriment, together enjoying fine mead as neither could stand up, for Zain had drunk beyond his limit and Gudrun had consumed some sixty cups of mead. There was great cause for worry, for if Gudrun should fall in a drunken stupor onto someone, none could lift him off. The servants kept a wide girth from Gudrun because of this, yet he called for more mead far into the night.

The gathering waged on deep into the night, for tomorrow would be a day of rest and recovery and battle plans would be made. For many, it would be the last night of their lives and they knew it, for there was a great happiness within the great hall and the city itself. Mads sat alone, off in the dark where the light of the candle was faint. He sat there with a cup of mead in his hand, drinking with dark eyes that stared into the fire as if it spoke back to him.

"Are you ready for this, ready for what's coming?" asked Alex earnestly to the group.

All had faced war and battle, for they were no stranger to death, but they would be fighting against death itself and they were all weary, although they masked their fear. The night went on and more food was brought into the mead hall, and it raised their spirits. Mead was abundant and it was not long before Gudrun laid upon the ground as a servant girl called for help. The crowd burst into laughter as they pulled her from undeath one of Gudrun's legs. Zain was also fast asleep against the wall, the crowd laughing and cheering as an old, mangy dog sat and licked his face as he too fell victim to the meads sweet embrace.

A group of heavily armed warriors, carrying spear and shield, brought out a large chest of coins which was delivered to Mads. He took it without saying a word of thanks and walked over to Arvid who was chatting with Alex about some of the southern kingdoms and the tribes of the desert plains. Mads approached them and opened the chest, and the silver shined in the light of the fires.

"What's that?" asked Arvid as he sipped from his cup of mead and bit off a piece of bread from a large loaf.

"What was split between many is now split between two. Our rewards for efforts made, take your share," replied Mads as he glared at him without blinking an eye.

Arvid was disgusted and repulsed. He closed the lid, pushing it away and back across the table. The blood of his fellow Northmen was on his hands, and albeit them being outlaws, murders, and bandits, he felt great remorse for enlisting their company for a bounty that proved folly and served no end but the end of their lives. It was blood money, and he was sickened by it. Mads looked back and forth between him and Alex before making no expression and walked away to Chieftain Grom, not even taking his own share, and leaving the coin behind.

"I hope you forgive me for what ive done," said Arvid as he sipped on his mead exchanging looks back and forth to Alex.

"Like a ship at sea in a heavy fog, it's impossible to navigate unless the stars above guide you. Its ok to lose sight," said Alex as she stood up and looked towards Chieftain Grom.

"There's no dishonor for a blind man to be blind," said Alex with a smirk as she left his company.

She stepped over Gudrun's legs and climbed up and over his belly as the warriors in the great hall laughed. As she approached Chieftain Grom who was tired and restless, she overheard the end of their conversation.

"Very well, luck be with you," said Chieftain Grom and at this, Mads left the great hall out the grandeur doors as the cold nights air blew in and whistled as the door closed behind him with a loud thud.

"What was that about?" inquired Alex as she knelt by the side of Chieftain Grom.

"Mads follows his own moral code. He cannot see any way other than his own way. I sent him nowhere, nor did he request anything from me. He simply told me of what he will do," replied Chieftain Grom, as a servant girl brought him a wooden bowl full of blueberries and a cup of mead.

"He leaves us on the eve of battle, like the smell of fresh flowers before the middays storm," said Chieftain Grom as he ate some blueberries and spilled some mead down his old chin and braided beard.

Alex left the great hall to try and persuade Mads to stay. He was a man devoid of emotion, and he could not shed a tear in compassion, but he was needed for he was an exceptional warrior.

As Alex exited the great hall, the bitter cold greeted her like a whip across her face. There were some drunken men who had ridden their horses up to the entrance and had grievance against Mads, for their former friends made up a portion of his party who all died at the hands of menacing beasts in the forbidden forests or evil demons that prowled the night and some to the undead in the cursed lands of Ang'daban. They tried to engage in insults, but Mads stood firm, staring back at them unphased with his dark eyes.

"Come down from your horse please," said Mads with a straight and serious face.

They continued to hurl insults at him, and he repeated his request with a smile of irritation at having to repeat himself.

"Would you come closer, please?" said Mads as one of the men on the horse continued to hurl insults at him, shouting obscenities which would be offensive to any man.

As the man leaned down and over the side of his horse's neck, he continued his rant. Mads quickly unsheathed his blade and cleft the man's head clean off, and it rolled down the embankment until coming to rest against a longhouse. His body fell from the horse as Mads quickly mounted it to face the other drunk man.

"Whose horse is faster?" asked Mads with sincerity as the man leapt from his horse and handed Mads the reigns.

Mads mounted it and said, "your water skin," and the warrior complied and gave him the goat hide waterskin without hesitation before quickly retreating inside the great hall.

"Goodbye little bird," said Mads as he slowly trotted away on his horse towards the southern gate, which led out to the curse lifted lands of Ang'daban.

The ground there was stained red, for the blood of the evil that had corrupted Reis was great. Alex shouted out to him as he rode off between longhouses into the light fog that gathered there along the ground.

"You had no cause to kill that man, nor was there cause in killing Katla," said Alex as she had some mind to let loose an arrow and dig it deep within his back.

"The man just now, no, but Katla I gave my word," said Mads calmy as he trotted out of view, obscured by the fog.

Alex returned inside the grandeur great hall and sought out the company of Chieftain Grom. She had stepped over many drunken warriors who now laid fast along the ground, succumbing to exhaustion. Some drunk with stomachs full of mead while others sought the company of women in plain view. Chieftain Grom was speaking with the other chieftains, and it was decided. Tomorrow they would gather and discuss the final preparation of the battle. Alex pleaded to know the meaning of the duel between Gudrun and Zoltar, and the mystery behind Reis and the evil that rose from her body and was subdued by Mirvi, but Chieftain Grom was in no mood for it, for he himself was awake at an hour beyond his strength. Chieftain Grom was helped away to his bed chambers, as were a great many of warrior who had ate their fill and drunk beyond their ability. On to dreams and a restful night, for the morning light would raise their spirits as the evening moon would test their mettle.

Alex returned to the high rampart walls, watching the tiny droplets of cold, wet rain turn into frozen snowflakes, for the air was chilly and she had goosebumps run up and down her arms. It was then her thoughts turned to the forbidden forest, Mirvi, and the bargain she made. Alex made her way to one of the tall watchtowers and stood next to the light of a mounted torch. Surveying the vast lands before her, Alex could feel a great wind come from behind here and at once, Mirvi appeared before her in an instant, like a flash of lighting which stretches across a dark moonlit sky.

20   WISDOM AND PRUDENCE

"What are you doing here?" asked Alex as she turned to face Mirvi who glowed like the twinkling of the stars.

Alex was eager to speak with her, for much had happened since their fateful meeting deep within the forbidden forest.

"Hoped to find you in the far north. Instead, I find you here along the rampart walls, drifting into thought and weariness," said Mirvi as she moved into the moonlight.

Mirvi's voice was gentle and comforting, yet Alex wondered if she was friend or foe. Shrouded in a heavy fog, like a beautiful fish that shimmered beneath the sun touched sea, Mirvi stood next to Alex as they gazed out and into the dark horizon. Mirvi glowed and reflected the moonlight as they looked to the curse lifted army to the south.

Gudrun joined them, bearing no weapon and outfitted in studded leather armor, for his other armor was rent and shattered from the battle with Zoltar. He walked closer, paying no mind to Alex for his gaze was set upon the splendor that is Mirvi. Captivated by wonder and glory, he stood there with a mead cup in his hand, and he looked to Alex and then back at Mirvi, saying nothing. Mirvi smiled warmly at Gudrun, and they heard heavy footsteps approach as guards brought up Chieftain Grom and they all stood there in her presence.

"Wise chieftain, much like your father and those before him. I am indebted to you for your help, for that evil has long since wandered these lands and wreaked havoc and dismay," said Mirvi as she floated there above the stout wooden planks of the watchtower.

"I am grateful that you honored your word, and I'm sorry Alex that I kept this secret from you. When you described what happened at the Exiles camp, that Reis rained lighting and destruction, I knew that it had happened, and she was completely corrupted by that evil thing. Yet it was Mirvi who revealed her purpose and together we sought to end that foul evil," said Chieftain Grom as he seemingly struggled for breath and coughed and hacked violently as the guards helped him rest there in the watchtower.

Gudrun stood firm, pondering the mystery of Mirvi as Alex listened yet did not understand what they spoke of. Chieftain Grom thanked Mirvi for her help and the two spoke of ancient kings and the line of Chieftain Grom back to the beginning for his line was strong and had been forgotten to the sands of time. Alex interjected with a question here and there before Chieftain Grom said he would explain what had taken place.

"Rest wise king, and I shall explain what has been, what is and what will be," said Mirvi as the heavy fog which shrouded her dispersed out of the watchtower and she glowed all the brighter.

Chieftain Grom sent away the guards as he, Gudrun and Alex sat and listened to Mirvi speak in a soft, gentle, and seductive voice.

"I have never known such evil as what is in the hearts of men. In ancient times, they were scattered until I gathered them from every corner and brought them here to this great forest. With my aid they grew to become a mighty nation, and in my presence many became mighty men of renowned. For in those days, I shined like a burning star, and I gave rise to the giants, titans, and marvelous beasts," said Mirvi in a commanding yet gentle voice.

Gudrun and Alex exchanged looks with one another as Chieftain Grom listened with intense focus.

"Now there was a time where men's hearts ran wild, and they chose to pursue their own selfish ambition. In that time,

they poured out their malice, their guile and a great many became malcontent. I am wise beyond measure, but I could not see their evil would affect me so. At a time of distant past, there between the perpetual darkness and light, I laid low the multitudes who gathered to bind me, and their likes have been scattered as far as east is from the west. I was in injured, and I suspect the wound sustained there made be vulnerable to the wickedness of men, and so I too had unfamiliar feelings and thoughts in the presence of mankind. Their evil bled into me, and I felt it grow as the days went on, for evil corrupts even the purest of things," said Mirvi as her light grew until they had to shield their eyes from her radiance, and they no longer felt the sting
of the bitter cold.

"I vigorously fought to subdue this newfound evil and casted it out only to find it had become the embodiment of raw chaos, evil and madness. This evil, which was far greater than the rest, fled and despite my best efforts it traveled north, beyond the Frozen Wastes. Seven other embodiments soon emerged, and I bound them in chains down in the deep, secret parts of the earth. To my dismay, it is bloodshed which breaks them free of their bonds, and of the seven, three have been loosed since ancient times. They are held captive, one here in the ancient tower in the heart of the seaside keep, one far to the north beyond Kazulgard and the other far to the east where the giants roam, beyond the eastern mountains," said Mirvi as her light was now blinding, and they all had to close their eyes and turn their heads away.

"Reis was corrupted, for the very presence of the evil sealed here deep below in the ancient towers can corrupt the most innocent of hearts to do their bidding. She moved too close, like a moth to the flame, to be consumed by the evil within herself much like the evil that Chieftain Grom took captive and brought back to the village of Grom, for there are greater evils and lesser evils like the one whom Chieftain Grom bound and kept secret underneath the village of Grom.

Once Chieftain Grom knew his daughter was no more, he struck a bargain as did Zoltar for they are truly wise and mighty men, like the men of old, for they seek peace for themselves and those they serve," said Mirvi as a great wind now came from behind her and the men were pushed to the walls of the watchtower, and they couldn't stand against it.

"For his help in destroying this lesser evil, Zoltar asked to be free of his curse, for he was the cause of his own ruin and downfall. He received only what he had earned for himself but suffered long through the ages for it, for his role in releasing the first embodiment of evil. Noble Chieftain Grom, you denied a request, but I give it freely to you. What do you wish, for it shall be granted to you without reservation," said Mirvi as the wind from her was subdued and her light dimed so that they could look upon her face.

"Would you save us from this evil that approaches to devour us as a wolf devours a sheep?" asked Chieftain Grom, for he and some of the others had doubt in their hearts as the day of battle came near.

"Men must show courage in these dark times, for the Vollgarim have been pushed back and defeated in the mist before. I will not interfere; it is men who must end this plight. Put away your pride, your malice, your anger, tongues that lie and deceive and hands that seek to spill blood. There is still good in the hearts of men and you must find it. Know that with bloodshed, the power of the evils grows. Those that spill blood only empower them, and through time will release them one by one. If it is man's destiny to be consumed by this evil, I will not interfere. Show me courage, show me strength," said Mirvi as Chieftain Grom looked on and tried to stand but struggled.

"Then restore me to my former days, so that I might stand and fight against this evil before my heart beats its last!" exclaimed Chieftain Grom.

Mirvi did not say a word, yet a golden mist engulfed Chieftain Grom and he changed before their very eyes. His thin, white hair returned to a thick, lustrous silver along with his impressive, braided beard and moustache. His wrinkly, veiny, and dark patched skin was smooth like a young man and his arm grew anew, powerful, and strong! His leg, which was maimed, had been restored and Chieftain Grom stood fast amongst them as he was a mighty sight. Mirvi had clothed him in an impressive gold plate mail armor with bracers of power and a helmet of gold which covered his head with two large spires and wings on its side. He was an impressive sight and indeed he resembled his youth, for in those days he was a formidable warrior, for he was brave and very cunning.

Chieftain Grom stood in awe as he raised his spiked mace which hung from a chain. It felt light as a feather yet could break bones, armor, and rend flesh, for it was notably strong. They were grateful and met one another with praise and good cheer while Mirvi locked eyes with Alex.

"Chieftain Grom, the bargain was honored but heed my warning. You will not last, the seaside keep will not last and the north will not last. Something is coming, and you are not prepared. Our bargain still stands Alex, venture north beyond the Frozen Wastes and find that which I seek. I will honor my word and grant you a request and restore your memories if you do so. Remember your father and hold fast to what is good and right," said Mirvi before she slowly started to depart, gliding out of the watchtower to the plains beyond the moat below.

As she slowly but swiftly moved towards the forbidden forest, she shrouded herself in mist and shadows and she moved like a shooting star across the plain.

"You said Mirvi uncovered her purpose, Reis as she was corrupted?" asked Alex to the now empowered and healed Chieftain Grom.

He walked to the edge of the watchtower before answering her, gazing up at the clear nights sky at what might be his last. He gazed at the stars as if he had never seen them before, turning to face Alex who was on edge.

"Reis was not fighting the Vollgarim on the mountain ledge when they attacked you and your party among the exiles camp. She was protecting Gudrun. The ruse between Zoltar and Gudrun sought to bring her out of hiding for she would surely appear to save him. The evils that Mirvi spoke of, those chained and bound in the deep, secret parts of the earth desire Gudrun," said Chieftain Grom as he began to leave the watchtower and return to his bed chamber.

"They seek Gudrun for what?" questioned Alex as she rushed to the edge of the watchtower, shouting down to Chieftain Grom who traversed the spiral, stone stairs downwards under the flickering flames of torches that lined the wall.

Chieftain Grom paused for a moment to shout up to Alex as Gudrun stood by her side with his hand on her shoulder.

"As a replacement. Think no more of these things, for tomorrow night we fight for our lives, for the men and women of these lands and for the days ahead. There is hope, as Mirvi said the Vollgarim have been beaten before and the Strange Ones said they will be weaker in form as they are still morphing into what they shall become. In truth, we know not of what Mirvi is, if shes friend or foe, for she is no ally in the war but an advocate that we should flee this land lest we find our doom," shouted Chieftain Grom as he continued and left their sight.

Alex and Gudrun stood there at the watchtower, not speaking a word but gazing out across the dark horizon. The stars that night shined bright, and several shooting stars soared across the dark, cloudless sky. Gudrun thought to himself what replacement Mirvi spoke of, and why this evil sought him out to protect him.

"I didn't know of Reis, only that Chieftain Grom asked me to fight Zoltar knowing that I may not survive," said

Gudrun for he too was kept in the dark from what Chieftain Grom and Zoltar were privy to.

Gudrun turned to face Alex, but she wouldn't look him in the eyes. Her focus was out along the horizon, for a heavy mist had formed at the barrier of the plains and the forbidden forest.

"They speak as if they don't trust me," said Alex in a saddened and dispirited manner.

She kept her gaze to the dark horizon as Gudrun patted her on the shoulder.

"You've changed since you returned from the north. Mirvi warned of bloodlust and there are none or very few who could stand against you, much like your uncle for I heard his bloodlust was not matched," said Gudrun in a soft voice to not provoke Alex.

"I am not my uncle!" she exclaimed as Gudrun rebuked her.

"You're not yourself!" he exclaimed as he recounted her as a young girl full of life and laughter, for she now lived with grief and inner turmoil since returning from the north, and the deep dark abyss which she would not speak of.

Gudrun left her side, as he would not concern himself further for tomorrow would bring its own challenges and difficulties. He left Alex there, standing in the watchtower alone with her thoughts as the cold, frigid wind from the angry sea swept through the village that was fast asleep. They all waited for the arrival of the bright sun, for the next evenings moon would bring death and ruin upon them.

21   LAST STAND AGAINST THE DARK

Chieftain Grom and a great many of warriors were awake before the red dawn as they watched the warm, golden sun stretch out from beyond the horizon. The vibrant seaside keep awoke with hope, for the days ahead were not written and they were all prepared to meet their doom in the glory of battle if need be. There would be no feast that night, no merriment in good company, nor good food or the cup of mead, as all prepared for the coming mist and took extra care as they prepared themselves under the command of their own chieftains. The air was warm, and the sky was filled with soft, rolling white clouds as the sun's rays pierced through them, shining its favor down on the seaside keep.

To their surprise, the Strange Ones who dwell deep under the mountains, far in the depths of the earth had appeared and with them, they brought a great many crafted weapons and armor. These were exceptionally crafted, forged and tempered for battle, for the armor was black as night, glimmering silver and gold and fit tightly and snug against the warrior's skin. The weapons were light and remarkably sharp, for many men sought to test their blades and at the slightest touch, their fingers ran red.

With the weapons and armor, the Strange Ones brought a great many horses which numbered in the thousand, enough for each warrior to ride, for the line of horses stretched as far into the southern horizon as they could see. The horses were brown and black, yet a lone white horse had been brought before Chieftain Grom. They were all adorned in beautiful battle armor, for their bodies were covered in silver and gold and the horses themselves wore crowns of imposing splendor.

Now there was several Strange Ones setting up what looked like a trebuchet. These machines of warfare were capable of hurling stone a great distance, and the Strange Ones set up several hundred throughout the city for the remainder of the day. The Strange Ones left, as quickly as they came, out through the southern gate presumably to return to the depths of the earth, yet seven stayed behind.

Alex and Gudrun stood there at the base of the ancient tower and were met by Arvid, Zain, and the other chieftains. Chieftain Grom rode his horse at a great speed through the town before joining them there. He dismounted and all were astonished at the sight, for he was no longer crippled but armored like the Valkyrie and spoke with great authority.

"We give thanks and praise for such generosity. Will you not join us in the battle?" asked Chieftain Grom as seven Strange Ones gathered around him and the others.

Covered in fur like a great wolf, they stood taller than any man. Bodies impressively large and broad, bound with muscle and fur of the darkest black. They wore no armor and carried no weapon, for one of them counted as a hundred of the mightiest men. One of them approached Chieftain Grom, standing high above him extending a hand in friendship.

"We once fought side by side, for we were allies in a great battle long ago. Each of us are commanders of a great many who dwell under the mountains. For in those days our armies fought a great beast that swam in the sea and walked on land. Much has changed, but the hearts of men have remained. You are different wise king, much like those before you. We will let it be known that men gathered here and stood against the tide, and that if you shall die, you will be remembered amongst those who fought against the evil that plagues this land, and while fear strikes your hearts, its courage that flows in your veins," said one of the Strange Ones as Chieftain Grom took it by the muscle bound hand which clasped far over Chieftain Grom's hand and around his forearms.

There at the base of the ancient tower, in front of the ancient, sealed doors were battle plans discussed. Chieftain Grom, the seven Strange Ones, Zoltar and his three beautiful guards, an Ogre King, the Undead King whose name was Jorthefire and his three commanders, Septimus, Zurn, Osric, Odd-eye, Arvid, Gudrun, Zain, and Alex stood in a large circle as Chieftain Grom instructed them each according to his will.

The Strange Ones breathed heavily as their fur swayed in the gentle wind. Zoltar and his three beauties listened

intently and carefully as did the Ogre King who stood high
with a crafted helmet of gemstones, a stark contract against
his grey, rock like skin which was hard to the touch and
unsightly to the eyes. Jorthefire stood eager, for he and his
army longed for death and knew they may find it, yet they
would fight on and let fate decide their destiny. His
commanders were mighty men who stood tall, wearing
ancient armor forged long ago in the fires of discipline and
loyalty.

Chieftain Grom instructed that Jorthefire and his army
should hold the southern gate and push back the mist
towards the mountains to the south. The Ogre King was
instructed to spread his forces between the south and
towards the eastern flank, towards the forbidden forest with
the rest of his forces of goblins and trolls. The Strange Ones
were left to their own devices, for Chieftain Grom was
grateful for their aid, both their efforts in battle and the
forged armor and weapons which now all warriors wore.
Zoltar and his three beautiful guards were to hold the
northern gate and the lands before them along with Odd-Eye
and his forces. Septimus, Zurn, and Osric were to hold the
eastern gate which was the largest and flattest of the
battlefields leading out into the horizon. Alex, Gudrun,
Arvid and Zain were to accompany Chieftain Grom and
stand along the rampart walls as it was filled with archers
spreading along its perimeter.

Their armies were comprised of the following: Chieftain
Grom, Gudrun and the nights guard numbered nearly two
thousand, Jorthefire's army was nearly ten thousand, The
Ogre King and his army of ogres, trolls and goblins
numbered several hundred, Zoltar's army numbered nearly
five thousand, Odd-Eye's army was nearly two thousand,
Septimus's army numbered nearly three thousand, Zurn's
army was nearly two thousand, and Osric's army was nearly
two thousand. Together, their total forces numbered some
twenty-six thousand brave Northmen.

Chieftain Grom dismissed them and wished them luck. They all exchanged words of encouragement as they prepared their men for the night, and with it, the coming of the Vollgarim. It had been a fortnight since Mirvi had warned Alex about a plight which would destroy the people and lands of the north, yet as she looked at their vast army, she knew they were not prepared for what may come. As the day grew on, so did their anxiety and trepidation, for even the bravest hearts sway against the darkness. The evening came fast and as dusk approached, so did the coldness and it began to snow ever so gently with tiny, white snowflakes falling from the sky which was growing more overcast as the final hour approached.

The chieftain's armies wore the gifted armor from the Strange Ones. It was an intimidating sight, for the armor was immaculate and flawless, not to mention the impressive and majestic weapons they now carried to battle. They rode out on their magnificent steeds, through their respected gates and stood in formation. The sound was great as the heavy unison footsteps trotted along the hard earthen ground. The horses neighed, snorted, and grunted as they lined up in formation, led by their own chieftains. The evening was exceedingly dark with a heavy overcast of grey clouds. The once bright, silver moon gave little light as they stood outside of the city, staring into the darkness beyond them. Chieftain Grom, urged by Alex, decided a stand be made outside of the city and that a retreat be called if need be.

Now the snow grew greater, and a coldness came from the north as the flames of the torches swayed in the wind. Braziers were brought out of the city and placed among the battlefield during the day to give some light and warmth, but they seemed to do neither there in the pitch black. As the sun finally said its last goodbye, and receding over the horizon, Chieftain Grom who now stood on the high rampart walls shouted out to the vast armies.

"We stand united as we have stood in the past. We stand together and will be remembered forever! Wisdom men! To remember the past. Courage men! To move forward without fear and dread. If your consumed by the darkness and have reached your end, look to the man beside you should your courage fail!" shouted Chieftain Grom and to this the men cheered with weapons raised.

Now each chieftain gave their own speech to their men, words of encouragement to bolster courage, for they knew the battle ahead will bring death and ruin. Alex heard a whisper, a quiet yet menacing whisper that was one but then turned to a great many all around her. Gudrun looked to her as she was visibly troubled, and she quickly departed the high, stony rampart walls towards the ancient tower that stood at the center of the city. As she walked through the frigid city, there were several warriors manning the great many trebuchets as she continued to follow the whispers. She came to the base of the ancient tower and leaned her ear against the sealed doors, and she could hear it clearly, the same whispering that she heard in the deep, dark abyss.

"There's still time, ride now with all whom you've gathered and flee to the north," said Mirvi as she surprised Alex, appearing out of thin air behind her.

Alex was startled and the whispering all seemed to fade away into the wind as she turned to face Mirvi, who stood there with the great ethereal elk that she rode out of the forbidden forest with some time ago, and a great ethereal wolf who rubbed its soft, white fur up and under Mirvi's arm, asking to be petted.

"We have nearly thirty thousand men, with troll, goblin and ogre and the great army of Jorthefire along with the Strange Ones who fight by our side. We will stand against this evil, for what could stand against us?" boasted Alex as Mirvi's expression turned to a frown.

"Are you boasting to me or to them, she who greets with fire?" replied Mirvi as she seemed to be saddened and crestfallen at Alex.

She floated there, for her feet were consumed by clouds of fire, as she simply turned away.

"I had hope, that you would be more like your father and less like your uncle," said Mirvi as she turned to shake her head at Alex.

"No more riddles! Tell me what you know of my father!" exclaimed Alex in anger as she was breathing heavy, consumed in fury as she drew her sharp, battle forged sword.

"Very well, it makes no difference now for you will be consumed by the darkness before the moon rests. Come with me, she who greets with fire, and see what has been and what will be," said Mirvi as she extended her hand to Alex, and upon reaching it, Alex fell into a deep sleep.

She awoke in the darkness with Mirvi at her side in a deep cave within a cave, deep in the earth beneath what is known. Mirvi provided the only light, for her body glowed and twinkled like a star, there in the deep darkness. Mirvi said nothing, and as she moved forward through the dark, Alex followed. She looked around but could see nothing beyond what was directly in front of her, for Mirvi said in these parts of the earth there is no light for light cannot exist, and things are not what they seem. As they moved forward it was not long before Alex could hear the whispers in the shadows. She suddenly could remember; she was in the abyss. Before she could speak, and knowing her thoughts, Mirvi began to speak.

"Come now and see what you already know. Do not fear, for this is the past and we move unseen and unhindered," said Mirvi, and Alex took it to be they were in a vision of things that had happened.

Alex recognized that place, for they stood on a great plain overlooking a great chasm. As they walked, Mirvi took her by the hand and they walked across the chasm, through the air, as the light from Mirvi was very great in that deep, dark place. Alex could see shadows in the distance and with them, sinister whispers, and menacing laughter that echoed in the dark. Mirvi took her by the hand and there appeared great figures of a ghastly sight.

"This is where I bound them, the seven embodiments of evil. For in those times, they took no shape, yet through the ages as bloodshed was spilt, they began to take form. They call forth ones of their choosing, and together they form what you see now," said Mirvi as they circled around them.

Each figure resided there in the darkness, in the pitch black as they conversed with one another in a tongue Alex could not understand. It was sinister and painful to listen to, and the menacing laughing and cries terrified Alex as she was frozen still; the reason Mirvi guided her by the hand. There was one figure completely covered in darkness as if it were the very darkness itself. Mirvi's light could not illuminate it.

"This is the origin of evil, the very first whom I casted out, for it fled to the north and its whereabouts are unknown. It takes no shape or form, yet its presence and will can be seen through the actions of the other evils. It moves freely, here and above while the others wait for bloodshed to be spilt to be freed to the surface. In ancient times, three have been freed and mighty men above fought to subdue them. The giants of old and titans came together to bind them in great towers, yet their evil presence causes a great madness to grow in the hearts of men," said Mirvi as they continued to move and take sight of the others.

They were the figures in her dreams, and Alex recalled them and the deep dark abyss along with the events of that day. Knowing her thoughts, Mirvi began to speak as she guided Alex over to a figure which laid along the ground, moaning in despair. Alex knew, it was her father.

"Yes, for on that day you and your father and a great many brave warriors found themselves in the deep, dark abyss but it was only you and your father who went this deep, no doubt drawn by the evil here. Gudrun is unmatched in these lands, a descendant of the giants and with a bloodlust that cannot be quenched. They seek him out, for if the evil merges with him, a great terror it would create. Much like your father, for the battle on that day was great and blood was spilt to impower and release another evil. Your father was a cunning warrior and sought after so they drew him here for the impending evils release. To their dismay, something happened they did not except," said Mirvi as she took Alex closer to see her father on the ground with a grievous wound that bled without end.

Alex walked over and knelt, trying to touch her father but her hand passed through to no effect.

"Yes, I remember. Better to fight and fall than to live without hope. My father's last words, I understand them now. He knew what evil he would become and as the evil sought to take hold of him, he smote himself with his sword. It was too late, for the evil took hold of him but he did not die, and the evil within him was only weakened. Little did he know, his sacrifice would weaken and contain one of the embodiments of evils," said Alex as she stood up and stared back at her father.

"Yes, what else do you remember, she who greets with fire?" asked Mirvi as she now circled around Alex, there in the deep darkness.

Alex began to look around at the figures and recounted the events, for Mirvi had restored her memory and brought light to that which was concealed.

"You yourself were corrupted, here in the depths in the secret parts of the earth. An evil grows within you, corrupting you as the madness grows within your heart and mind. Ingenious really, for you've gathered some thirty thousand men to the slaughter to impower the release of another great evil here," said Mirvi as a cloud of fire all but consumed her, and Alex could no longer see her behind the flames.

Alex was confused and angered, knowing now that she had unwillingly done the bidding of these evils. Was it unwillingly or willingly? She asked herself. She was not sure of anything anymore. With her memory restored and the mystery revealed, she sought to leave this place for the madness took over and she began to scream and shout. She realized that it was she who killed the two visitors, Weohstan and Oslaf, outside the village of Grom, along with several of the nights guard before she departed the village of Grom, and she slayed many exiles when they were encamped there, for the evil in her took hold and drove her to a madness that she could not remember.

"In time you will go completely mad, for the good in you is at war with the corruption, in constant tension but it will not last. You must decide, will you stand against the evil like your father, or succumb to it like a great many others," said Mirvi as her words echoed from behind the flames of the fire, as the sinister laughing and menacing words of the evils there began to echo throughout the darkness.

"The future is uncertain, but I will not intervene. If it is the fate of man to slowly succumb to the darkness, then so be it," said Mirvi as the flames engulfing her were subdued and she took Alex by the hand once again.

"What should I do? I do not know anymore," said Alex as she was emotional and knowing the fate of her father, very distraught.

"Go to the north, to the far reaches were a great many of your peoples are. Seek out what has become of this origin of evil. Now, I have shown you a mercy and granted you knowledge of things that were and shown you your father. Will you do as I ask?" asked Mirvi in a soft, gentle voice.

"I will do as you ask but grant me a request at the time I ask," replied Alex who stood with her hands covering her ears, closing her eyes tightly not to hear or see the evils there in the darkness.

"Agreed," replied Mirvi and at once Alex awoke to find herself there at the base of the ancient tower, sitting on the ground, leaning against the ancient, sealed doors.

It was Gudrun who found her, and soon after the ornate alarm bells of the watchtowers rang their mighty tune. The mist was forming, for it was thick and heavy and crept and crawled out of the forbidden forest and along the southern and northern horizons. Gudrun tried to pull Alex to her feet, but her mood was distraught and her will was shattered, for she told Gudrun what she discovered with Mirvi, in the secret parts of the earth.

"No time for your dreams, the mist approaches and with it, death and glory," said Gudrun to Alex as he pulled her to her feet and carried her as she struggled and pleaded with him to listen.

By the time they reached Chieftain Grom and the other men along the high, stony rampart walls, the mist had descended halfway between the forbidden forest and them. Chieftain Grom ordered for the moat to be lit a flame, and at once it was in a fiery blaze. The mist rushed forward and consumed the city, up and over the fiery moat without any hinderance. The moat provided an abundance of heat and the flames danced high and fierce, yet it proved to be no barrier to the mist, for it was not simply fog but this heavy mist foreboded some new terror to come.

Alex pleaded to them that the battle was folly and that they must flee, lest they be taken by the darkness, but they did not listen. Nay, for Chieftain Grom called for his horse and that all men along the rampart walls put away their bows and arrows and take a steed of their choosing and ride out into battle. Alex pleaded and tried to tell them of what she knew, but they would not heed her advice. Flags and banners were raised, and the chieftains prepared their men for a charge into the mist.

Chieftain Grom mounted his beautiful, armored white horse and called for the men to follow, as he, Gudrun and a number of warriors rode out of the eastern gate and formed a formation among the rest of the chieftains there. It was pitch black and the mist that engulfed the city now made the air thick and heavy. Snow continued to gently fall as the ground was now slightly covered in a smooth, white layer of snow which looked almost to be ash.

"How cunning, to unite the armies of the north here, for there is nowhere to retreat, and Gudrun too for many evils have taken mighty men but none of the descendants of the giants," said Mirvi as her soft glow appeared out of the mist.

Alex rushed to the watchtower and Mirvi followed, as they peered out into the darkness from the tall stony, rampart walls. The air was cold, and you could hear a whisper from a far. Mirvi stared into the horizon as the flames from the fiery moat casted their shadows and highlighted the vast armies on the plain before them.

"Now you will know why men fear the darkness, now you will know why hearts sway in the night," said Mirvi in a sinister voice as Alex looked at her then back out into the darkness.

From Mirvi came forth a great wind and it pushed back all the mist from the city walls to the edge of the forbidden forest, and further north and south into the horizon, but only for a moment before the mist returned and pushed back into the city. Alex could see the Vollgarim, and the monstrous creatures that dwell within the mountain for their numbers were great, far greater than the armies amassed here. Should the armies of the north men number nearly thirty thousand, they were outnumbered, for the myriad of Vollgarim before them numbered some two hundred thousand.

A great rumble came and with it, the stomping of many animals as both wolf and bear, boar and fox, deer and elk, and all manner of animals came rushing towards them. Running around and through the heavily armored armies in their formations, they sought refuge in the keep, for something drove them out of the forbidden forest, the verdant rolling hills to the north and the great sun scorched plains to the south. Verily, a great many animals rushed over the cliffs edge along the southern plains for they would rather plumet to their death than to be shredded and eviscerated by the Vollgarim. Alex saw that the first of the Vollgarim would reach the southern gate, for it was Jorthefire and his army that would meet the Vollgarim first with spear and shield and sword and axe.

At first it was a great howl of the wind and the piercing cold, like the door to the heavens was left open and its draft felt. This distant thundering of a marching army only grew, for soon the air was filled with the howling wind and the grunting and moaning of the Vollgarim. It was very dark, for they could only see them should they stand but a few paces in front of them, as they anxiously waited for the battle to begin.

The Strange Ones instructed the warriors inside the seaside keep to fire the trebuchet and as the men did so, the nights sky was filled with giant boulders of flame, launching them towards the southern plains as they lit the sky up like falling stars. Their bright red glow illuminated the dark clouds above and came crashing down on the great many who charged forward. The howl of the wind intensified until it was deafening, and the Vollgarim appeared.

"To battle men! To victory and death!" shouted Jorthefire as his army cheered and shouted but to his dismay, many of the horsed reared up and threw a great many riders off.

Indeed, they were frighted as were a great many who turned to flee back towards the keep. Before a proper charge could be made, the Vollgarim attacked and overran a great portion of the battle formation. Jorthefire fought on with great zest and gusto as his battle cry and unnerving laughter could be heard among the screeching and gnawing of the

Vollgarim. Indeed, many of the men who were formally undead met their end as they laughed and cheered, for it was death they longed for and death they found. Having no fear of their end or the Vollgarim, they fought on, throwing spears and maiming the monstrous creatures who stood as tall as giants but were menacing and wild.

Jorthefire's three commanders fought on, as they encouraged their men and charged into the fray. One of them was slain as a great number of Vollgarim overwhelmed him, and not being able to bite and gnaw through his crafted armor, pulled his arms and legs out of his body. He let out a moan and then a laugh before succumbing to his injuries as he shouted for the men to battle to the end. Another commander led a group of warriors towards a hulking monstrosity before they were met with a mighty swipe of its arms, casting several to the side. A commander was lifted into the air and crushed in the palms of one of the beasts, not before casting his spear through the eyes of the monstrous giant like beast. It came crashing down and with it, the commander was slain for his bones were crushed and he had all but found the peace he longed for. Jorthefire's forces recomposed and gathered themselves to form a line with shield in hand and spear in the other, for the Vollgarim continued to crash against armor and shield without rest.

One of the Strange Ones leapt from the high, stony rampart walls across the fiery moat and began its attack. It was wild like a beast, and it bite and tore many Vollgarim to sunder. It cleaved many Vollgarim's head from their bodies and it retrieved one before leaping back up over the high, stony rampart walls. Alex rushed to its side, for it had minor wounds that it paid no mind. Alex could see the Vollgarim clearly and indeed they had changed.

It had the flesh of a man, for the Strange One tore it to pieces but it did not bleed. It appeared to be like a man who had died and started to decay. This Vollgarim has a black skull with bright white teeth, no eyes to be seen and yet it could see. Its arms and legs had flesh in some places, while in other places the bones were exposed, or it had skin broken apart, decaying. Its body was bloated, and some skin had turned a bright red, contrast to the pale or dark black skin.

"They are changing, they number like the grains of sand along the shores, yet they are in a weakened state as they are changing into what they will become. For in ancient times, they stood on all fours like a bear and moved like lighting with heads that could swallow men whole," said the Strange One before leaping back over the rampart walls, back into battle without fear.

The Ogre King and a number of ogres led a ferocious charge, for their stampede laid waste to a great many Vollgarim as they targeted the tall, monstrous, giant like beasts. With a swing of the mace, they crushed their bones and only a few ogres fell in battle, for the Vollgarim climbed them, gnawing and biting as their numbers were many and although a great many were slain, many more continued to charge towards the city. Goblins and trolls climbed on the ogres, and from their mighty shoulders they casted rocks and stone and shot bows and arrows which were laced with poison, although they made no affect against the Vollgarim.

Zoltar and his three beautiful guards led a charge as the wind howled and whispered and screeching approached. They charged into the darkness of night, unaware of what horror was just out of sight. The trebuchets were fired to the north, and the fire from those boulders lit up the battlefield. The men fought on as the fire casted shadows amongst them. Zoltar slayed a great many, for he was fierce as were his beautiful guards. They stood back to back, fighting the oncoming horde of the Vollgarim. Luck would have it, that Zoltar was nearly crushed by a falling boulder of flame, but he was pushed aside as one of his beautiful guards was crushed. He rushed to her side to say goodbye, but she was already gone, the light in her eyes faded and sent Zoltar into a rage.

Odd-Eye, who had been waiting behind the initial charge, then gave a battle cry as he and his warriors rode in flanking the horde of Vollgarim, giving Zoltar and his men time to regroup and mount their horses. Many Vollgarim were slain, for Zoltar was fierce as was Odd-Eye who saved many warriors as the Vollgarim descended upon them. Odd-Eye cleaved many Vollgarim in two, and as the battle raged on, so did their courage. Odd-Eye cried out for victory as he and his men gained their second wind and charged forward against the horde of Vollgarim who toppled over themselves as they rushed in. Strange Ones jumped and leapt through the battlefield, and they slayed many of the horrid, giant like beasts alone, for each of them counted as a hundred mighty men. They stood with arms wide open, and heads raised to the sky. The Strange Ones roar was mighty and indeed, many men screamed a battle cry that rang like a mighty trumpet throughout the battlefield.

Septimus, Zurn, and Osric were gathered out beyond the eastern gate, for they prepared as the Vollgarim charged forward. Horses reared and ran, casting many riders off as some of the men also turned to flee. With their line broken, they stood shoulder to shoulder, shield to shield, waiting for the darkness to come. All at once a horde of Vollgarim appeared as they crashed against shields, and a great many jumped and crawled up and over one another to reach the mighty men of the north.

Chieftain Grom and Gudrun led a charge with a battle cry that could be heard on the highest peak of the highest mountain. They charged forward, swinging axe and sword without fear of the Vollgarim, without fear of the darkness. Now there came to be a break in the charge, and the men gathered themselves as formations were made and the lines were held. Chieftain Grom had ordered all to stand fast as the warriors took a moment to catch their breath, exchanging looks of courage and also fear. They stood fast as the sound of crashing steel against shield, battle cries along with moaning and groaning faded, for the horses neighed softly as they pulled against the rider's rains violently, for they had fought amongst men but never against this horror.

"Death!" shouted Chieftain Grom as the entirety of the armies gathered cried out in unison three times.

"Glory!" shouted Gudrun and again the entirety of the armies gathered cried out in unison three times.

They waited there in the pitch black as the roar of thundering footsteps approached, as did the frigid wind which whistled and howled as the marching footsteps grew near. Whatever fear which was felt was now lost, and the men showed great courage and the desire for battle, for when the Vollgarim and the hulking monstrosities came into sight, Gudrun let out a cry that echoed across the battlefields.

"Charge!" shouted Gudrun and as he raised his sword, the mighty armies of the chieftains charged forward and met the Vollgarim with the blade, spear, axe, and shield.

The noise of the battle was great for horses neighed, shields were shattered and cracked, swords cleaved and hacked flesh, the moans and groans of battle raged, the cries of pain and the screams of fury and the screeching and gnawing of the Vollgarim filled the cold nights air. There were four giant monstrosities who had the face of men but hair wild like a lion's mane. One of them called out to Gudrun, for it was one of the ones in the cave in which Gudrun had killed one of their kin. They charged Gudrun who stood firm ready to swing his mighty sword.

The seven Strange Ones appeared and jumped over Gudrun, climbing the monstrosities with great speed and agility. Two Strange Ones held the monstrosity by its wild mane, pulling its head to the cold, hard ground as the other Strange Ones grabbed and twisted the monstrosities head until the neck was broken and it laid motionless along the cold, snow covered ground. Another monstrosity approached and as it reached for Gudrun with those mighty, horrid hands, a Strange One grabbed hold of its palm and severed its fingers from its hand. It reared its hand away, screaming in agony and as its mouth was open and wide, another Strange One leapt and took it by the fangs, pulling its jaws apart until it became unhinged and fell to the ground with a crashing thud. Gudrun let out a mighty laugh and cried out charge and the men followed suit and pushed into the crashing waves that was the Vollgarim.

All of the trebuchets fired and the sky was lit anew, for the burning boulders crashed far into the distance like the sounds of great thunder. The battle was for the survival of these men, their families who hid behind the city and for the future of the north, for no war horns were sounded and no banners were held on that day, it was a battle for sheer survival. The Vollgarim continued without rest until at last the sound of screeching ended, the howl of the wind faded and all that was left was the panting of exhausted warriors and the gentle neighing of horses in the dark.

"Victory men! Victory!" cried out Chieftain Grom, as did the other chieftains shout in unison and the entirety of the armies gathered there, for the horde of Vollgarim had been defeated by the hands of the north peoples.

The Strange Ones came to Chieftain Grom and spoke with great authority for they served no king but he who dwelled under the earth.

"Wise king, seek shelter in the city for an evil comes. An evil as dark as night and bright like the sun," said one of the Strange Ones as the other Strange Ones began to roam the battlefield to take the wounded back inside the city.

Chieftain Grom sounded a war horn for a retreat and the other chieftains, and their lieutenants sounded their own. A great march began, for horses galloped and men retreated into the seaside keep. The wounded were quickly gathered, and the battlefield was soon devoid of warriors, save those who met their end and fell valiantly in battle whose names would be sung with praise and glory.

The night was pitch black and the only light came from the torches and braziers which were spread throughout the city. The mighty moat flamed on for the flames grew high and the sound of the fire was great. Tress were burning and breaking, and the crackling and snapping of the fire continued far into the night, for all warriors stood inside the keep waiting for orders from Chieftain Grom. Chieftain Grom stood there along the ramparts with Gudrun and Alex to his side along with the Strange Ones.

It came to pass after a short time, when the warriors regained their composure and the injured had been carried inside the city, that a great light appeared on the horizon. At first, Alex took it to be Mirvi and yet she had recalled this flame, as did Chieftain Grom and some of the warriors who fought in the north against a terror that has no name. Septimus rushed to their side, and they all watched as they could see a fire far in the distance. The dark clouds receded like a scroll that was rolled up and the moon light casted its silver light across the battlefield. The number of slain was great, for not a man or horse could walk through in some places without having to step or climb over the dead.

They could see it clearly, what appeared to be a fire was a great evil that they had fought before, the flame that has no name. Septimus pointed and cried out, for it was the evil that almost ended the line of Chieftain Grom. Alex clenched her fist, for she fought against it and had long suffered since. Chieftain Grom looked on as he remembered the taste of defeat at the hands of this evil.

This evil, it had the appearance of a man but was twisted and gruesome. It was a hulking figure, bound with muscle and flame. The snow-covered earth melted with each step it took and the very ground became like a cinder of a long burning fire. The hard, blood-stained earth glowed like a hot coal as the evil came closer across the battlefield. It bore no armor nor weapon, but its claws could rend armor and flesh alike. It had the body of a man but the face of a lion and the horns of a ram. Its face was scarred, and its fur was wild and white as snow. It had several arms, each large and powerful.

Septimus recounted the tale, for all knew of the courage and bravery of Alex as she fought this beast when so many others would not dare or died trying.

"Any man who moved too close was burned, for their armor smoked and smoldered and their skin and blood boiled. It was Alex who removed her armor and with only her sword, she fought with the beast. As she fought, her body ignited into flame, yet she continued to wage battle tirelessly and determined until she wounded the beast. It retreated towards the Frozen Wastes. Alex pursued it, along with a great number of our bravest," said Septimus as they looked on and when they looked for Alex, she was nowhere to be found.

"There!" shouted Gudrun as it was Alex who walked slowly out through the eastern gate towards the evil. They all watched as the gates were ordered closed and Alex walked out across the body ridden, blood-stained ground. As she approached the evil it let out a menacing laugh, deep and sinister as Alex stood there at the boundary of the burning earth. Mirvi appeared behind her as the two stood to face the evil that has no name. It stood there, dark as night and bright as the burning sun as it began to sing.

> *The dread beneath your skin*
> *A sweet melody that pulls you in*
> *deep within your heart, broken yet you stand*
> *I call you forth and you do as we command*
> *A burning ember that corrupts thy heart*
> *Charred, seared and afire from the very start*
> *You started a war and the battle raged*
> *Piece by piece, carefully staged*
> *Follow me now, back to the dark*
> *The taste of blood is sweet, you find it bitter in your heart*

We have finished what you have started
Come now and depart from what Mirvi has
thwarted

Alex stood there, her bright azure eyes glared at the hulking figure as she raised her sword and thrusted it into the cold, hard earth. She slowly removed her immaculate gold and black armor to reveal a scorched and scarred body, for the flames from this evil were intense as the sun itself. She stood there in a thin cloth skirt, picked her sword up which was crafted by the Strange Ones and charged forward as the men along the high, stony rampart walls cheered and shouted.

The night was black as was the battlefield and the evil fiend retreated into the darkness and mist. The only light came from Mirvi, who stood firm along the blood stained, corpse ridden ground and the fiery moat which circled the city. Alex pressed on into the darkness, seeing the earth scorched and smoking as she searched for the evil. Its dark, hideous laugh came from out in the darkness and as she approached her body caught a flame. The evil rushed in and took hold of her with one of its several arms. Its hand wrapped around her waist and lifted her in the air, pulling her close to its face.

The face was that of a lion, for its dark eyes gave way to a menacing laugh and as it bellowed, she could see its jagged fangs as its fiery mane swayed in the cold, frigid wind. The evil which has no name pulled her close until her head was met with one of its horns. Alex could see the scars on its face and as she tried to swing her sword it casted her out and across the earth. She rolled across the snow-covered ground and her body burned and stung as the evil retreated again into the darkness, out of sight.

Chieftain Grom ordered for all the trebuchet to be fired at Alex's location and they soared and struck the ground around her, lighting up the earth there in a fiery blaze. The fire there raged but the evil remained hidden in the dark. Its menacing laugh could be heard, echoing in the darkness. Alex stood among the burning boulders, as the evil stepped through the shadows to reveal itself. The fire casted a shadow and its silhouette was impressive and imposing. The Strange Ones appeared around Alex and nodded, for if Alex was the bravest of the north, she was the least among the Strange Ones and their kind. At once they leapt, each grabbing hold of the evil and its large, powerful arms. Alex charged and thrusted her sword into the chest of the evil one who has no name. The Strange Ones burst into flames along with Alex, for the evil moaned and cried before casting them all aside, for it was strong beyond measure and none could hold it. Alex rolled across the cold, snow covered ground as the Strange Ones fell and landed on their feet, rolling in the snow for their bodies had been lit a flame.

"Very well! Resists if you can, for however long you can, she who greets with fire! You should have heeded the warning, for blood has been spilt and another has been released. I have come for that which sleeps and slumbers in the dark!" said the evil who has no name as it pulled the sword which had been plunged deep in its chest out, but it did not bleed.

The evil casted the impressively crafted, glimmering sword to the side as it walked quickly with haste past Alex who burned anew as the evil passed by. She moaned there softly, clutching her side as her breath was knocked out of her. The men on the rampart walls casted a volley of arrows at the evil but to no avail. The Strange Ones came to Alex's side to tend to her, picking her up and putting out the fire before carrying her back inside the city. The evil which has no name broke down the eastern gate, shattering its iron bars with the crash of its powerful arms. It tore the gate a sunder and charged onward and roamed through the city. Men fled lest they be burned by the ancient terror, as it crushed longhouses and ripped through the great mead hall. It set the city ablaze as it moved through unhindered as the men all rushed to retrieve their families, for the city hosted the warriors along with their families, both woman and children and the young and the old.

The time passed and soon the sun began to rise and with it, a haunting sight. The battle was won, but also lost. The great sun scorched plains to the south, the verdant and rolling hills to the north and the once farmlands and fields of wheat to the east towards the forbidden forest were a sea of corpses. Bodies stacked and torn asunder, for despite their efforts and the victory at hand, some twenty thousand brave Northmen were slain in the glory of battle, never to raise sword or mead cup again. Even worse was that the stench of death and the sounds of battle brought forth Fangore, and its mother.

Septimus cried out as Fangore was roaming far in the distance, eating the corpses of many while its mother stood, snarling back at the keep. If Fangore was an impressive sight, she was dwarfed by her mother. Some of the ancient things of the earth had lived since the times of the titans, and some could not be slayed by the sword or spear, nor could they be burned and consumed by fire, nor did they need sleep to rest or food for nourishment, for they existed and would exist to serve no purpose beyond their own, and one of these ancients was Fangore's mother. She resembled Fangore but was much larger, bearing no tail but in the place of a tail a second head. She needed no mate for she birthed at will, and she stood there far across the horizon with her sights set on the city and all those who dwell in it like sheep huddled in a barn.

"There is no escape, for if we should flee, we would be consumed by Fangore and its mother. The sea is folly for the Leviathan roams like a lion who stalks its prey. Is it our fate to defeat the Vollgarim only to be eaten by an ancient or consumed by the fires of this evil which now walks among us?" said Chieftain Grom as he was troubled for the future was bleak and the hearts of all in the city were broken and their spirits shattered.

The great evil which had no name had casted its flame on the better part of the city, for the homes were destroyed and the rampart walls crumbled under the intense heart of the evil. It approached the ancient tower and cried out in an ancient tongue, screaming a menacing roar that echoed throughout the town. The flames from the beast grew as if the sun had fallen amongst them, and it broke the ancient, sealed doors and descended into its depths.

The Strange Ones burst forth from the earth, near the now burning, blazing, and crumbling great hall and as they poured out, they brought forth great machinery of finely crafted mechanisms. For from the darkness rose a great many ships for they were Zeppelins. They instructed all to enter the flying ships, lest they be destroyed.

Now Alex stood firm, and despite her flame licked skin and battered body, she cried out for Mirvi. Not as soon as she spoke, Mirvi appeared in all her glory, glowing and in an instant Alex's flesh was restored. Her skin was burned to a light pink in some places and bloodied in others with several bubbles which oozed and exploded, for the burns were deep and her body was hot to the touch. In an instant her skin grew anew, and she stood recomposed and thanked Mirvi, knowing that if her courage should hold, Mirvi would honor it with restoration, for she shows favor to those who stood against such great evil, at whatever the cost.

"All is lost, she who greets with fire. Had you heeded my warning and accepted my proposal, things would not be as they are now," said Mirvi as the city burned, and the warriors were herded into the flying Zeppelin machines which the Strange Ones had built.

Zeppelins, machines intricately crafted and meticulously built, for they were ships which sailed the skies and had been used in ancient times when the land bore no sea and the fountains of the deep still slept.

"I will go north and do as you ask. You say my people are there?" asked Alex as she stood there as burning embers floated in the air along with ash and dark clouds of doubt brought on from the fires.

"Yes, a great many, for when you fled from your homelands a great many were destroyed by the Leviathan and yet a great many survived and landed in the far reaches of the north, where the sun does not shine and the mountains of fire erupt and spew their molten breath," responded Mirvi as her eyes glowed and she smiled warmly.

"Very well, grant me a request and slay the Leviathan, all of them!" shouted Alex as Mirvi looked on with a confused expression.

"The Leviathan are here to protect you against that which you cannot see. Should you destroy them, you will leave yourself unguarded from an evil to come," replied Mirvi as she asked Alex if she was sure this is what she wished.

Alex agreed and Mirvi began to ascend towards the clouds as Alex could see the fire in her eyes and the sparkle of her armor. Mirvi said nothing but as she drifted towards the stars, Alex could hear a voice inside herself which told her to honor her word. Like lighting, Mirvi reached the sky and flew across the sea. Alex rushed to the western rampart walls facing the ocean and saw the expansive sea part as Mirvi flew across its surface. The ocean parted and the waves reached great heights, for Mirvi descended into its icy depths towards the Leviathans. A flash of light came from beneath the sea and the sea collapsed back in on itself. The waves were great, tall, and fierce as the sea began to stir violently. A great groan and grumble like the death cry of a great beast could be heard across the sky and with it, the water turned a bright red. The frothy and foamy waves crashed against the sandy shores below and the foam turned a bright red as white, foamy bubbles splashed the shore and receded back into the ocean.

Now the better part of the city had boarded Zeppelins as the injured were drove in like sheep and then the remaining families and warriors boarded and settled there. Chieftain Grom called out to Alex as he and the other chieftains all stood aboard one mighty Zeppelin. Alex departed the rampart walls, not before seeing the ocean recede into the distance as the waves along the horizon grew to a great height. Alex made her way through the crumbling and burning city to find the Strange Ones entering the chasm from which they poured out of the earth. Some stayed behind to pilot the Zeppelins but one of them, hulking with seared fur and a scarred face looked to her and spoke.

"Mighty girl, much like your father and those before him. You fight as they did, long ago when it came crashing from the stars. Honor your word little one, honor them," it said before leaping into the dark, deep chasm below and with it, the last of the Strange Ones disappeared back into the deep parts of the earth where none have entered since ancient times.

The earth shook and it bellowed a great roar from deep underneath the city. Alex stumbled as the earth opened as if its mouth sought to swallow her whole. She leapt along the surface for it broke, cracked, and opened violently before she boarded the last Zeppelin. It rose into the air and accompanied the others, for many men were lost and of the nearly thirty thousand warriors who fought, a fraction remained. The Zeppelins rose into the sky, in between the earth and clouds but not much higher than the tallest trees as they could see the earth beneath them shake and roar violently. Parts of earth collapsed and fell to great depths. The rampart walls came undone, and rock and stone flew along the ground, for the great hall itself was sucked into the earth with a mighty clash of wood and iron.

The mighty Fangore and its mother roamed free across the battlefield, devouring bodies until they were sated. They fled however, back into the depths of the forbidden forest and no doubt to the far reaches of the eastern mountains from whence they came. Lo! The mighty Leviathan rose from the sea, for it swam and then crawled up along the shores, for the waters there receded into the horizon. It was a sight and in plain view, a serpent of old, for it had lived since ancient times and while it was impressively large, they could not see an end to it.

They rode high into the sky on the ancient, crafted Zeppelins as clouds gave way to the rising orange sun. As the earth opened, the ground gave way as it crumbled and sank and before them was a great chasm whose depth could not be measured. The ancient tower remained and as high as it rose into the bright sky, its depth was greater, for its foundations were deep in the earth, deep into the darkness below, for they could not see its beginning. The ancient tower spiraled down into the unknown as the Leviathan came forth from the depths of the sea.

It was slender and long and had the body of a serpent, yet it walked on four legs which were powerful and flexible as it breached the sea and stood where the seaside keep had once stood. It had a tail in the likeness of a whale, and not one but many of these which came forth from its back. Its head was concealed, like that of a turtle hiding in its shell and as its head emerged its face was armored, but its eyes glowed bright green with a translucent face. It swam through the sea and walked on land before rearing up as it seemed to breach the clouds. Mirvi came from behind with a great gust of wind and the Zeppelins flew and sailed with the great wind onward north, to the lands of Zoltar.

The Leviathan was fleeing from Mirvi, for the sea had already run red from the blood of others. As the Leviathan wrapped its body with great wings that stretched forth and concealed it like a mighty shield, its translucent face glowed and its eyes grew fierce. The sky turned red, and a mighty flash could be seen across the sky as far as east is from west. All the warriors on the Zeppelins shielded their eyes for the light was blinding and when the light subdued the Leviathan was slain. Its body cleaved into pieces for it fell apart there and its body fell into the depths of the chasm below. What once was the great seaside keep which had lasted through the ages was no more.

So ended the battle of the north and as they flew north towards the lands of Zoltar, they peered out of the Zeppelin at what they thought would be their last stand against the Vollgarim. With the seaside keep a crumbled and destroyed ruin, fallen into the depths of the earth and the battlefield full of death and decay as bodies of fallen warriors were scattered about, they sailed onward as the ancient tower fell over the horizon and they gained sight of the mighty mountain chains of fire and ice. Alex, whose stomach was growling and empty, looked over the edge of the Zeppelin and Zoltar stood beside her and began to sing, for the sun was bright but their spirit's dim.

Violent is the sea where my fears are bound
The sun glares at me as I sink and drown
We stood together for our swords swung true
We fight for honor, we fight for you
We fight on, for our destiny is not fixed
Never turn your head or close your eyes
There is no illusion, only truth shrouded in lies
She who comes across the unknown
She who stands like a mighty cyclone
The sun will rise, and the sun will fade
It comes for you, for the choice has been made
I hear the voice aloud, calling out to me
She gave way to titans, yet there is no destiny
My fears are bound beyond that which is known
Watching me close, yet I'm not alone
Forget the peace inside as you watch and wait
Giving way to the light of redemption or hate

A poignant reminder for the battle never ends
We long for glory and honor, yet we seek
destructions end
A familiar sound but it haunts me
It was not always so, and thus it must be

22   BETWEEN THE LIGHT AND DARKNESS

The Zeppelins arrived late in the day as the sun would soon bid them all a final farewell. Its yellow and orange glow was far off in the distance, surrounded by an overcast purple, pink and light blue sky which was full of puffy, slow-moving clouds. The vast green forest and spiked, jagged mountains were dark, hiding in the shadow of the sun as they could see the great castle of Zoltar, built in the very rockface of the mountain. The lands here were mountainous with numerous curving and winding fjords below. They sailed there, high up in the heavens as they passed emerald rivers running through the great many forested plains below. The fjords were very calm and still as Alex could see the waters below which gleamed like a sea of glass, shinning gold as the sun set.

Zoltar has instructed one of the Strange Ones to land in a clearing where the fjords meet the mountains and as they descended into the shadow of the valley, the surviving warriors and their families were met with the sounds of children who frolicked and played cheerfully, for their master had returned. Alex and the party were vexed but Zoltar explained that he was not the gruesome and ravaging monster they had perceived. Lo! He saved a great many children, for when the Vollgarim began to rise, he took children from all the north to spare them, for he could move in the darkness against the Vollgarim, unhindered like the bat which screeches across the moonlit sky. Many families were reunited with their children, and they gave thanks to

Zoltar, for he was most feared among the people of the north, but it wasn't merited for Mirvi had cursed him long ago and he bore the mark for countless generations.

Zoltar's castle sat high upon the mountain and as they ventured forth through the dark black forest below, they were greeted by his servants, and all were welcomed in. The castle was impressively built in the distant past, a remarkable sight as its towers went high and the glow of the fires, torches and braziers lit its face a warm yellow glow. The moon was full, and the sky was lit a great silverish hue and the forest below was shining in the moonlight. The grey, slow rolling clouds high above began to divide, like a scroll that was rolled up and the stars shined and twinkled ever so brightly. Many shooting stars soared high above and there was a peace among the men of the north that lasted throughout the night.

A great feast was held, for it had been an age since the men of the north were completely gathered together in a single place. The grand hall was vast, for it formed a great circle with many tables and chairs, crafted from wood of the finest oak, ash, and spruce trees. At its center sat Chieftain Grom along with the other honorable chieftains as they gazed to the ceiling above which was made of glass. They could see the bright moon and the gentle rain as it fell and pelted the smooth clear glass above them. Torches were lit throughout the grand hall and a great many candles hung above them, all lit using the oil from fish, seals, and whales. Abundant food and mead were prepared as well as stews, soups, bread, and fruits.

The merriment lasted well into the night, and all took party in the gaiety, for the mead was strong and the food was plentiful. They cheered and sang songs of praise for chieftains and brave warriors alike, recounting the battle and honoring those who fell. There were several wounded and many injured, and the servants there tended to them in the traditional fashion. Of the chieftains, some had been injured for their armor was tough but the teeth and claws of the Vollgarim were formidable.

A warrior had been injured, and he suffered a deep wound to his fat belly. He paid it no mind and played proactively with the blond, slender servant girl who tended to him. She prepared a very strong onion soup, and he drank it heartily knowing its purpose. After a few minutes, the servant girls knelt to smell his wound and they spoke that it had the smell of the onion soup. His death was certain, for they say that should a warrior have the onion soup sickness and his wound bear its stench, his wound was deep, and he should surely die. He was brought mead for the remainder of the night and despite his fate, he gripped his sword tightly as he drunk mead until his eyes closed and he faded into dreams of glory. Indeed, there were many injured but despite their grim fate, they were cheerful, and their spirits didn't falter.

Now it came to pass that when the hour was late, Zoltar stood and spoke, and all eyes and ears were granted to him. He was cheerful, for his curse had been lifted, yet he spoke as an austere man for he no longer had the desire for the comforts and luxuries the castle gave him. Having lost one of his three beauties, for they were his lovers through the millenniums, and rather losing them to age, he took them to be a part of his curse. He relinquished his castle to Chieftain Grom, to do with as he pleased and released all servants and those who dwelled in it to return to their homelands. Chieftain Grom spoke, for he was old and had no sons or daughter, and despite being restored to his youthful prime, he too desired peace and contentment over the life of a chieftain. He passed his authority to Alex, for she was the closest to a daughter he had wished for.

So it came to pass that Alex ruled as chieftain, for she was a mighty and fierce woman and all respected and honored her that night as a woman from the north and not that of an outlander from across the sea. She sat next to Chieftain Grom as she leaned over her grandeur chair, grasping his arm with hers as a young child might do with their father. They sat and spoke of better days and what the future might bring as the fires raged and the cheerful, merrymaking dwindled as the night went on. The days ahead were bright and verily for thirty days the fjords ran red with the blood of Leviathan.

Osric set sail, returning to his small, smokey volcanic island across the sea as several of the others gathered their caravans and ventured out into the safe forests, back to their homes to rebuild their villages and start anew. Ravens were sent and returned, for all arrived safe and there was no sighting of the Vollgarim or of the dreadful Fangore and its mother. Zurn prepared to leave as well, for his homeland was not too far south from where they stood now.

"You could stay old friend, least for a little while longer," said Alex as she hugged Zurn goodbye, there on the shores of the fjords.

"Hope to see you again little one and should the Vollgarim return with their horde of fangs and claws, remember your old friend Zurn. For I do not ask how many the Vollgarim are, but where do I find them!" shouted Zurn in jest but in truth, he was a fearless and wild man.

They embraced for a moment before he boarded one of the great ships along the small, grey and black pebble ridden shores. Crafted like a dragon with sails that blew and tossed in the strong wind, he waved goodbye as he sailed across the fjord and out of sight.

"Mighty big ship, think hes compensating for something?" asked Gudrun to Alex but he said it in jest, for he knew Zurn could hear him.

They both laughed and waved goodbye as they knew it may be some time before they would all see one another again. It was then a great wind blew from the forest and Mirvi appeared as she walked in splendor to the sounds of gentle waves along the shore. Alex greeted her with a smile, for she was accompanied by a group of ethereal wolves which rubbed and nudged Alex with their soft, white fur that sparked in the sunlight.

"The north stands, and my oath will be honored," said Alex as she continued to play with the wolfs, kneeling down as she scratched and rubbed the wolf behind its ears.

"Theres no time, for you have sat here idle and evil knows no rest," said Mirvi as she glared at Alex who continued to play and dance with the wolves.

"The kings of the south are coming, all united together as they make way to the giants who dwell in the east. The evil that slept in the ancient tower at the seaside keep has been released, venturing south its corrupted their minds and brought anger and malice from within their hearts," said Mirvi as Gudrun crossed his arms there along the rocky shoreline.

Flux accompanied him, and he frolicked and played with the mighty ethereal wolves but growled menacingly at Alex, much again to their surprise. Mirvi explained that the remaining numbers of the north people would prove pointless to attack, for much blood would need to be spilt for the rise and release of another great evil which is bound in the depths of the earth. The evil which slept in the ancient tower at the seaside keep has gathered the people of the south, the kings who dwell across vast desert plains which are stark and flat and devoid of life, across the endless sands with hulking orange hills. Together they march against the giants who still dwell past the colossal eastern mountains, for their purpose is twofold. One to break free the ancient evil which is bound in the depths of the ancient tower there, and two to bring about the death of a great many of the southern kingdom's warriors. For on that day of battle, a great evil will be released from its chains along with the evil who is already bound at the base of the ancient tower," said Mirvi as she glowed a heavenly light.

"We would need an army to protect the giants and keep the ancient tower sealed. I will honor my word and venture north, for it my people are gathered there, I will unite them and together we will make a stand against the southern kingdoms," exclaimed Alex as she stood, and Gudrun gave a nod in agreement.

"I've done it for you, she who greets with fire," said Mirvi and from the edge of the forest, Alex's people appeared. There number was great, and she saw many riding on ethereal wolves, their bodies and faces covered in red and black as they were robed in exotic and unusual animal skins, carrying wooden spears in hand as the beat of drums were loud and deep, and the ululation was long, wavering, and high-pitched.

Alex saw her uncle, alive and well and they embraced each other in tears. The people of the north came down from the elaborate castle and greeted the gathering of Alex's people. Hospitality was extended and they met them with friendship and humility. The lands to the north beyond Kazulgard were shrouded in darkness, for now as the winter season comes, so does the sun depart and its shine is not felt for several months. In truth, Alex was grateful, for she knew the journey to the furthest reaches of the north was unheard of. A desperate and dangerous venture without question, for to enter the Frozen Wastes and journey into the unknown could not be fathomed.

"I revealed your father who is bound by his choice and delivered your people and uncle safely here at your side. A mercy granted to you for you each choose separate paths, but it is the choice of your father than grants you this mercy, for in his life he fought the evil, and in his demise, he slowed their will and impeded their plan," said Mirvi as Alex and her uncle turned to face her, still holding one another in happiness at their reunion.

"You are not what you seem, she who greets with fire. What you are, I do not know. Time will tell, for should you honor your word and march to the east where the giants roam, I will guide you for the mountains along the eastern ridge are impassable and you will be liable to fend off Fangore and her mother," said Mirvi as she stood there, watching as the gathering moved north and back inside the great castle.

"I will honor my word," said Alex as she hung to her uncle's arm as they walked out of sight.

Gudrun stood there as the lovely gathering moved on and Mirvi, who floated on clouds of fire came and stood next to him. She placed her hand on his shoulder as the two felt the wind in their hair and the cool evening air left him chilled.

"I was rather hoping to be done with battle, for I've seen plenty and have drunk my fill of mead," said Gudrun with sincerity, for he longed for peace and wished to grow fat and live to a ripe age, trading the sword and axe for the plow and ox.

"As long as those who dwell in the depths remain, there will be war. Little did Alex's father know, that by binding himself with one of the evils, they would be collectively weakened, for if others choose the same path their reign of terror would cease," said Mirvi as she slowly walked away and out of sight.

Gudrun stood there as she walked on and into the shadowy forest, as the ethereal wolves followed suit and nudged up against him as they departed. With the clouds moving swiftly overhead and the sound of thunder on the horizon, he joined the rest of the party back inside the great castle to which a feast was held that night to welcome Alex's people. It was quite a gathering, for the people of the north wished to know the history of Alex's people and how they came to survive the Leviathan and dwell in the most unhospitable lands to the north, full of ice and mountains that spouted fire and flame along with unspeakable beasts.

That night when all rested and the howling of wolves were heard deep within the forest below, Gudrun found Alex sitting in her newly appointed chieftain chair in the center of the great hall. She sat there with a troubled brow, as her eyes met his across the vast great hall.

"Thinking ahead to the battle in the east, are we?" questioned Gudrun as the large chair beside her squeaked and cracked as his heavy frame sat in it.

"Tomorrow morning, we will prepare the remaining ships and depart from these lands. We sail west to the lands of my forefathers" said Alex as she pushed her hair away from her face and leaned back in the chair with a deep sigh.

"Is that why you wished Mirvi to destroy the Leviathans, that we should flee and abandon this grand castle and our people here?" asked Gudrun as he leaned in making gestures with his large, powerful hands.

"I am staying behind, there's something I must do. Gudrun, give me your word you will look after the people should something happen to me," said Alex as she glared at Gudrun.

"On my honor I will but talk no more of this nonsense. On the morrow, we sail together," said Gudrun with a pat on her shoulder as he stood up to depart for the night.

Alex couldn't sleep; indeed, she was troubled, and her eyes didn't rest as she watched the morning sun break the dark night above her. With the rise of the morning sun, all prepared and boarded ships and set sail bound across the sea, free from the Leviathan's grasps. It was a sad departure, for Gudrun and Alex exchanged words and a wave of the hand as his ship left the shores and traversed through the calm fjords out to sea. A single ship was left behind with a handful of men, along with Alex's uncle.

Together they rode on their majestic steeds, deep into the north beyond the frozen pines. They arrived at Stormgarden, and indeed it had been long burned to a cinder, yet the ash remained as tiny, dark flakes floated in the air and the wind whistled through the settlement. Further north they went until their dark eye lashes were covered and frozen with snow and when they rested for the night, their cheeks would freeze to the animal hides which they slept on. It was a bitter cold land, and during some part of the year the sun shined continuously but they were deep in the winter months and the sun during this time hid below the horizon, for it was a land shrouded in darkness.

They came upon it, the lands of Kazulgard and as they did their horses reared and neighed with apprehension. Alex and her uncle came upon a chasm in the ground, a cave that went deep into the earth. They alone ventured into its depths with torch in hand until a wind swayed and bent the light of the flame violently as a familiar voice was heard. It was one of the Strange Ones, and their eyes appeared like tiny fireflies in that darkest of places.

"No further, lest you be overtaken by the darkness," one of them said as their voice echoed in the deep and Alex's uncle jumped with fear and waved his torches flame to get a glimpse of the creature.

"I fear no man or evil, nor creature or beast or that which dwells in the deep darkness," said Alex as she carried on as the Strange Ones walked at her side.

"The light will soon cease to guide you, and you shall find no comfort in the depths below. Only suffering and anguish, for that which is bound takes no pleasure in company," said a Strange One as they halted in place as Alex and her uncle carried on.

Soon the temperature dropped, and Alex's uncle shivered and quaked as the air whistled and howled before a great wind came and blew the light of their torches out. Alex could hear an all too familiar sound, the feint menacing laughter, and whispers in the shadows as they carried on in the darkness.

"Our king will know of this, who shall we say defies the darkness and ventures into the secret parts of the earth?" cried out a Strange One whose voice echoed in the darkness.

Alex burst into flames and the Strange Ones shielded their eyes as she carried on in the dark, to the astonishment of her uncle and the Strange Ones. Alex walked on as her uncle sought to catch up to her, for she was the only light in that place that twisted and turned, and the Strange Ones wondered if she sought to venture forth into oblivion.

"Better to fight and fall than to live without hope, " said Alex aloud as her thoughts were on her father. She carried on, her uncle close behind, as they ventured into the darkness as they heard the menacing laughter and sinister whispers beyond the umbra.

Made in the USA
Monee, IL
14 January 2023

25305992R00135